Blazing

Triskelion Motorcycles Book 1

Robin Andrews

Blazing
Triskelion Motorcycles Book 1
Robin Andrews

Published by STE Entertainment LLC

Copyright 2020 STE Entertainment LLC
Print Book ISBN: 978-1-7345279-6-4

Triskelion Motorcycles logo and cover art designed by Brandon

Dedication

I have three children and I love them all equally. But they all have aspects that make me appreciate them differently. This book, for reasons that will become self evident, is dedicated to my middle child. My son, Brandon.

Brandon is the child that is probably the most like me as far as personality and character. Growing up, he was the one that I wanted riding shotgun if I had to do a long drive because we could talk about everything and nothing and the trip seemed less exhausting and definitely not boring. In high school, he always got recognized for having the most spirit during homecoming events. I can remember helping him dye his hair blue, rainbow, and bleached blonde with hippie symbols in various colors dyed into his hair. He was the one that created an outfit that was half blue and half white for his school colors. And by half I literally mean half, the shirt was half blue and half white, the pants were half and half but on opposite sides, his face was half blue and half white, and so on. This boy literally goes all out for anything he believes in and has a heart that is so open and loving.

Fast forward several years from high school and he is now a stay at home dad, with one child who is Autistic and one child who has medical challenges. And he's an amazing dad. He doesn't always see it, and yes, like all of us, he isn't perfect. But you can see how those kids light up when he comes home from running an errand.

Not, that he has much of it, but in his spare time, he loves to create things and build things. He has expanded his children's play structure and added more slides and a tire swing and new levels and platforms for them to play on. He makes dragon eggs and magic wands to sell online. He is amazingly creative.

He's the type of person that steps up when someone needs him. Which brings me to why this book is dedicated to him. I had a set of premade covers that I had purchased for this series. I paid for them with the understanding that when I was ready for them, I could let the person who made them know and my name would be added and any personalization I needed would be done. I contacted her about a month before I really needed the cover and she responded with "I'll get right on them." And that was the last I heard from her. I got no covers, I got no response to messages or emails, she totally took my money and ghosted. I was getting down to the wire. A book needs a cover. My son stepped up and made me my cover and I happen to think it turned out pretty amazing. He took a look at what I was supposed to have from the other person and without infringing on any sort of copyright that she may have had, he made a cover that was similar but not exact and I am so thankful for him being willing to do that for me. He didn't want a credit because he doesn't think he really did much, but I completely disagree.

Prologue

"Okay, here's what we know," Bryan said, sitting across from Pete Hallowell in the coffee shop where they had agreed to meet. Pete was an attorney/brewery owner that the Lawson brothers had done a job for a few months ago. He had recently asked Bryan to see if he could find the guy who had been an abusive jerk to Pete's sister. "Your guy is definitely in the area. And he's been here for a while, from what we can tell. Fortunately for us, your parents are like most wealthy American families, and they have an alarm system and surveillance cameras at their home."

"This guy has been in my parents' house?" Pete was livid.

"Not in their home, not even at their home, really. He always stays across the street. The closest he has ever gotten is their mailbox." Bryan tried to be reassuring. Although he knew if it was his family, that would not have been a reassurance to him either.

"That's supposed to be better?" Pete asked.

"Well, better than having access to the home, yes, this is better," Bryan stated.

Pete had to agree with that, to a point anyway. So he gave a reluctant nod for Bryan to continue.

"He never approaches the house. He waits for your parents to be gone. As a side note, your mother spends way too many days at the country club. She leaves most days by nine-thirty, he waits until she is gone, and he checks the mail." Pete gave him a puzzled look, so he continued, "Our guess would be that he is hoping your sister is mailing something to your parents, Christmas cards, birthday cards, even just a normal letter. He's hoping to find a return address or at the very least a post mark."

"Thank goodness my sister is a tech freak then," Pete replied. "If she can't do it on a smart phone or computer, you would never hear from her."

"That brings up the other issue we have," Bryan continued. "He never takes anything, but apparently, he has opened your parents' cell phone bills. Most likely trying to see if she is still on their contract. She's not, by the way. Your sister may be a tech freak, but she has what most people call a burner phone. It generally can't be traced. It's pre-paid, and she has the tracking and GPS off. She's pretty smart about it all, definitely someone who doesn't want to be tracked down easily. I think Trevor got a hard-on when he realized just how technologically adept she is."

"Yeah, you tell your brother to keep his hands and eyes off my sister," Pete threatened.

Bryan raised both hands in a sign of surrender. "Nothing will happen with any member of my team unless it is one hundred percent consensual." Bryan had seen a few pictures of Pete's sister in the file, and he wouldn't mind having some consensual time with her, but this was business, and he would do his best to remain professional. They would probably hand the information to Pete, and he would know the score and he or one of his friends would always be at Sophie's side. Hell, he might even ask her not to come to the party for her own safety. "We are fortunate that your parents don't get a detailed bill. Most people don't anymore. A detailed bill may have listed her number on the list of calls going in or out. With the number he still wouldn't have been able to track her, but he could terrorize her with phone calls."

"How much do you charge for bodyguard services?" Pete asked.

So little brother was prepared to hire someone to keep his sister safe. That kind of made sense, though. As far as he could tell, most of the brewery owners had paired up with a woman in the last year or so. Pete would have to entertain guests and keep an eye on his pregnant wife. He probably figured it was easier to just hire the job out than trying to figure out how to handle it himself.

"We usually charge by the day. It's a set fee for the time she isn't in a secure location, like your parents' house or whatever," Bryan replied.

"Oh, hell no!" Pete exclaimed. "This guy knows where they live. I want one of your brothers staking out my parents' house in case this guy shows up. But I want one of you with her 24 hours a day while she is here. I'll find a place for her to stay where you can keep her safe. Maybe my friend Walt. He lives in a huge house on the east side. I don't know, but I want one of you with her every minute she is in town."

"Okay, you're the client. Whatever you say goes, man. How is your sister going to feel about having a babysitter?" Bryan asked.

Pete shook his head, thinking about exactly what his sister would think about being babysat. "Well, you can be her date/bodyguard," Pete suggested. "I can't imagine my sister objecting to having you around. I can't imagine many women complain about you being their bodyguard."

It was true; women didn't complain when any of his team was assigned as a bodyguard. The problem was that most men didn't want their wife or girlfriend being guarded by a tattooed former Green Beret who rode a Harley. They usually got private investigator assignments or bodyguarding some old guy who thought everyone was out to steal his wealth or off him for his money.

"However you want it set up," Bryan agreed. "I'll have Riley and Trevor handle the surveillance and keep eyeballs on your parents' house. I'll also have Trevor set up a facial recognition program and keep a scan of the area."

Pete stood up and put out a hand to shake with Bryan. "Sounds good. I'll text you her flight information when I know it." And then he left.

Bryan headed back to the motorcycle shop to fill his brothers in on their assignments and to get working on a bike. Whenever he felt like a job was going to be tricky to handle, taking apart a motor or restoring an old bike always gave him time to shut it all out for a few hours.

Chapter One

One week later

Bryan stood slightly behind Pete. He didn't want to interfere with the reunion of the two siblings. He had been out of the military for years, but he still had the tendency of standing with his fingers interlaced behind his back, eyes forward, spine erect, shoulders slightly forward. It was how he tended to stand anytime he had to wait for someone or something. A few minutes later, he saw the young woman from the pictures in the file that lay open on his desk back at the shop. He had to admit, those pictures had captured her basic look, but they really hadn't fully done her justice. She was much more beautiful in person. She had rich mahogany-colored hair that was braided in a long tail down her back. She had lightly tinted sunglasses on, but he knew that she had eyes the color of precious emeralds; he had gotten lost in them for several minutes at the office one day. Her skin was a pale olive color. He wasn't sure what her heritage was, but he would bet there was some Mediterranean connection in there somewhere, maybe Greek. By the time he pulled himself out of that whole wrong line of thinking, she was hugging her brother.

When Sophie pulled herself away from her brother, she noticed the mouthwatering piece of eye candy standing slightly back and off to the side. To be honest, she had noticed him yards ago as she approached, but she had told herself that there was no way this guy was with her brother. He was probably waiting for some girlfriend to get back from her latest trip to Maui or something. She hugged Pete and then asked, "Who is Hottie McHotterson there?" while using her chin to indicate Bryan.

Bryan had also been in the military long enough to have almost perfect hearing, and the character to not acknowledge that he had heard her statement. He just moved closer in position and politely waited for Pete to introduce them.

Pete just shook his head before telling his sister, "This is Bryan Lawson, your date for the party."

Bryan held out his hand and said, "Ma'am" with a slight dip of his chin.

"Oh, God, don't call me ma'am. That just makes me feel old, and if you're my date, the last thing I want you thinking of me as is an old woman," Sophie said with a scowl.

"Not that kind of a date, Soph," Pete said, shaking his head. "He's a trained bodyguard."

"Now why ever would I need a body...oh, you know," Sophie said.

"Yes, I know, and I think I probably know a lot more than you know," Pete stated irately.

Bryan kind of stepped between the two siblings. He had been doing that with his own family for years. Ever since their parents had died, Bryan had been the mediator and the one to keep them all together. "If I may, I believe this explanation is more suited for a private location, and I think I might have a better way of explaining," he said, looking between the two.

Pete nodded agreement, and Sophie just stood there stunned. Bryan put out an elbow for Sophie to take so he could direct them to the baggage claim area. After they picked up her bags, they went to a coffee booth in the airport and took their beverages to a more secluded group of chairs in the terminal.

"May I proceed now?" Bryan asked, looking pointedly at Sophia.

"Sure, as long as you don't call me ma'am again," Sophie said with sass.

"Thank you, Sophia," Bryan said with his deep 'no argument needed' voice. This woman was going to be a challenge. Not because he didn't like her sass and brashness, but because he did. He loved a woman with a bratty side, especially when he could be the one to spark that sass and then punish them for being a brat. Punish in only the sweetest of ways, of course.

"She doesn't like to be called Sophia," Pete began.

"Oh, you hush, little brother," Sophie said with furrowed eyebrows. "As long as he doesn't call me ma'am or some other old lady term, he can call me anything he wants." She turned her eyes toward Bryan and said, "Pardon my little brother's rudeness. You were saying?" Pete had been absolutely right, normally she hated being called Sophia, but for some reason, Bryan saying it didn't bother her at all.

This woman was going to be the death of him; he had to remain professional. He was going to ask Trevor to put that on a repeating cycle of text messages to his phone. REMAIN PROFESSIONAL every thirty seconds or so should keep him out of trouble.

"Right, I was saying," Bryan began. "We have been keeping an eye out for Larry Ribinsky." Sophia's eyes immediately changed from light and flirtatious to serious and scared. "Pete hired my firm to run some facial recognition and things like that to see if we found him anywhere in this area. We also ran the same test for a one hundred mile radius of where you live. We didn't expect for him to be in Colorado, but we wanted to take precautions."

"And did you find him?" Sophie asked. She didn't know what she would do if he knew she was in Colorado. That had become her safe place.

"We did," Bryan confirmed. "He has been seen around your parents' mailbox on several occasions."

Sophie was puzzled. "Why would he be around the mailbox?"

"Hoping you mailed them something," Pete said somberly.

Sophie was just kind of sitting there staring at the floor with her arms wrapped around herself in a hug. How could he still be out there looking for her? Hadn't he done enough to ruin her life years ago? What did he want, another chance? That was never going to happen. She had hoped after he called the ambulance and went on the run, he would just disappear into some small backwoods town in Oregon or Washington and live his life. She had always been worried that he would hurt another woman like he had her. But it wasn't like she would have been able to stop him from doing that. She might have been able to get him arrested, but her dad and her brother were attorneys, so she knew not all bad guys went to jail. She also knew that even if they did, they got out eventually and they might take revenge on the person they thought put them in jail in the first place. "Why would he still be doing that? What does he want?" Sophie said softly.

"That's what we need to find out," Pete said. "And until we know, you have to have Bryan or one of his brothers with you at all times."

She looked to Bryan, so he tried to give her a rundown of how things would go. "You can't go to your parents' house, obviously. We don't know for sure if he keeps an eye on the house other than just checking the mailbox, but if he looks at the papers at all, he probably has a good idea that you might be in town. Your parents announced the marriage and celebration on the social pages, and while I'm pretty sure Larry doesn't care much about most of what is on the social page, knowing who your parents are, he may be keeping an eye on it in case your parents post anything involving you. Pete suggested his friend Walt's home as a safe location for you to stay."

Sophie did not want to believe what she was hearing. That man had given her enough pain and torment in her life. She could not have him walking back in now—correction, she could not have him walking back into her life ever. She didn't realize she had sort of zoned out and sat shaking her head thinking of all the reasons that man needed to stay out of her life. She finally realized that she was not paying attention when she heard Bryan saying something.

"Sophia, it will be all right," Bryan was saying softly. "I promise you we won't let anyone hurt you. You have my promise that my siblings and I will do everything necessary to keep you safe from this man. He will not get within ten feet of you."

Bryan sounded very sure of himself, and he and his team were probably very well trained, but that didn't change the feeling of cold terror anytime she thought about Larry. She couldn't even think or hear his name without a chill running up her spine.

Pete had noticed the look of sheer terror on his sister's face. He still could only imagine what all that piece of scum had done to his sister. He knew what the hospital reports said, but he was sure they could only comment on the injuries that were fairly recent to when she had arrived. His sister had been with the man for months; obviously there had been injuries that were healed prior to her stay in the hospital. The look of fear on her face told him that he had done the right thing. He needed her to stay as far away as possible while still allowing her to be here for the reception. He knew she really wanted to be here, and their mother would be disappointed if Sophie didn't make it. Their mother would understand if Pete told her about Larry, but he was hoping to keep that piece of information away from them. The Lawson brothers were already taking care of checking his parents' mail and making sure he wasn't hanging around their house anymore. He just needed to keep her safe for a few days until she could make her way back to Colorado. His parents didn't need to know all of what Pete knew, although he was planning to tell them that he had Bryan involved just in case her ex decided to try to make contact. He needed to make this seem a little less terrifying to her somehow.

"You remember Walt, right?" he asked, and at her slight nod, he continued. "He's married now, to this really super sweet former ballet dancer. Her name is Rayne. They have a big five-bedroom home, and they are looking forward to your visit. You won't believe this, but Zak has actually settled down too. He's not married yet, but things are pretty serious between him and his girl, Skye. They got engaged at Christmas. I'm sure you'll meet them all soon. The guys are all looking forward to seeing you again." He wasn't going to say that they hadn't seen her since just after she got out of the hospital. She remembered that time as well as he did. Talking about it would only give her more to think, and he needed her to move her focus from the past to the present.

Bryan could tell that Sophia was getting lost in the past, and that would do no good for any of them. He needed to get her on the move so that she didn't have time to dwell on the past. The present needed to hold all her focus for the time being. He gave an imperceptible nod to Riley, who would appear to be reading the paper to anyone that might pass by. What he was really doing was watching for any sign of the perpetrator in the general area. Trevor was outside in his truck with his computer running facial recognition scans on the feeds coming from the security system he had tapped into when they had arrived a few hours ago to get the lay of the land for the easiest path to get Sophia off the plane and into their truck. Riley tapped out a message on his phone and then gave a small nod back. Riley had sent a text to Trevor telling him it was time to pull up to the exit closest to their current location. It just so happened that the exit closest to them was a door that would normally sound an alarm if anyone opened it, so hopefully Trevor had taken care of that too. "It's time for us to go," he stated simply.

"I'm not done with my coffee," Sophie complained.

"Then take it with you." Bryan issued the command in a way that would tell anyone that no argument would be tolerated. "It's time for us to go. Sophia, you need to learn to listen to everything I say and do as you are told. This isn't me trying to be some bossy arrogant prick. I'm doing what I have been trained to do to keep you safe. When I stand up, you will stand up. I will put my arm around you like we are a couple and we will head for that door over there." He gave a chin nod to the exit.

Sophia challenged him by asking, "And how is setting off an alarm going to keep us from being noticed?"

"My brother has taken care of the alarm on the door, so that won't be an issue. Pete, you follow us out. Riley will be trailing behind us until we get outside." With that, he stood up, and fortunately, Sophia stood too. He put his arm around her, and they headed for the door.

Sophie wasn't sure exactly how she felt about Bryan. He came across as a bossy asshole, but he really did look good doing it, and she had to admit, having his big muscular body pressed up against hers wasn't a bad thing at all.

* * * *

Pete breathed a sigh of relief when his sister followed Bryan's directions. He got up and followed them out to the waiting vehicle. Bryan opened the door and helped Sophie up into the big four-wheel drive pick-up. As they had arranged, Pete climbed into the front seat with Trevor. He spotted Riley walking casually to his Harley that had been propped near the wall in the little alcove area where the garbage bins for the businesses inside were hidden out of sight from the average passerby. To most people, he would just look like some guy from the local motorcycle club heading for his ride, but Pete had been around these guys enough to know that Riley was always surveying the area.

From what Pete had seen during their meetings and interactions, Bryan was the take-charge leader of the group. That made sense since he was the oldest and from what Pete had heard, he had been the only adult in the family when their parents had died. He had taken responsibility for his three younger siblings. When Trevor had become an adult and was able to step in as head of the household, Bryan had joined the Marines and become a Green Beret. Pete didn't know how things had gone from there as far as the Lawson kids went, other than the fact that both brothers had joined the Green Beret when they became able. Trevor was definitely the tech guy on the team. Pete had been amazed at what he could find just with a few keystrokes of his computer. Riley seemed like the quiet loner type. He was as good as his brothers when it came to skills and knowledge; he just seemed like he would feel more comfortable in the background.

When they got into the truck, Bryan introduced Sophia to Trevor. "Sophia, this is my brother, Trevor. He's the tech guy on our team for the most part, but don't let that fool you. He knows how to do the dirty work too. Trevor, meet Sophia Hallowell."

Trevor tuned around in his seat enough to reach his hand out. "Ma'am," he said with a nod.

Sophie shook his hand but then said, "Good lord, not another one. I am not that old. I would be willing to bet that I am not any older than Bryan here. Why does everyone think I'm old?" She let out a huff of frustration.

"It's not your age, Sophia," Bryan assured her. "We are all former military, and it's a term of respect. Although our father had taught us to be respectful long before we joined up."

Trevor turned and pulled away from the curb and headed his truck for the east side neighborhood that Walt and Rayne lived in. He looked in the rear-view mirror, and as expected, Riley was a few car lengths behind them. Trevor hadn't seen anything in or around the airport that made him suspicious, but Riley was back there to help assure that they didn't have a tail.

When they arrived at Walt and Rayne's house, they pulled right up to the front door and parked in the circle drive. Walt had received a pretty decent security upgrade thanks to the Lawson brothers. He now had motion detectors and surveillance cameras in several locations on the perimeter of his home. The front door opened, and three people stepped out. Pete went to stand by Autumn. He put his arm around her waist and drew her toward him. "Soph, I'd like you to meet Autumn, my wife." Pete beamed with pride.

Autumn stepped forward and gave Sophie a hug. "I've heard so much about you. It's wonderful to meet you."

"I feel the same way," Sophie agreed.

Walt stepped forward and gave Sophie a warm embrace. "It's so good to see you, Sophie." As he pulled away, he reached his hand to Rayne, who stepped forward and put her hand out. Walt said, "This is my wife, Rayne."

"It's a pleasure to meet you, Rayne," Sophie said with a smile. "When Pete told me Walt had gotten married, I told myself she must be someone pretty special if she got Walt tied down."

"I wasn't that bad," Walt protested. "Zak's the one who amazes us all."

"I heard. I didn't think anyone would tame him, at least not for a couple more decades." Sophie laughed.

The roar of a Harley picking up speed out on the road could be heard as the group walked inside. "I thought I was going to meet your other brother?" Sophia asked.

"You will, in a little bit. He'll circle around the block a couple of times to be sure there wasn't a tail on us, and then he'll be here. We didn't see anything suspicious on the drive over, but that also helps it seem like he isn't associated with us if he doesn't follow right behind us," Bryan explained. "We really don't think this guy is sophisticated enough to know to follow us and all of that, but we don't take any chances."

It was nice to know that they were going so far to try to protect her. She really didn't understand why Larry would go to any trouble to find her. They hadn't seen each other in years. Yes, he had seemed to think he owned her when they had been together, but when he had left that day, it didn't seem like he would ever look back. He knew what he had done would be on record with the hospital and the police. He was a fool if he thought he could get her back. She had no intention of trying to get him arrested for what had happened years ago. But she would not hesitate to involve police if he tried to touch her again now.

"I've made some sandwiches and snacks—well, Mrs. Steele and I did." Rayne smiled. "Why don't we head into the kitchen and grab a bite?"

Bryan wanted to wait until Riley was back before they went into the plan for the next few days, so he followed the group into the kitchen and grabbed a plate.

"So tell me all about this brewery," Sophie stated, looking from Pete to Walt. "I hear it's pretty successful."

"We do all right," Walt agreed. "Jason runs the business side of things. We are all pretty sure we owe our success largely to him; however, don't tell him I said that. His ego is big enough." Walt chuckled.

"Has he got a girlfriend?" Sophie asked. "Seems all of you boys are settling down now."

"That's a good question," Rayne stated rather somberly.

At Sophie's puzzled look, Pete tried to explain. "Jason has been dating Rayne's best friend for about a year now, but it seems pretty superficial. They are always together when our group hangs out, but it doesn't really seem like it's getting more serious. None of us is sure what is going on in Jason's head."

"I've heard a woman did a real number on him a few years ago, although I don't know the details," Rayne stated. "I just wonder if he'll ever be able to figure out his issues."

The two friends looked at each other. They were pretty sure they knew what Jason's issue was, but it wasn't their place to say anything.

Before she could ask, Pete told her that Jeremy was still playing the field; no woman had trapped him yet. At those words, Autumn gave him an elbow to the ribs.

"Trapped him, hmm? I don't think I was the one to suggest eloping," Autumn said with a grin.

"Trapped in all the best ways possible, love," Pete said, then he gave Autumn a kiss on her temple.

"Mm-hmm," Autumn said with a shake of her head, but she was smiling, so it was obvious it was all being said in fun and in love. That was the part that got Sophie the most. It was so obvious that these men loved their women beyond reason. She hoped she could find that someday, although with her predilections she wasn't sure that would ever happen. It was nice to dream, though. She looked up and realized there was another very large, very muscular man with tattoos standing in the room. Where had he come from? She found herself drawing closer to Bryan.

Bryan had noticed when Riley had come into the room. Of course, Trevor had too, but none of the others had. Most nonmilitary people wouldn't have heard him come in. Bryan also noticed that when Sophia had seen the newcomer, she had moved closer to him. That was a good sign; she was already seeing him as her protector. That was a valuable and necessary aspect to the whole bodyguard thing. He could tell that for the most part, Sophia was a strong and independent woman who had not let her past affect her everyday life. But when there was a perceived threat, he needed her to rely on him for protection. At least for as long as this operation lasted.

"Everyone," Bryan said when the conversation had quieted a bit. "This is our brother Riley. Some of you have met him already. Riley is our stay in the shadows and observe guy most of the time. He has really great instincts when it comes to the spy game."

Riley stepped forward and shook hands with everyone. The ones he knew he greeted by name, the ones he didn't know he greeted with 'sir' or 'ma'am.' Bryan heard Sophia say, "Oh lord, another one" softly. He just smiled; this was going to be an interesting few days. He had absolutely no doubt that Sophia would challenge him in numerous ways; hopefully, that would not include times when he really needed her cooperation for her own safety.

Once they had all had a light lunch, Bryan suggested that they move to the dining room table where they could make sure everyone was up to speed on what was going to be happening the next few days. After everyone was seated, he began. "Okay, first, there has been a security upgrade to Walt's home. The intercom system that Walt had installed previously has been upgraded to include all of the bedrooms and several positions here on the main floor. In addition to that, the system will connect to our system and will alert us if anyone uses the intercom. They also have a panic button that will alert both my team and the police." He looked around and everyone seemed to be on board so far. "Our hope is that they are never needed, but if you think you hear something, or you think you see something moving out in the bushes, things like that, use the intercom. One of us will check it out. If you know you see someone in the house, find an open exterior door or window, or something that is a definite threat, use the panic button first, then call us on the intercom." Everyone nodded their agreement, so he continued, "There is a code on the doors that has to be entered if you are coming or going. Everyone has been taught how to use that except Sophia. She and I will go over her responsibilities separately."

Trevor began speaking when his brother was done. "At the family-only dinner tomorrow night, we don't expect any trouble, because it's private and by invitation only. However, Riley and I will be there. We have an in with the catering staff and will be helping in that aspect. If you see anyone that isn't on the guest list, let us know. We believe that the club will not allow anyone past their security, but it has happened on occasion, so we want to cover all bases." Again, everyone nodded their understanding.

"I don't want this to sound like some huge military op," Bryan began. "And we don't really believe this guy has much ability to really be a problem, but we always cover every possible aspect when we do bodyguard work. As far as we know, this guy is just some lowlife who thinks he can have another chance with the one that got away, so to speak. We really don't believe any of you have anything to worry about other than possibly Sophia, but it's best if the women don't go anywhere alone. If your husband isn't going with you, one of us will. No offense, but this guy seems like the type that would potentially try to find a woman he considered weak if he did want to try to get into the house or have access to Sophia."

Riley stepped forward from the position he had taken in the corner. He opened his folder and began the itinerary for the weekend. "Tonight, the rest of the owners of the brewery will be coming over for a cookout in the back yard. I believe tomorrow the women are scheduled for a spa day beginning at ten hundred hours."

Bryan interrupted him by simply saying, "Rye."

"I apologize, the ladies will have their spa day at ten o'clock in the morning. Bryan and I will be watching the entrance to the salon. It is closed for the day to any customers except those related to the wedding party. When the ladies finish, everyone will be prepared and dressed for the family dinner. The men will rendezvous with the ladies at four-thirty in the afternoon, and you will travel as a group to the dinner. Trevor and I will already be at the country club in our positions as catering staff. When the family dinner is over, everyone will go to their respective accommodations for the evening. At ten o'clock on Saturday morning, a brunch is planned here at the Jensens' home. The wedding celebration is scheduled for three in the afternoon on Saturday. Everyone will travel as a group by limousine to the reception. It is imperative that everyone arrive at the same time and leave at the same time, unless you have contacted one of us to inform us that you need to deviate from this plan. It's much easier for us to keep our focus on Sophia if we don't have to consider where anyone else might have gone."

Sophie took three things from that whole speech. First, it was very obvious that you could take the man out of the military, but you couldn't always take the military out of the man. Although Riley was the only one that seemed to be that formal, Bryan and Trevor didn't seem to be quite as militaristic. Second, everyone was going to a whole lot of trouble to try to keep her safe, even though she really didn't think there was as big of a need for that as everyone else seemed to think. And third, she didn't mind when Bryan called her Sophia, but it bothered her when anyone else did, including Riley and Trevor. That was an odd thought.

When the debriefing, as Sophie thought of it, was over, she asked if she could be shown her room so she could relax and get unpacked before the dinner this evening. Bryan was more than happy to show her the room chosen for her to stay in.

As they walked up the stairs and then along the hallway, Bryan pointed out which room was which. The master bedroom was to the right down a short hallway from the top of the stairs. The bedroom directly at the top of the stairs would be taken by Pete and Autumn so that Pete could have time with his sister. The first room down the hallway to the left of the stairs would be Bryan's and finally, her room was the room at the end of the hallway beyond Bryan's room. She walked into the room and waited for Bryan to set down her luggage and walk out the door. She went to look out the window at the backyard below. How was it possible that this brief visit that was supposed to be for a happy occasion had turned into the latest military black op? That's what it seemed like to her. She felt like she was some world leader who knew where the nuke buttons were. It was just her, and while she did know what hell Larry had done in her life, she wasn't really sure any of this was necessary. Just before Bryan fully closed the door, she called out to him. "Bryan."

"Yes, Sophia?" he asked, stepping back into the room.

"Will I be able to spend any time with my parents other than at parties?" she asked.

Bryan could see the look of sadness in her eyes. He was pretty sure that she didn't see Larry as the threat the rest of them thought he might be, but he was sure the sadness came from having her weekend so controlled and dictated. Sophia was probably a free spirit most of the time who didn't have a ton of worries in life. She had taken the steps necessary to distance herself from her former life and had obviously been able to heal enough to move past it. Having it come back to haunt her like this was likely very difficult for her. "Yes, Sophia, you will. Right now, the plan is that you will be able to go to their house on Sunday, but the location is tentative. We have to play that part by ear. We are trying very hard not to let your parents, most especially your mother, in on what is going on. If it becomes an issue of your safety, we will change the location, but yes, you will be able to spend time with them before you go back to Colorado Monday afternoon."

Sophia didn't say anything more, so Bryan walked out the door again. Just before the door shut fully, Bryan heard the soft gasps of breath that were a sure sign that she was crying. He stepped back into the room again and walked up to Sophia's back. He placed a hand on each arm and turned her gently. Sure enough, there were tears running down her cheek. He pulled her to his chest and tried to console her with his strength and with his words. "It will be okay, Sophia, trust me. I know this isn't easy for you, but we will do everything we can to make this a safe and happy time for you to celebrate your brother's marriage. Please don't cry, Sophia. It will be all right." He stood holding her until her soft gulps of air subsided, and he no longer felt warm tears dampening his shirt. He held her a little longer too, wanting to be sure she was okay. This woman was definitely going to be a challenge for him between her spunky side and her soft side. The alpha male in him was going to have to be very careful.

Chapter Two

All the Five Sloth guys had arrived with their significant others except for Jeremy, who was apparently flying solo tonight.

Sophie had heard one of the guys harassing him about not bringing 'the girl that had been attaching herself to a barstool every time he was on duty.' He turned a little red and excused her absence by saying, "Yeah, we're not at the point of her wanting to come and hang out at a 'family function,'" making actual air quotes with his fingers.

Sophie thought she saw a look pass between Jeremy and Riley for a minute, but it was gone as fast as it was there, so maybe she'd imagined it. She had decided on a tight pair of jeans and a form-fitting long-sleeved shirt with a vest over the top. She was going to take every opportunity she had to try to get Bryan to notice her as more than the client/potential victim. It had felt so right being in his arms earlier as she had let the stress and strain and worry flow from her body. Not that it was completely gone, but she did feel a lot better than she had since Bryan had informed her that Larry was still actively looking for her. She was going to do her level best to have fun tonight. She was in a fenced-in yard where no one from the outside world could see her. She was surrounded by friends, old and new, and three of the buffest, most badass men she had ever met in her life. She was going to enjoy the evening to the fullest extent possible under the circumstances.

The evening was filled with laughter at old stories Sophie shared with the ladies about the antics of the guys growing up. Everything from the first time Zak had asked her if she had any condoms because he thought he might get lucky on his date later to times they had asked her to buy alcohol when they were still underage.

"Hey, I was trying to be prepared in case," Zak said, trying to defend himself.

"You were what, thirteen at the time?" Sophie asked. "Did you actually get lucky that night?"

"No," Zak said, shaking his head, "but I could have."

"That's the playboy I know and love," Skye said, giggling.

The group all laughed, but Jason spoke up and said, "At least we don't have to have anyone buy us alcohol anymore. We make our own just the way we like it." The Five Sloth guys all raised their glasses of beer and gave a hearty sound of agreement. It kind of sounded like they were still living out their frat boy days.

Sophie's mind kind of drifted off to the fact that her bother had all these guys who had been his friends forever, and she was sure they would do anything for each other. That was another thing that Larry had cost her. She'd had to give up her friends when she was dating him either because he didn't like them for one reason or another or because she knew that they would see right through her claim of being fine and happy. She had distanced herself from her family and friends. Even now, she lived in Colorado away from her family because she didn't think it was safe to come back to Michigan, and apparently she had been right. It wasn't safe for her here.

Colorado was a nice enough place, and she had made friends with some of the people in her small town. But she still kept everyone at arm's length. She had friends, but not really anyone close. She hadn't dated anyone since Larry either. She just couldn't trust someone to not hurt her that way again.

Being in a protected backyard, Bryan didn't stay immediately by her side every moment. He went and got food or a beverage. He had even offered to bring her whatever she wanted. Although he wasn't always within arm's reach, he always seemed to be watching her. Whenever she looked up, he was there, never far away, but always watching. Sometimes when she had been talking, she had even sensed his gaze on her. He was obviously very good at his job of watching over the client. A part of her wished that he was watching her for other reasons, like maybe he found her as attractive as she found him. But she told herself that was a silly wish. He was being very professional, watching her so that he could learn about her mannerisms and things so that he would be better able to understand her in an effort to keep her safe. There would be no weekend fling with the hot bodyguard for her.

She hadn't had a relationship or even a sexual encounter in so long that even a weekend fling would be welcome at this point. She pulled her attention back to the conversation going on around her. It would do no good to fantasize about her hotter than hell bodyguard.

Despite the fact that there was definitely a sense of caution around the group, Bryan was glad to see that for the most part, everyone was having a typical good time backyard barbeque. It wasn't really warm enough for the full backyard effect. It was only early April in Michigan, which meant the days could be in the fifties, but the nights still got quite cold. Walt's backyard had a large, mostly enclosed structure that many would call a three-season porch. He also had kerosene heaters keeping them all warm. Bryan didn't need a heater to keep him warm. Every time he looked at Sophia, he got plenty warm. Whenever he looked at her, her gaze turned to him as if she had felt his eyes on her. He thought long and hard about what it would mean to allow himself to cross that line with Sophia. As long as it was consensual, he was sure Pete wouldn't be upset about it. They were two grown adults, and if they chose to fool around a little, it wouldn't be a huge issue. As long as he could continue to do his job and be professional with guarding her, having a little fun shouldn't be a problem. Although Bryan wasn't the type of guy that usually had one-night stands, he also wasn't the type of guy who thought every sexual encounter had to be part of a long-term commitment with potential marriage on the horizon. He had always dated a woman for a while before they had gone that far. He had always been respectful and had never taken advantage of any woman, even though he got offers frequently for a one-time thing. He had to know a woman a little to be able to enjoy sex with her. Although he did have to admit that it wasn't a matter of time, like they had to date for a certain number of weeks or whatever. It did have to be about a connection and a feeling that there was something there. Oh, he knew in his life it had never been love. He hadn't ever loved a woman, but he did have to care about her and feel like they knew each other on more than just a sexual desire level. On the other hand, Sophia was only here until Monday. Maybe it wasn't a good idea to start something that he would likely never be able to see through to its completion. Whatever that situation might be, he wasn't sure that three days would be enough time to really see how compatible they could be.

Out of the corner of his eye, he saw Riley pulling his cell phone out of his pocket. He was reading a text. A minute later, he was obviously typing out a reply. Then Jeremy appeared to receive a text message and looked at Riley. There was a small nod between the two of them. Something was up; his senses were firing off all kinds of alarm bells. But if he didn't want to panic everyone in this backyard, he needed to try to act like he didn't know something was going on.

A minute later, Jeremy stood up and held up his cell phone, then he said to the group, "Hey, I need to head to the brewery. Apparently there is some sort of commotion going on. It's probably a drunk or something, but I want to go check it out. You guys all stay and have fun. I'll let you know if it turns out to be anything."

Almost immediately, Riley came closer to the group too. He looked at Jeremy and asked, "You want me to come along? Like you said, it's probably nothing, but I can be pretty convincing with drunks."

"Sure." Jeremy agreed. "If that's not going to be a problem here."

Bryan wasn't sure exactly what the two were cooking up, and until later when he could get a debrief from Riley, he wouldn't know. But he did know that he had to play along. "Yeah, yeah, go ahead, Rye. I'm sure we're good here. Most likely we will be going inside soon anyway."

With that, the two of them took off, the roar of Riley's Harley fading in the distance.

"Yeah, it is getting a little chilly out here," Rayne agreed. "Why don't we head inside for the dessert?" The group all settled in to the big relaxing TV room that Walt had set up and got comfortable to finish their evening.

When all of the guests had left, Bryan took Sophia upstairs to make sure she fully understood the intercom system and the panic button. "But I'll be right next door. If you need anything, yell my name and I will be here," he assured her.

Sophie went into the bathroom attached to her room and got ready for bed. She kind of wished she owned something sexy to put on. Maybe she could fake hear something in the night and get Bryan to come in to 'rescue' her. But the shorty pajama pants and tank top that she slept in weren't really anything that would seduce any man. As she was crossing the room, she thought she heard low voices out in the hallway. She walked over and opened the door slightly so that she could hear the conversation.

"Summer texted me. She was pretty sure our perp was just sitting at the bar, sipping a few brews, so she wanted me to come scope it out," Riley was explaining. "I didn't know how to leave without causing concern, so I texted Jeremy and had him make up the whole possible drunk scenario."

"And?" Bryan didn't sound overly happy to be receiving this report.

"And when Jeremy walked in the guy was sitting there, but when he saw me walk in, he fairly quickly paid his tab and hit the road," Riley said. "Either he knows we're watching him, or he just didn't like the look of someone that could kick his ass if he got out of line. I don't know which it is, but it was definitely our guy, and he didn't stick around long enough for me to make any contact with him. I wanted to avoid a scene inside, and by the time I got outside, he was gone. It's a fairly busy night at the pub. I had to dodge a few people before I made it to the parking lot."

"But you're sure it was him?" Bryan asked through clenched teeth.

"Yeah, man, positive," Riley explained. "Summer has his picture; you know she wouldn't have contacted me if she wasn't sure it was him. She doesn't have our military training, but being who she is, she remembers faces."

"Right, sorry, I was just hoping there was a chance that maybe this was a guy who looked like our guy but really wasn't," Bryan said.

"I totally understand, brother, but he knows the brewery connection at the very least," Riley said. "We have no reason to believe that he has any idea where any of the owners live, though. He asked the bartender on duty if he was one of the sloths. When the guy told him no, he asked if any of them were there tonight. The bartender simply told him that they all had other obligations tonight, but he would be glad to help with whatever he could. The guy didn't really have much to say after that. Like I said, he hung around for a while, maybe hoping to see something or hear something, I don't know, but he didn't get any information out of anyone."

"Good, he is still just fishing then," Bryan stated.

"Yeah, and I know this won't make you any happier than it made me, but Summer tried to chat him up a little, you know. Like flirt or whatever. She said he told her he wasn't interested, he already had someone." Riley went on, "As far as we know, he isn't in a relationship, so it's possible that somewhere in his sick twisted mind, he still sees Sophie as his."

That was when Bryan noticed Sophia's door was open slightly. He was positive he had closed it when he told her goodnight. If she had just heard that conversation, it was not going to sit well with her. He tilted his head slightly and moved his eyes toward her door. Riley caught the movements and realized what Bryan was trying to tell him. He started to turn to go back down the steps. As he turned, he said, "I'll let you know if I hear anything else."

Bryan debated over whether he should just go straight to Sophia's room or if he should wait and listen to see if she really had been at the door. He heard her door close softly and heard her feet padding across the room. He knew he needed to get ahead of this situation before she let her imagination get the better of her. Just because the guy knew that her brother was one of the owners of the pub it didn't mean that he had any idea where Sophia was or where any of the owners lived. He really did seem like a guy who had very little intelligence and very little skill. It wouldn't take much for someone to know that Pete was part owner of the brewery. Hell, it was one of the most popular microbreweries in the area. It had been in the paper several times. The owners weren't exactly secrets.

Bryan walked down the hall the few steps it took for him to get to Sophia's door and knocked softly. The others were all settling in for the night; he didn't need to draw added attention to what was going on by alerting everyone. He didn't get a response, so he opened the door slowly while knocking again softly. The room was mostly dark, except for the light of the moon coming in the window. But he could make out the shape of Sophia sitting on her bed with her knees drawn to her chest gently rocking back and forth. He walked over and sat on the edge of the bed and put a hand out to touch her shoulder. She didn't stop rocking, and she didn't make a sound.

Sophie had heard Bryan knock on her door, and she had heard him open it and walk in. She had felt him sit on the edge of her bed touching her shoulder. That didn't mean that she could unfreeze her body and say or do anything about it. She felt numb. What had she ever done to make Larry so completely obsessed with her? She hadn't been young and naïve when she had met him. He had just come across as something that he wasn't, and by the time she realized that, she'd felt trapped. He had moved her to Oregon, away from everyone she knew and loved, most likely trying to make her more dependent and committed to him. She didn't know how long she sat there just going over and over the thoughts in her head. It might have been minutes; it might have been an hour. But, eventually, she became aware of Bryan again. Still sitting there, still with a hand on her arm, trying to lend some level of comfort. It registered in her head that he had been speaking softly to her, she hadn't really been aware of the words, just the slow deep timbre of his voice trying to reassure her that he was there and he wouldn't let anything happen to her.

Sophia looked up at him, and Bryan could see the total confusion and fear in her eyes. He wasn't really sure why he did it, but he leaned over and lifted Sophia into his arms. He sat up on the bed with his back against the headboard and sat Sophia across his lap. Never in his life had he seen a woman so lost and confused. The Dominant part of him just wanted to hold her until her world was all right again. He wasn't really conscious of his movements, but he was stroking her hair and saying things like "Hush little one, it will be okay" and "It's okay, Sophia, I've got you, I'm right here."

Sophie started to feel warm again, not frozen in terror and numb. She started to hear and understand just what Bryan was saying and how he was saying it. She was pretty sure that he was a Dominant. And oh, could she use a Dominant in her life at least for one night to help her forget everything that was going on in her world. She had to at least try to get him to give her this one night. She turned toward him and asked, "Would you please help me take my mind off of all of this?"

Bryan heard her question and he was pretty sure he knew what she was asking of him. He just didn't think it was a good idea to give it to her under the circumstances. First, she was the client, and second, she probably had no idea just what she was asking and just who he really was. "No, Sophia, that's not a good idea. You're my client, and we are very different people." How did he explain it to her without hurting her further? His lifestyle choice wasn't one that a lot of people agreed with. He had had more than one girlfriend tell him that he was way too intense and too kinky for them to want to stay with him.

"Why, because you think I don't know that you're a Dominant? I don't know about the lifestyle?" Sophie was becoming more and more agitated by the moment. "I was openly involved in the lifestyle before I met him. In fact, the fact that he came across as a Dominant was why I was drawn to him. I found out he was just a controlling abusive asshole, but I enjoyed the lifestyle a lot before him." She stood to her feet beside the bed. "Floggers? Love them. Canes? One of my favorites. Edge play makes me melt." She was adamant about wanting him to know just who she had been.

Bryan stood beside her. He did not touch her; that would be tantamount to agreeing to her crazy request. "No, Sophia, this is not a good idea. You think you want this now, because of what you heard earlier. You're scared, and you think that if you get dominated you can forget for a while. I won't be a part of that."

Sophie figured there was only one way to try to get him to understand. She removed her tank top and shimmied out of the little shorts she had been wearing and went gracefully to her knees. She spread her legs far apart so that she knew he could see her pussy, and she placed her hands palm up on her thighs. She kept her head bowed in a submissive pose but made sure it was loud enough for him to hear when she said. "Please, Sir, help me float, help me forget. Please, Sir, use me in the way that you see fit."

As soon as Bryan heard those words, he knew he was probably damning himself to hell for all eternity, but he couldn't help but give in to her oh so sweet and submissive request. She needed to forget even briefly the abuse she had suffered with a man who was domineering and not dominant. And she needed to do it with someone she felt she could trust. He muttered, "Oh, hell." And then he leaned over to tilt her face up to him with a hand under her chin. "Yes, little one, I'll take care of you for tonight."

Chapter Three

Sophie tilted her head a bit so that she could sort of rub up against his hand like a kitten would do. She closed her eyes and let herself trust that he would do what he had said: he would take care of her.

Bryan sat on the side of the bed and looked Sophia in the eyes. "Your request is going to be difficult to meet under these circumstances, but I promise you that I will help you as much as the limitations allow. I can't really use any implements of pain. Normally, I would not have an issue with pulling out my belt to give you a spanking. But I don't think your brother would be okay with hearing that coming down the hall. I don't have my kit here, so we are limited as to what we have to use. But if you promise to listen and obey, I do think we can get you to float."

Sophia started to speak, but Bryan interrupted her. "I have already realized that you can be an incredible brat, Sophia." When she started to speak again, he put one hand up to pause her. "That's not a bad thing. I love to spar with a brat, on most occasions. However, this is not a place where that is possible. If we were in private and you wanted to brat off, I would take great joy in being the one to curb your smart mouth. But in this house, we can't do that; we have to be very careful about what noise we make. I don't think your brother or his friends would take very well to hearing me beat your ass with my belt or even with my hand for that matter." He did not miss the flare of heat that passed across her face at that statement. Too bad he couldn't test that theory.

"If you want this, you need to be obedient. I am sure I can improvise for a gag, blindfold, and even mild bondage with things I am sure I can find in the room or in your suitcase, but I can't do impact play. You said you enjoyed edge play, so we can experiment with that. But it is of utmost importance that if you really want to be able to fly, you remember that if you brat off just to get a spanking, you will be highly disappointed." At her nod, he continued, "Good, then we will see just how obedient you can be." He stood and walked across the room to where her things had been unpacked from her suitcase. He found a scarf that would make a fairly decent gag and another that would make a passable blindfold. The curtains actually had rope-like tie backs, so those would do for a form of bondage. But, really, it was far more about the mental aspects of it than it was the actual implements. He walked back to the chair in the corner. Before sitting down, he removed the gun that had been at the center of his back tucked into his waistband. He placed it on the small table. He then removed his jacket and took off the shoulder holster and placed that gun on the table too. He noticed that although Sophia was still in her position on the floor, she had shifted enough to be able to watch what he was doing. That was fine; he wanted her to be aware of the guns so that there was no concern with her safety. He sat in the chair and removed the gun and his ankle holster. Then he looked Sophia in the eyes. "Okay, we use the traffic light system. You know what that is, right?" If she said no, he was going to realize that she was trying to bullshit him, and she knew nothing about the lifestyle. But she nodded her agreement.

"Normally, I do like a submissive that is quiet and knows her place; however, since this is our first time together and we are using modified types of play, I am allowing you to speak when you need to. If something feels off, say so, and if anything frightens you, say red." He was staring her right in the eyes; he could see that she was listening intently. He could also see that just talking about this was starting to make her sink deeper into her submission. Just the sound of his voice was making her eyelids droop a little lower. "If you agree to be open and honest with me in everything I ask you and let me know if anything triggers a bad memory, we can begin." At her nod, he said, "I need to hear you, little one."

"Yes, Sir. I am ready to begin," Sophie said. Oh God, was she ever ready to begin. She was way past ready to begin. She was years beyond being ready to begin. To begin her life again, to begin submitting when she chose to. She knew she would never be a slave or whatever one wanted to call the women who submitted twenty-four hours a day, but in the bedroom and even beyond the bedroom at times, it fulfilled something in her to be able to give over control to a dominant man. Of course, she still had her obstinate side. She didn't often just submit without questions or a challenge here and there. But she had learned that with the right Dominant, that was all a part of the relationship. With a man who loved the bratty side and knew how to give it enough rein to be a challenge, but not enough to let her really get away with anything it could be an amazing combination. She was tired of letting Larry take that away from her. She had no delusions that she and Bryan would be a couple. She was going back to Colorado in a few days. But if he could give her this tonight, and maybe even for the next few days, it would hopefully release something in her that had felt broken for oh so long. She realized that he was patiently waiting for her to meet his eyes again before giving her a command. When she met his eyes, she felt the connection she had only ever felt when she had been willing to let go and submit.

"Very good, little one," Bryan said with that oh so deep and commanding voice. "Now, crawl to me and remove my shoes and socks."

Sophie's mind immediately thought of a smart mouth comment to respond to that command with. After all, they didn't call her a smart mouth masochist for nothing. But she also realized his statement earlier was very true. She usually just mouthed off to get a spanking or some other punishment which would be very hard to do in the current situation. She would just have to trust that he would know how to take her where she needed to go without the use of a belt or paddle. During that little struggle in her head to keep quiet, Sophie had crawled to his feet. She sat in her submissive pose again and began untying his shoes. He had worn a dress outfit, most likely the professional businessman's attire. She would bet he was much more casual when he wasn't on duty. Although, admittedly, the jacket and looser pants had made it far easier to hide all of those guns. When she had his first shoe untied, he lifted his foot so that she could remove the shoe and sock. She set them aside to do his other foot. When she had both of them off, he told her, "Now, fold my socks neatly together and place them on top of my shoes. Set all of it under the edge of the table."

How did this man know her so well already? One of the things that had always been a huge draw for her was when the Dominant gave very specific instructions on how to carry out a task. Bryan instructed her to crawl back to the side of the bed and remain in the crawling position while facing the bed. Sophie could hear him moving around, most likely disposing of his jacket and maybe some of his other clothing too. She sensed rather than heard him approach her. She had to say that his military training had done a great job of teaching him how to move with little to no sound. He knelt on one knee beside her and ran one finger slowly through her soaking wet slit. "Lovely, little one. I will of course need you to communicate with me, but this also tells me so very many things about you. What we have done so far has gotten you aroused. That's a very good thing."

"Thank you, Sir," she said softly.

"I need to know some things from you before we continue, Sophia," he stated very matter-of-factly. "Do you have any limits that might come up while we are here? I don't need to know every limit you have, because some things obviously aren't in play while we are here together. For example, I don't need to know if you are against blood play. Even if it was something I did, I wouldn't do it here. I will also tell you that I have a hard limit against true degradation and true humiliation. For example, I will make you crawl, I may even make you exhibit yourself to me when it's safe to do so, but I will not call you names like whore. I will not ever make you embarrass yourself in front of others. Therefore, if you are to trust me, if I tell you to lift your skirt, for example, you would do so, knowing that I would not ask if I did not know that there was no one else who would see it. Is that understood?"

"Yes, Sir," Sophie agreed.

"Good. Now, any hard limits beyond what I just mentioned?" Bryan asked.

"No, Sir."

"And I need to know if you are agreeable to sexual intercourse being a part of our play. I will admit that it would be hard for me to do, but I can take care of you without going that far," Bryan stated.

Just hearing him talk about sex made her even more wet. "Yes, Sir, I am fine with that. I am hoping for it actually." She could only imagine what his body would look like when she could see him. When they had picked her up at the airport, she had seen evidence of some tattoos, and it was very obvious that he was very muscular, but she was dying to see what he looked like without all of those clothes on.

"Good. Any form of sexual intercourse, or are there limits?" he asked.

Oh, God, if he was asking that, it meant that he was considering oral and anal as possibilities too. That would be just too amazing to have found someone who loved both as much as she did. "Yes, Sir, I am fine with any type. Admittedly, I love all three areas of penetration." She was trying to say it without sounding too slutty or overly anxious.

"Good. Now, as far as safe sex. I am reasonably certain you haven't had sex in quite a while. It's been a bit for me also, and I have had a physical and was tested. I am clean, but I still need to know what all you are comfortable with. I generally keep one condom in my wallet just in case, but since I was coming here for what I had mistakenly thought to be simply a body guarding job, I didn't bring more. It would be a little awkward at this point for me to text Riley or Trevor to ask if they have any, and again, I am pretty sure your brother and Walt would both string me up if I were to ask one of them."

"I understand, Sir." Sophie was kind of taken back by his openness and willingness to just put all that out there, but on the other hand, it wasn't like they were dating and had all the time in the world to work out the details. They had tonight, and hopefully the next couple of days if he would agree to that, to see how much exploring they could do. "I am on birth control, but still prefer the added protection of a condom if at all possible to prevent pregnancy. As far as things that don't cause pregnancy, I am fine with not using a condom if you know you are clean." Geez, this sounded like a negotiation that her brother or father would do in court. She just wanted to move on and get to the good stuff already.

"Great, and I saw that look, Sophia. I know this isn't the fun part of the night, but these things do need to be discussed, even if you don't want to. For that small eye roll that you just gave me, your punishment is to crawl up onto the bed and spread your legs for me. Once you are in position, you will begin to masturbate, but you are not allowed to orgasm. You will continue to masturbate while I recite the alphabet," Bryan stated.

That shouldn't be so hard; she could masturbate slowly. She didn't have to give it her best effort and hopefully he would say the alphabet at a reasonable pace. "Yes, Sir," she agreed and got into her position on the bed.

"Oh, and Sophia, no half-hearted effort on this. I noticed the vibrator in your belongings, and if I need to, I will include that in your masturbation efforts."

Okay, so apparently, this man was at least part sadist. It was confirmed when he nodded for her to start and said "A," then proceeded to hum a song. Then he said "B" and started to whistle that same song. This man was going to drive her insane. By the time he got to C, she had realized that she really needed to go slow because if she didn't, she was going to orgasm way too fast. She tried to make her fingers move at a pace that he would think she was giving her best effort, but she didn't actually have to touch her sensitive clit on every swipe. She could spend time on the edges a little, make it seem like that was just part of how she liked it.

After he said "C," Bryan kept watching Sophia intently. This time, he began to sing the song he had been using to time his letters. He knew from lots of experience that the song took just under two minutes to get through fully if you sang it at the proper military pace. "From the halls of Montezuma to the shores of Tripoli, we fight our country's battles in the air, on land, and sea." He could tell that Sophia had changed the way she was moving her fingers, no doubt trying to take attention off of the areas that would set her off the fastest. He would let it slide for now. He had all night and he could sing the Marine Hymn as many times as he needed to for him to win this war of wills.

By the time the infernal man got to H, Sophia was really struggling. No matter how hard she tried, she would end up touching her most sensitive flesh. She had been masturbating for years, and she knew how to make it feel good. What her mind couldn't wrap itself around was doing it but trying to not make it feel so good. She knew she wouldn't make it to the end of the alphabet; she might as well surrender now so that she could finally have that sweet release. "May I please come, Sir?"

"What was that, Sophia?" Bryan asked, pausing his song. "Are you giving in on me? You want this done so quickly?" He knew he was taunting her. He was totally ready to let her have her orgasm; he was more than ready to move on to other things. Watching her finger herself hadn't exactly been like a cold shower to his libido. But he wouldn't look very dominant if he gave in that easily. He walked to the side of the bed and leaned over her. "You want this done, Sophia? You want that release?"

"Oh, yes, Sir, please?" Sophia panted.

"You do remember where we are, Sophia," Bryan stated. "If and when I allow you to orgasm, you have to do so very quietly, no screaming out. We don't need the whole house knowing that you've had an orgasm." That was definitely a mind fuck because in about sixty seconds he was going to give her a mind-blowing orgasm that she would not be expecting. Fortunately, he had picked up her soft tank top from the floor and had it poised and ready for his devious plan.

"Yes, Sir, I remember," Sophie said. Why was he prolonging this? She needed this orgasm already or she was going to end up screaming out of frustration. That would be a really bad thing in the current situation.

"Good girl. Then yes, Sophia, you may come for me." And with that, he pinched and twisted her nipple quite hard. She began an orgasm that was more intense than she ever had before in her life. He was prepared for the scream that proceeded to come out of her mouth. He simply placed her shirt and his hand over her mouth and it very adequately quelled the volume of her sounds. Bryan had no doubt that if they were in a home that was of a lesser quality building material wise, the sound might have been slightly audible through the walls. But this house was one of the more elite types with lots of insulation and quality materials. Besides, his was the room right next door, and she had definitely not been loud enough for it to travel down the hall.

"Naughty, naughty Sophia. If I hadn't been prepared, Trevor would have heard you downstairs," he taunted. He was sure that she wouldn't actually feel any shame over her actions, but it was all a part of the mental game they were playing. "Now, if you want this to continue, you must learn to be more subdued. Is that understood?"

Sophia nodded silently. Her eyes were pleading with him to please continue.

"Very good. You have no objections to being gagged, do you, Sophia?" he asked. He always used the submissive's name as much as possible when he was playing; it kept them more completely focused on him. At her head shake, he removed the T-shirt from her mouth and placed the scarf he had found around her like a gag. "Now we will begin our next adventure." He removed the tie rope from the curtain and used it to secure her arms to the headboard. He tied them in a manner that her circulation wasn't cut off, but she wasn't able to move her arms much at all.

Bryan walked over to where her vibrator lay in her suitcase. He turned it on to a low speed and placed it against her soaking wet slit. He didn't place it directly on her clit; this was all about strategy, after all. He found the panties she had removed earlier and helped her get into them. They would hold the vibrator right where it needed to be. He knew that the slow speed of the toy wasn't likely to take her to orgasm of its own accord, but he had plans for that. He leaned closer to her face and said, "Now, Sophia, you may move in any manner necessary, but I want you to bring yourself to orgasm two times. You can take however long you need to, but keep in mind that the best is yet to come, and that can't happen until you complete your task." He saw Sophia's eyes go wide, and she started to shake her head slightly. "Oh, Sophia, you aren't going to disappoint me now, are you? I'm sure you have more in you."

Sophie knew that she was very multiple when it came to orgasms; she just wasn't sure that she could achieve it with the vibrator placed more outside than directly against her inner flesh. If she had the use of her hands, it would be an easy thing. But that wouldn't be the way to keep her mind focused on this game they were playing.

Bryan stood at the foot of the bed and watched as Sophia did her best to move her hips and wiggle to try to get the vibrations where she wanted them. It was very enticing to watch her gyrations; the movements were like the most erotic of dirty dances. Bryan knew he wasn't going to be able to wait long before he got some relief of his own. He removed his shirt and did not miss the heated flare across Sophia's face when she got her first look at his upper torso.

Sophie was trying really hard to concentrate on her movements; she needed to get those two orgasms over with so that they could move on. She was desperately hoping that moving on meant that Bryan was going to fuck her long and hard. It had been so long. She had kind of thought that she had resolved herself to the fact that sex wasn't really all that big of a deal. She hadn't had any real sex in several years, and even then, Larry hadn't been the best lover in the world. Apparently all it took for her libido to not only restart but to go to full speed in seconds was a sexy dominant bodyguard. When he took his shirt off, she saw what she had been pretty sure would be true. He was an absolute work of art. His muscles looked like they were carved from granite. She had seen the hints of tattoos, but without his shirt, she could see the full effect. He had a tribal type design that covered his entire right shoulder and bicep area. She could see that it must continue onto his back the way it arced over his shoulder blade. Just seeing the man half naked drew her focus away briefly, but it quickly sparked her need to get back to the task of making herself come. She looked from his amazing torso back up to his eyes. She could see the fire in them. There was no doubt, that what she was doing was thoroughly arousing him. She glanced down and her thoughts were confirmed by the large bulge in his jeans. She locked eyes with him and sped up her efforts to get her release. When she finally got there, she clamped her mouth down on the scarf in her mouth and let out a long whimper, but she did not cry out. She kept her sounds low enough there was no way anyone would have heard them. When the fog cleared a little, Bryan had moved from the foot of the bed to the side of it.

He leaned over and stroked Sophia's cheek gently. "Good girl, Sophia," he praised. "That was much quieter. I knew you could do this for me. You deserve a reward, little one. Would you like a reward?" Hell, who was he kidding? It wasn't as much a reward for her as it was for him. He was going to explode if he didn't get some relief soon. But he wasn't going to tell her that; it had to seem like she was being rewarded for her efforts to remain quiet. At her fervent nodding, he unbuttoned his pants and lowered them enough to free his cock from the confining space. Sophia's eyes heated even more as she watched him. "Turn your head this way, Sophia. I want my cock in that bratty mouth of yours."

He untied the scarf as she rolled her head in his direction. She opened her mouth and eagerly leaned toward him to be able to take him more deeply. He felt that warm space close around him and knew that this couldn't last long. This one would go quickly for him, but he knew he would better be able to take care of both of them if he got this first orgasm. Then he could focus on taking more time for the rest of their encounter. He started pumping himself slowly into her mouth so that she had time to get used to the feel of him and he could feel the moisture all around his heated flesh. He reached one hand down and removed the vibrator. He replaced it quickly with his fingers, stroking her gently at first, but as his thrusts into her mouth got quicker, so did the stroking of his fingers. He was on the verge of orgasm, and he was pretty sure that she was too. He thrust his fingers inside of her and kept pace with his hips, forcing himself into her mouth, not that she seemed reluctant in any way.

This time when Sophie orgasmed, she made a noise that would have woken the whole house if it hadn't been muffled by the large cock that was currently shooting hot semen deep inside her mouth. She swallowed it all and used her tongue to clean all of it up as well as she could from the odd angle of being tied to the bed. Bryan got up from the bed far too quickly as far as Sophie was concerned. She barely had time to register that in her brain, though, because she was being lifted at the hips and soon found herself face down on the bed.

"On your knees, Sophia. I want that gorgeous ass of yours in the air," Bryan commanded. He placed his hands on her hips in case she struggled to get up. Without the use of her hands, it might prove difficult for some women. But not for Sophia. She was obviously very nimble and in shape because she positioned herself quickly. He knew that he couldn't cause any slapping sounds, but that didn't mean he couldn't pinch her flesh or bite it, for that matter. When she was settled into her position, he leaned over and bit her flesh, then quickly soothed the pain with softer licks. He wasn't sure what her pain tolerance level was. So he would start with small bites and lots of soothing and go from there based on her responses. Judging on her moaning and wiggling, she wasn't minding this mild pain at all. He deepened the bite and added suction. She would definitely have marks on her, but hopefully she wouldn't be showing her gorgeous body to anyone but him for the next few days.

"These marks are going to look wonderful on you, Sophia. My marks on your body. I will enjoy seeing them if you give me a chance to spend more time with you this weekend."

"Yes, Sir," Sophia said. Her voice was definitely a sure sign that she was sort of floaty. "I want that too, please."

So she was okay with his plan to continue this brief interlude. That was good to know. He continued to bite and nip at her for a few more minutes before he could tell that she was definitely hitting a level of what most people referred to as subspace. That place where you aren't fully aware of the world around you. It's all about your mind sort of leaving your body and existing in a dream-like state. He stepped away long enough to get the condom from the pants he had discarded after his blow job. Her moans sounded kind of like a protest, but it was half-hearted at best. He put it on and got back behind her. He slowly eased himself inside her. She said it had been a while for her. If his guess was correct, she most likely hadn't been with anyone since she had gotten away from her abuser. It was hard for a woman to know who she could trust after a situation like that. He was sure that her trusting him was based mostly on the fact that her brother trusted him with her life. It wouldn't be a stretch for her to feel safe with him sexually if she knew he was a trustworthy person in general. He would make absolutely certain that he did nothing to betray that trust. Which meant he needed to get more condoms in case this continued. He brought his mind back to what he was doing. It wasn't that his mind wasn't focused on her as much as it was focused on what he could do with her now and over the next few days. He only had until Monday, and it was already late Thursday night, or hell, it may even be early Friday morning by now. That wasn't much time, but it was all they had.

After entering her slowly and fully, he kept still for a few moments to allow her body to adjust to his size. Then he started a slow rhythm. He could see the color starting to change where he had bitten her or given her hickeys. She would bruise beautifully if he ever had the chance to use a belt or a flogger on her. He had to remind himself that wasn't very likely to happen, not with the short time frame and the fact that they were basically surrounded by her family and the guys who had grown up with her. They weren't likely to be able to step away for a few hours of uninterrupted play in the small dungeon area of his home.

He picked up the pace until he could hear the soft sound of his skin slapping against hers. He didn't dare go any faster or harder for fear of someone hearing something down the hall. That was okay, though; they were both definitely getting close to their release. He wanted to make sure that she went over that edge first, though, so he took his thumb and pressed firmly into the darkest of the bruises starting to form on her bottom. That made her begin to moan even more. Her face was mostly buried in the pillow, and she wasn't being loud, just a low moan deep in her throat. He was getting so close himself that he needed to push her further. He reached down between them and firmly pinched her clit. As he had suspected, that quickly brought on a very hard and deep orgasm, which in turn sent him over that edge. As they both rode that high for a few brief moments, he thought again how much he would love to have more than just a few days with her to explore her submissive side. She seemed to be in alignment with most of the things he enjoyed in his BDSM activities. He wasn't looking for anything serious, but if two people had so much in common with what they enjoyed in the D/s area, it was always nice to have time to explore it and get both of their needs met for a while.

Bryan realized that Sophia had sort of collapsed and he had collapsed on top of her. He moved so his weight was off of her but held her close. This was their first time together, and some submissive people crashed really hard after they had been floating. He wanted to make sure that she was back to herself fully and was aware of her surroundings before he went back down the hall. He freed her hands and tossed the curtain tie aside.

Sophie slowly became aware of where she was. She knew she was in a bed at Walt and Rayne's home. Her brother and his wife were just down the hall, and she was in bed with a man who had just given her something she hadn't had in more than four years. He had taken her to a place that she loved to go. She had been able to reach what some called subspace because this man knew what he was doing, and she knew she could trust him. She had been able to let herself go.

"Sophia, are you okay? Talk to me. Did I hurt you?" Bryan asked with concern in his voice.

Sophie became more and more aware and realized that she was crying. It had come from the release and the relief that there was someone out there that understood her and thought she was okay. Larry had told her so many times that she was twisted and perverted to want the things she wanted. Oh, he hadn't had a problem with hitting her in an abusive way, but he thought it was wrong of her to want it in an erotic way. The fact that he was concerned that he had done something wrong and the fact that he was asking if she was okay had been so foreign to her for such a long time. It was making her cry all the more. She could see the concern on Bryan's face, but she couldn't speak. She had to find a way to show him that it was okay. She reached down and took his hand, brought it to her lips, and kissed it. She caressed her cheek against it. It was something she had seen years ago. A submissive who had been given a good scene by a Dominant would kiss the hand that had doled out the pain as a symbol of thanking it for what it had given her. She had to hope that he understood.

Bryan felt the light kiss and the caress on his hand. He was pretty sure that was her way of saying that she had enjoyed it, but he had to be sure. "So you are okay, just emotional?" he asked. When she nodded, he lay back and drew her more tightly to himself. "I would give anything for you to have never had to experience whatever that lowlife did to you, but I promise you, he will never get near you on my watch." He held her like that for a long time until her crying stopped and her breathing got heavier. She wasn't asleep yet, but she was close. He kissed the top of her head and said, "I should probably head back to my room so no one wonders where I am. That is if you are sure you are okay, Sophia."

"Mm-hmm, thank you, Sir," Sophia said softly.

With that, Bryan got his pants back on, replaced the curtain tie, and left the room to walk quietly down the hall. Shortly after he got to his room, he got a text from Riley.

You sure this is a good idea?
No, but it's pretty much a done deal now.

No, he wasn't sure this was a good idea at all. In fact, he was pretty sure it was a really bad idea, but there was just something about Sophia that connected to something inside him. He couldn't explain it, but that didn't mean it wasn't there.

Chapter Four

Sophie woke up from the best night's sleep she'd had in years. It was amazing what a few orgasms and a trip to subspace could do for a girl. She realized that what had woken her up was a knock on her door. She heard Pete's voice. "Hey Sophie, you awake. You girls need to leave for the spa in about an hour. I thought you might want to eat."

"Yeah, I'll be down in a few," she responded. Thankfully her brother had not stuck his head in the door or he would have gotten an eyeful. She had fallen so deeply asleep after her encounter with Bryan that she was lying there totally naked with not a cover or a sheet over her. She heard Pete walk away and made a dash to the bathroom. She would have to have a quick shower. Fortunately, the spa day would take care of her hair and all that. It was her understanding that today was for pampering and haircut or color, mani-pedi and whatever else. The actual hair style and makeup and all that would be done the following day right before the reception. She rinsed herself off as quickly as she could, put her hair into a messy bun, and threw on the outfit she had planned for the day. It was a simple slacks and blouse outfit. Easy and comfortable. She went downstairs and found everyone hanging out around the kitchen and breakfast bar area. There was a large spread of everything from omelets to yogurt to fruit. She grabbed a yogurt and a plate of fruit. She knew she would be served a large meal at tonight's family dinner, and there was sure to be a lot of food tomorrow at the party. Autumn's family was Hispanic, and they rarely had a party without lots of food. She needed to pace herself or she would gain five pounds over the course of the weekend. Although, if Bryan did what he implied, she might also be getting some decent exercise. She was just sitting at a stool when he walked up to her. He had a plate of eggs and bacon. It wasn't piled as high as she would assume a man his size would have, but it was a decent portion of food. He placed the plate in front of her. She looked at him quite puzzled.

He just raised his eyebrows before leaning in a little so no one else could hear. "Eat this, Sophia, or you will have to abstain from the wine and champagne that I assume will be flowing at the spa. I will not have you getting sick or drunk this weekend. I need you at the top of your game so I can be at the top of mine." He really didn't sound like what he suggested was optional.

Sophia just glared at him and said, "I can't eat all that!"

"You can, and you will, or no alcohol for you. A bit of yogurt and fruit isn't enough to have in your stomach when drinking." He gave her a look that told her she was better off trying to eat as much as she could at least. He leaned in to add, "Oh, and Sophia, no waxing unless you are calling 'red' on any more fun this weekend."

How did this man know so much about a woman's grooming habits? She just looked at him and when he returned her glare, she backed down and started eating the eggs he had placed in front of her.

Pete walked over and said, "This looks pretty intense. What's going on?"

"I was just talking to Sophia about how we are going to sell this to your parents. If I am going to be able to guard her adequately, she basically needs to be on my arm anytime she isn't in a secured establishment. I know you don't want your parents knowing the real reason for my presence, so we need to have something to tell them that won't cause any suspicion. Any ideas?" he asked, turning his attention to Pete.

They were both looking at each other at a loss for what to use as a cover story. So Sophie spoke up. "I think it's easy. We don't have to tell them that we know Larry has been around. They know that I moved halfway across the country to avoid him. We just say that I asked Rayne or Autumn to hook me up with a hot guy that would scare Larry away if he did try to show up." She made it sound so simple, basically because it was. "We tell them that I am acting like Bryan is my boyfriend so that word will get out that I am taken."

The two men looked at each other and debated her idea. "It's plausible. They would believe that she was just being cautious. It's not like they don't know that him showing up at any point could be a possibility," Pete said, mostly to Bryan.

"It would also lend credibility to her acting like I am her guy," Bryan responded, again, to Pete, not her.

"Am I chopped liver here?" Sophie asked. "It's my idea and it's a damn good one. You just both need to realize it." They looked at her and then back at each other and finally agreed that it should work. Sophie just went back to eating her eggs and bacon. She was going to need the fortification of food so that she could get the fortification of alcohol later. It wasn't that she didn't appreciate the lengths that her brother had gone to, but she did have a brain in her head. Men could be such a pain sometimes.

When they arrived at the spa, Sophie saw Riley across the street. To anyone who didn't know him, it would seem like he was working on something on his motorcycle. She didn't know where Trevor was, but she was sure he was somewhere nearby, most likely in his truck or a local building monitoring security cameras in the area on his computer. In order to not make it look odd to Sophie's mother, the guys had ridden along with their ladies. The limo they had rented for the weekends' festivities was as large as a small house. As each guy got out of the car, he turned to put out a hand and help his partner out. Sophie's mother was waiting at the curb. They had been texting with hereach other all morning and she knew her mom was so happy to have her home even if it was just for a brief visit. She had to do her best to keep any drama away from her mother. She let Bryan help her out of the car the same way the other guys had with their ladies. He leaned in and gave her a brief kiss on the cheek, more for the opportunity to talk to her than to give her an actual kiss. "Trust my brothers and me, Sophia. You may not see us, but we are here, and nothing will happen to you," he assured her. "And I meant what I said about the wax."

Sophie rolled her eyes and walked into the embrace her mother was offering her. "Who is that, Sophie?" her mother asked quietly as they embraced. Far be it from her mother to make a scene or say anything loud enough that Bryan would hear her.

"Let's just get inside and I will explain, Mom," Sophie said. She didn't want to seem panicked, but she did not want to stand out on the open sidewalk any longer than she needed to. She didn't believe that Larry would be aiming a sniper rifle at her or something like that; she just didn't want to be on a public street any longer than necessary. The more exposed she made herself, the more likely it was that Larry might see her, or someone would tell him that she was in town.

When they got inside, Sophie stepped aside with her mother. "His name is Bryan," she explained. "I asked Pete if Rayne or Skye knew of any hot guys that could be my date for the weekend. I just thought it might be a good idea if I looked 'taken' in case anyone who knows Larry is still hanging around town." At the mention of Larry's name, her mother had tensed up. Sophie tried to reassure her by saying, "It's not that he's a threat, I just wanted it to look like I'm taken just in case he hears any rumors about the wedding." Sophie hated lying to her mother. She knew Larry was a threat, but it would do none of them any good for her mom to worry about it. Sophie just had to believe that Bryan and his brothers would keep Larry far away from her for the rest of her visit. It had freaked her out a little when she heard he had been at the brewery the night before, because that solidified the fact that he was still looking for her for some reason, but she didn't think he would ever get close enough to try to take her.

The owner of the spa greeted them and introduced the ladies that would be taking care of them for the day. Each was assigned according to what services they were planning to have. That little brat voice inside of Sophie almost won out; she was tempted for all of two seconds to get a Brazilian, but that would ruin her fun for twenty-four hours, and she only had a little over forty-eight hours left of her visit. She didn't want to make herself untouchable to Bryan any more than he seemed to want her to be untouchable. She had enjoyed her night last night. She hadn't been able to just let go like that in years. No, there was no way that she was going to spoil that fun, but she could have a different kind of fun. She decided to go for the wax, just on her legs. She could taunt Bryan with that for a bit, maybe get him to give her a little taste of punishment. Yes, a wax it should be, and she also decided on some highlights for her hair. She didn't want a full color change, but some accents would be great. She really hadn't done anything like this since she had gotten away from Larry. She hadn't wanted to draw any attention to herself. She didn't wear makeup; she kept her look simple and plain. It was time for that to change. At least for a few days, she could pamper herself and look pretty.

After dropping the ladies off, all of the guys except Bryan had headed to the brewery for a guys' day. Bryan headed to Trevor's truck, where he had his base of operations set up. He was around the corner watching feeds from security cameras in the block around the spa.

He climbed into the truck and saud "Tell me what you've got."

Trevor never looked up from his computer as he stated, "Nothing on the security cameras. Unless this guy is much better at spying than I think he is, I don't think he would know where the ladies are. He has shown up on the feed at the parents' house, so he's most likely assuming that's where she would be. I ran a check. He doesn't own a gun or have a gun permit, at least not a legally obtained gun. We both know that doesn't stop someone who wants one bad enough. Do you think you could convince her to wear Kevlar?"

"Uh, no," Bryan stated. "I've seen the dresses she's wearing both tonight and tomorrow, and I think a bulletproof vest would be an accessory she wouldn't agree to."

"I don't know, brother, from what I hear, you definitely have an 'in' with the girl," Trevor said, laughing. "You could probably talk her into it."

Damn Riley and his super hearing. They all had it really, though. "Yeah, okay, we had some fun. It's nothing more than two people gaining a little relief from each other. She overheard what happened at the brewery last night and it freaked her out a little. So I went in there to try to calm her down. She just needed to fly a little, so I obliged."

"Fly a little?" Trevor said, glancing up very briefly. "She's a sub?"

"More like a SAM, but yeah," Bryan continued. "I think before this guy came into her life she was into the lifestyle. She wouldn't be the first woman that mistook an overbearing domineering man for a Dominant and didn't see the difference until it was too late."

"That's true," Trevor agreed. "Just be careful, man. She's only here for a few days, and I don't think we can afford to piss off the brewery guys. They are a great reference for future jobs. Not to mention the fact that if we ever need a lawyer we're pretty much set."

Bryan knew he was mostly joking about needing legal representation, but in their line of work, it wasn't completely unheard of to face some legal issues at some point.

A few hours later, the limo pulled back up in front of the spa, and the guys got back out. Bryan had changed into the suit he was wearing to the party. The ladies had changed while they were here so the limo could take them directly to the country club. Bryan wasn't really worried about tonight. They would be inside in a private room at the club. It was tomorrow that was the logistical nightmare. That was outdoors on a fairly open lawn that had a deep row of trees surrounding it. At some point, further back, there was a fence to keep people from just wandering onto the property, but it would be easy to climb over if someone actually wanted to be there. Hell, they could only do so much about watching who came in and out of the parking lot. He could pull right up to the front door. He wasn't a member, so he wouldn't be allowed in, but he could get on to the property easy enough.

Bryan was distracted from his thoughts when Sophia walked out the door. She had definitely used the spa day to change up her appearance. She had highlighted her hair so that the dark mahogany had strands that looked almost a deep blond. Her face had been beautiful with no makeup, but what she was wearing was subtle but added color and definition to her high cheekbones and made her eyes stand out. The dress she was wearing was stunning on her. She had been beautiful before she had walked into the spa, but she was a goddess now.

Sophie hadn't missed the flare in Bryan's eyes as he had taken in her appearance. So apparently she had done exactly what she had hoped to do. Now to just set her other little plan in motion. When the limo pulled away from the curb, she said, "Wasn't that so relaxing, ladies? I mean, the waxing isn't really all that fun, but the result is so worth it, am I right?" She did not miss the glare that came her way from the man across the seat from her. He had always insisted on being closest to the door so he was the first one out to assess any danger or threat.

The other ladies made comments about their day, but Sophie didn't really hear them; she was too busy waging a war of wills silently with her gorgeous bodyguard. Oh, this was going to be a fun evening for sure.

Chapter Five

As they got out of the limo at the base of the steps of the entry to the country club, Bryan was the first one out as usual. He was on extra high alert. Trevor and Riley were already inside performing their catering duties, so he was on his own for this part. He had no doubt that the brewery guys would do their best to keep Larry from getting close to Sophia, but they weren't trained like his brothers were to watch for any movement in the trees or the glint of a gun. God, he hoped the guy hadn't found a way to obtain a gun. After he had looked around to make sure he didn't see anything out of the ordinary, he took Sophia by the arm and ushered her inside. He said something to the others about needing to brief Sophia on the protocols for the evening and ushered her to a small storage closet. "Did you or did you not disobey me and get waxed?" Bryan demanded.

Oh, she really did like it when a man got all dominant and controlling, in the right way. "Waxing, well, yes." She was so totally playing the dumb act for this one. "When you said no waxing, I assumed you meant my pussy, and I would never dream of disobeying a direct order. I did get my legs waxed. I assumed you would prefer them stubble free." She gave him her best *but I'm so innocent and naïve* smile.

Bryan pressed her fully up against the wall. "You like testing me, don't you, little one? You don't think I know just what a brat you can be?" He leaned closer to her ear so that his breath was warm against her neck. "But you see, Sophia, bratty girls deserve punishment. Give me your panties." When she hesitated and looked a little bewildered at his comment, he reiterated. "Now, Sophia, remove your panties and give them to me."

Sophia bent so that she could reach her panties from under her dress, then she efficiently wiggled out of them and handed them to him. He wadded them and put them into his pocket. He leaned down and placed his hand on the inside of her ankle and then ran his hand all the way up the inside of her leg as he stood. His hand brushed briefly against her pussy. "You're right, Sophia, your legs are so soft and smooth, and, your pussy is just as I remember it from last night. Good girl, Sophia."

"Can I have my panties back then, since you know I didn't disobey?" Sophia demanded.

"Oh, no, the panties weren't punishment for waxing. The panties were because you decided to challenge me in front of everyone when I couldn't do anything about it. No, Sophia, you will not be getting your panties back anytime soon. In fact, you may not get them back at all," Bryan stated. He made sure her dress was back in its proper position and then adjusted his tie and suitcoat before escorting her out the door and back to the rest of their group.

The brat part of Sophie wanted to stomp her feet and tell him he was a bully, but the rest of her knew that she was in for so much fun the next couple of days. Bryan had proven to her that he would not back down, even if they were in a semi-public setting. He was just what she had always looked for in a partner. Too bad they only had two more days and most of that would be spent with friends and family.

They were seated at the table for the groom's family. Which meant Sophie was going to spend the next couple of hours with her parents, without her panties. It also meant that her mother was going to take every opportunity possible to match make for her and Bryan. It didn't seem to occur to her mother that she lived in Colorado and Bryan lived here in Michigan. That was apparently a moot point as far as her mother was concerned.

"So, Bryan," her mother began, "what is it that you do for a living?"

"Well, my brothers and I own a motorcycle repair shop," Bryan began. Sophia's mother looked a little like most mothers did when they realized that that meant he probably also rode motorcycles. The clothing he had worn all day had covered his tats nicely, but he would bet if Mom ever saw him without a shirt, she would swear him off as a really bad match for her sweet little girl. Not that it bothered him, he wasn't looking for a relationship with Sophia—well, not more than they were able to have over the next couple of days anyway. He had definite plans for her for the time there weren't social obligations, but he would escort her to the airport Monday, wish her well, and go back to his solitary life. His focus would be what it had been for years now: family and business. Someday he would move past that place, but it wasn't today. He continued on, "We also do some private investigating work, that type of thing."

It was then that Peter Sr. jumped into the conversation. "That's right, you and your brothers are the ones who helped my firm take a serial rapist off the streets. I want to thank you for that, it meant a lot to my son and all the women you helped feel safe again." What he didn't add was that he knew that his new daughter-in-law was one of the women who could feel safer because the Lawson brothers had helped capture and prosecute the sick bastard.

Bryan just gave a brief nod of understanding. Sophia's father might know, but her mother obviously did not. "It's all in a day's work for us, Sir. We were glad to play a part in that investigation."

Sophie was putting two and two together, and she was definitely coming up with four. Bryan and his brothers had been the one to protect Autumn and bring her attacker to justice. She was finding more and more to like about this man all the time.

The dinner proceeded as Bryan would have expected any country club dinner to. Formal dinner served by men and women in traditional black slacks, white button-down shirts, and black aprons with the logo of the club on them. Trevor was nearby with a coffee and water cart to refill glasses and cups as needed.

The conversation at their table remained pretty much casual. They were seated with Walt and Rayne and Jason and Sunni. Bryan was pretty sure there was some conflict going on between the later couple. Sunni seemed more focused on Rayne, and Jason seemed more focused on Walt than they did on each other. Bryan could definitely sense the tension.

When the toasts and speeches began, Bryan felt Trevor move in closer in position to them. To most people it would look like he was just making sure he was close by so the guests could ask for a refill without having to interrupt the toasts. It didn't sit well that Riley was nowhere to be seen either. It was possible that he was just in the kitchen helping with his duties as a caterer, even though the supervisor knew he wasn't really part of the staff. He didn't like the way things were feeling, so he quietly scooted his chair closer to Sophia and put his arm around the back of her chair. When she glanced at him to see what was going on, he simply stated, "Just being cautious; relax." Sophia leaned into his chest and relaxed against him. Damn, this woman felt right pressed up against him. Her body fit into his perfectly, and the fact that she wanted to rely on him definitely did something for his ego.

It was about ten minutes later when he saw Riley again. He had obviously been doing some running or some physical exertion. He no longer looked as neat and tidy as the other servers. Riley looked towards Trevor and gave a brief shake of his head before stepping back into the hallway. When he saw Riley again, he had righted his uniform and tie and no one would be the wiser that he hadn't looked that way all along.

Something was up, and Bryan wasn't sure what it was. But he couldn't very well step away without raising the suspicion of Sophia and the brewery owners. They all knew exactly why Bryan was here, and anything out of the ordinary would most likely put them on alert.

When the festivities were winding down and some guests were leaving while others were still mingling and talking, Bryan caught Riley's eye, and Riley gave a brief head motion that signaled that he needed to convey some information. Bryan checked, and as expected, Trevor had stepped closer to Sophia so that Bryan could step away for a moment. He excused himself from their group and walked out into the hallway with Riley.

"So what's going on?" he asked as soon as they were out of earshot of the other guests and staff.

"There was someone looking in the window. I spotted him so I made my way out and around hoping to catch him. But he got spooked and ran for the woods. I lost him in the trees." Riley sounded very disappointed in himself. They were all usually pretty good at catching up to a runner, but the thick wooded area that the country club loved as a barrier did not make for an easy place to track and chase someone.

"Was it our guy?" Bryan asked, on full alert now.

"I can't say for certain. It was dark, and he was several feet ahead of me, but unless we have someone else here who has a stalker, it has to be him," Riley stated.

"I know, I'm not trying to be a jerk. It just gets me that he is able to get so close," Bryan said.

"Height and build is consistent with our perp too," Riley added. "If I was going to place bets, I'd say it was him."

Bryan began pacing in the hallway. He needed to figure out just what had to happen to keep Sophia safe. Riley remained there, but quiet, letting Bryan process his thoughts. Bryan had always been the thinker and the planner in their group. Trevor was the tech guy, and Riley was sort of the dumb muscle. Not that any of them ever treated him that way, but it was how he felt. Finally, Bryan looked back to Riley. "You have your bike here?"

"Yeah, it's in the back of the parking lot, near the employee entrance. Why?" Riley asked.

"You mind me using it? I have a feeling that this is going to freak Sophia out a little. I want to take her somewhere that she can just let go and not have to think about all of this, and being around a group of people is going to be hard for her. She will want to put up a good front, but her mind won't be able to be in a good space to hang out with her brother and his friends. I'll be the one to explain it to the client, though. I'll tell them we suspected he was at Five Sloths last night and we don't want to take any chances. I'm taking her to a safe house so there's no way he can locate her. I'll make sure I have her back in time for the brunch and hair and makeup thing tomorrow," Bryan explained.

"You don't think we can keep her safe at Walt's house?" Riley asked.

"Naw, man, it's not like that. I know the three of us could keep her safe pretty much anywhere. What we can't keep her at Walt's house is out of her own head. You texted last night and asked if me going to her room had been a good idea. The answer to that is I don't really know. I saw her door open a crack when you were debriefing me on the situation at the brewery. I went to check on her and she was sitting with her knees drawn up to her chest rocking and crying softly. Knowing this guy was at Five Sloths did that to her; what do you think it will do when she knows he was watching her through the window? The protector in me couldn't let her just sit there and rock. She'd given me some pretty good signals that she is a sub or at least was before this asshole took advantage. When she took off her clothes, got in position, and asked me to take care of her, I couldn't say no. Tonight will be no different when she hears all of this, and I don't know that I can keep it totally quiet and still take her where she needs to go. I'm pretty sure only you know that I was in her room last night. I can't really do much with her brother a hundred feet away and without the rest of the house hearing us. And being quiet isn't always easy when a sub really needs to let go."

"Yeah, I understand. However you want this to go," Riley said and handed Bryan his keys.

Bryan put out his hand for their usual brother handshake and pulled Riley into a one-arm hug. "Thanks, man. And if this all comes back on me, it will be only me. No one else needs to know that you had any clue what Sophia and I were doing."

"You know we got your back, man. If one of us goes down, we all go down," Riley said, giving one final pat on Bryan's back before pulling away. "I'll ride in the limo with the group then and make sure the house is secure. Give me a call or shoot me a text if you decide to come back early at all so I can make sure the alarm is off."

"Great, thanks. When you guys are in the car or back at Walt's you can tell them more in depth that we think the guy might have been outside. That's why I took Sophia to a safe house. I just don't want that aspect discussed until I can tell Sophia in private. She will want to seem strong for her brother, but it will mess with her head. I'll just tell them that I need to go over security protocol and things with her for tomorrow so I'm taking her to a safe location or something like that. I don't know, hell, it's not like she's a kid and I have to have her little brother's approval to be with her. But after the way things went with Larry years ago and Pete feeling like he was not there for her, I can see him wanting to be protective of her now."

"For what it's worth, I'm pretty sure Pete trusts that you won't treat her like that guy did. He knows you're a good guy," Riley assured him.

"Yeah, but you know how brothers can be about their sisters." Bryan smiled.

"What, you think we give Summer a hard time over guys?" Riley laughed.

"Nothing more than they deserve, Rye, nothing more than they deserve." Bryan chuckled. "She is my little sister, after all."

They walked back into the group, Bryan took his place at Sophia's side, and Trevor stepped back and helped clear tables. Bryan told Pete that he was going to be taking Sophia with him; they had some protocol they needed to go over before they were going to be out in the open tomorrow. He promised that he would keep her safe and that he would have her back to the house as soon as he felt she was ready for 'the big show.'

Pete looked at his sister. "Are you comfortable with that, Soph? I'm sure Bryan could do it at Walt's house if you want him to." It was pretty obvious that he was kind of torn. He wanted his sister to feel totally safe with her bodyguard, but he didn't want her feeling overly close to her bodyguard. Bryan could totally understand that; she was going back to Colorado Monday afternoon.

Bryan was pretty sure he was the only one that really recognized the smoldering look in Sophia's eyes. She was guessing that he was taking her somewhere so that they could play, and that was definitely at least part of the truth. She just wasn't going to like the rest of what they needed to do. "Oh, yeah, I'm totally fine with it. I trust him. You guys don't need to hear all the directions on where to stand, and which side of him to walk on and all the other things he wants me to do to keep me safe," Sophia assured them. "It's already pretty late, and I'm sure we will take a while, so don't worry about us. I'm sure Bryan knows how to work the alarm system."

He held out his hand for Pete to shake and offered his promise, "I'll keep her as safe as I would my own little sister." Jeremy kind of coughed when Bryan said that. Bryan wasn't sure why; maybe Jeremy had a little sister so he knew what it was like to feel protective of one. He wished everyone a good night and took Sophia's hand and headed through the kitchen and out the employee entrance. As promised, Riley's bike was right there in front of them.

"Wait, we're riding a motorcycle?" Sophia asked with disbelief.

"Yes, it's Riley's. I assure you that I am a safe biker," he offered.

"But in case you haven't noticed, I'm wearing a dress," Sophia protested, "and thanks to a mean brute, I'm also wearing no underwear." The last part was said more quietly just in case there was someone else close by.

"I am well aware, Sophia," he agreed. "Just think of it this way: you will be sitting tight up against me, your pussy will be well hidden pressed up to my ass. Now, get on. We can't stand out here in the open." He handed her Riley's helmet and got on the bike to help her up behind him. He was counting on two things as he started the motorcycle and rode out of the parking lot. The first was that Riley had chased the perp far enough away that he had been too scared to come back, and that the helmet would hide Sophia's identity, at least until he had her in the safety of the Triskelion Motorcycle shop.

As they pulled up to the shop, he hit the button to open the door to one of the smaller bays. They used the smaller ones as more of a personal garage and the larger ones for bikes they were customizing or repairing. His bike was sitting in its usual spot, near the office area of the big garage. Trevor's was there too. They all had other vehicles that were more conducive to being on the job, and for the simple fact that Michigan winters were hell for motorcycles. He helped Sophia off the bike and then he got He removed her helmet and placed it on the seat of Riley's bike. He took her hand and walked her to his bike. Ever since he had met her, he'd had some pretty vivid pictures in his brain of her in various positions on his bike, but none of them included sitting like a normal rider would.

"This is my motorcycle, Sophia, and I have so many plans for you tonight. Now, remove the rest of your clothing so that I can help you get onto the bike. Leave the shoes on, though; the heels might make it easier for you to reach." His eyes were heated.

So were hers when she asked, "Reach what?"

"Oh, the floor, the running board, whatever it is I may need to put your feet on for all of the wonderful torture I have planned for you." While Sophia was removing her remaining clothing, he went and grabbed the rear wheel stand. It would hold the motorcycle in a more upright position than the regular kickstand. It had a wide enough base that he wouldn't have to worry about the bike tipping over with Sophia on it. He also grabbed his kit from under the bench. He had way more toys at home, but these would work for tonight. When Sophia was undressed, he helped her onto the seat of his Harley. He pulled a length of rope from his bag and tied it securely around her wrist, then he wrapped the other end around the handlebar and pulled it until she had to lie forward on the gas tank to be able to reach. Her feet were still on the running boards but just barely. Keeping the heels had been the right thing; besides, a woman in heels was always a sight to be seen and enjoyed. He repeated the same with her other hand. He could already tell that this would put her in the perfect position for oh so many wonderful and nasty things. He went back to his bag and took out the three packages that he had gotten at the adult toy shop. He hadn't used them; he always bought new when he had used one of the toys in his kit. He gave the toy to the sub after they were done playing. Although he was going to keep the things he used on Sophia until she was ready to go back Colorado. He wasn't sure if they were going to get more freedom to enjoy private time together or not, but he wanted the clamps, the butterfly, and the small anal plug to be ready if he needed them. He would wash them and put them back in his kit until she was going to the airport. He set them aside for now, along with a small bottle of lube and took out his soft deerskin flogger. He began trailing the falls softly over her back. He couldn't have her flying, not yet. They really did have some things to talk about. He watched as her body physically relaxed into the pattern he was making around her spine and shoulders. He kept the movements and his voice both soft as he began with the things she needed to know. "Now, Sophia, I need you to stay with me for a few minutes. I do have things that we need to talk about. But I promise that once we get the unpleasantness out of the way, I will make this very pleasurable for both of us. Do you hear me and understand me?"

"Yes, Sir," she responded softly.

"Good. Now you need to know that we believe that Larry was outside of the country club tonight. We aren't positive, but Riley saw someone outside trying to look in through the windows. Riley gave chase, but he lost the person in the woods." He had watched her body stiffen at his words. He just continued to keep the flogger going in gentle, massaging strokes. "It may not have been him; someone else at the party may have attracted unwanted attention. It's even possible that it was paparazzi. Your family is associated with two very prominent businesses in the area. But just in case, I need to make sure you understand some things for tomorrow."

He began using a soft thudding pattern on her back, nothing that would be painful at all, but would feel more like a deep tissue massage. "We have no reason to believe that he has a gun, but if you hear anyone yell the word gun, you get to the ground immediately." Her body wasn't really relaxing at all anymore, but he understood that, and until she knew the full score, he couldn't let her get out of her head and float. "I can promise you that I will always be right at your side. If you need a drink, ask a waiter. I'm not going to be like a typical date tomorrow. Normally, I would go get my girl a drink, but not tomorrow. If you need to use the restroom, I will walk you there and back. I can promise you that he will not get close enough to touch you, but I cannot guarantee that he doesn't have a gun. We don't think he wants to harm you, but we can't know that for sure. We believe that what he really wants is to try to get you back, or at the very least talk to you and spew more of his bullshit lies hoping that you will continue to not press charges or do anything to harm his freedom." He changed his pattern and rhythm. He wanted to help her destress, but he needed to keep her on her toes for a little while longer. "To everyone tomorrow we will seem like the kind of couple that can't keep our hands off of each other and that we can't bear to be apart. You will be holding my arm or my hand or I will have my arm around your back. We will appear to be the typical young couple in love to everyone who doesn't know the true story. Do you have any questions about tomorrow, Sophia?"

He could see the tears on her face. He had known they would be there, and he knew he couldn't prevent them. She softly asked, "Why?'

"Why what, Sophia? Why do you need to stay so close? What are you asking, Sophia?" He had a feeling that he knew, but he wanted to be sure. He stopped his flogging and leaned closer to her face. He kept his hand firmly on her shoulder. He wanted her to see and feel that he was right there with her.

"Why won't he just leave me alone? I'm nothing special. As much as I don't ever want another woman to be treated the way he treated me, there is a part of me that just wishes he would find someone else to be obsessed with," she cried.

"I understand that, Sophia, and I can't explain why. Other than the fact that some people are just obsessed with things they shouldn't want or can't have." He assured her, "All I can promise is that my brothers and I will do everything in our power to keep you safe tomorrow. Although if we told your brother about what happened tonight, I am sure he would understand if you decided to not go to the party." He was certain that suggestion would go over like a lead balloon, but he had to try.

"No, I'm going. I only have one brother, and he's only getting married once. I'm not going to let fear keep me away, and I trust you and your brothers to do everything you possibly can. I just have to remind myself that I have to keep control of my own life. I can't let him ruin things for me anymore."

Bryan bent further and turned so he could look her in the eyes. "Good for you, Sophia. I promise to keep you safe." At her small nod, he continued, "Tonight, however, I would like for us to both be able to focus on something else, at least briefly. I would like to show you all of the wonderful things I can do to you on my Harley." He gave her a wicked smile, and she gave a small smile in return.

"Yes, please, Sir," she said softly. "Take me out of my head for a while." Those words were music to his ears.

Bryan took her right breast in his hand and leaned forward so that he could draw her nipple into his mouth. When it was fully aroused, he opened the nipple clamp and tightened it down on to her tender flesh. Tight enough it wouldn't fall off, but not tight enough to cause serious damage. He moved around to the other side of the motorcycle and repeated the same process on her left nipple.

Bryan stood up and started to flog her in earnest, especially on her gorgeous ass and outer thighs. He tempered the hits if he was hitting a less fleshy part, but he was going for a nice deep pink on the parts that could handle it. It took several minutes of his constant attention before he saw her body again relax into the curve of the motorcycle. He wanted her relaxed, but still able to respond and assist a bit with her movements when he repositioned her. He stepped away and retrieved the bottle of lube and the other toys he had set out for use.

The small butterfly-shaped vibrator had straps that could help hold it in place against her clit. It was made to be stepped into like a pair of underwear, but it also had a way of unhooking one end of each strap so that he could put it into place and then reattach the strap. When he had it positioned where he wanted it, he turned it on to a medium speed and tucked the remote in his pocket. He leaned his face close to Sophia's ear and said, "Tonight, I want you to fly as much as you can, little one. No need to ask permission, no need to even think, just fly." And with that, he removed his shirt and resumed the flogging.

Sophie watched as Bryan removed his shirt. The night before, they had been in semi-darkness; this time, the motorcycle shop was well lit. She could see and admire the definition to his muscles. She could clearly see the ink that covered the top of his right pectoral muscle and went up and over to cover his upper arm and right shoulder blade. She made up her mind right then that she was going to spend every minute she could getting to know every inch of this man's body. She was going to memorize it for her dreams and fantasies for the future. Colorado was a beautiful place, but she had kept herself mostly isolated apart from a few acquaintances in the small town she lived in. The memories of Bryan and their time together would keep her warm on the long lonely nights ahead. If it weren't for Larry, she might even consider moving back to Michigan and seeing if Bryan was open to being a somewhat regular play partner for a while. But Larry had already proven to her that she wasn't safe in Michigan; he was already making her life miserable. She needed to let go of those thoughts for now, though. Bryan had promised her that he would take her soaring without ever leaving the room, and she intended to enjoy that to the fullest extent possible. She closed her eyes and gave in to the sensation of the sound and feel of the flogger hitting her flesh and the persistent vibration between her legs. The clamps were just the tight tension, enough to cause a little bite, but not so much that the pain would take her over the edge too quickly. She pushed Larry out of her mind as best she could. He had no place in this room or in her head space for the night.

Bryan could tell the moment that Sophia had made the conscious decision to shut Larry out of her mind for the next few hours. Her eyes closed, and she had a contented smile on her face. Her body relaxed fully onto his bike. It was the most amazing sight he had ever experienced. He wanted a picture of this for his memories after she left. He pulled out his phone and silently clicked the picture. He would show it to her in the morning when she was more in control of her thought process. If she didn't want him to keep it, he would delete it off of his phone, after he had stared at it long enough to burn the image into his memory. In reality, the picture was far more artistic than it was pornographic. Nothing showed except the lovely curves of her body draped over the seat and gas tank of his Harley. You couldn't see anything that would be incriminating. Her face was only partially visible because of the way her arms were tied to the handlebars. No one who didn't know every curve of her body would be able to tell that it was Sophia. "You are so beautiful like this Sophia," he praised. "I've never seen a more erotic or enticing image in my life. I was right to think seeing you like this was going to be amazing."

Bryan adjusted the speed of the butterfly according to her reactions. He wanted to keep her on the edge without taking her over long enough that her brain was focused on one thing and only one thing: being able to find that release. When he had taken her to that edge and pulled her back several times, he took mercy on her and finally pushed her over the precipice.

While she was riding the waves of her orgasm, he got the small anal plug and the bottle of lube ready. He stepped closer to her again and said, "Now, Sophia, you told me that you were looking forward to me using all three of your gorgeous holes. As much as I would enjoy that, if it's been so long since you have had any sexual contact, I don't think we will be able to get to the point of trying anal sex; however, I do have a small plug I want you to wear for me. You can do that, yes, Sophia?"

Sophia softly agreed, "Yes, Sir."

"Good girl, Sophia." Bryan praised. He opened the small bottle and slowly squeezed the lubricant between the cheeks of her ass. He used his finger to spread it around and to begin to massage the tight ring. As she relaxed more, he used the tip of the plug to rotate against her opening. The more relaxed she became, the more he slowly pressed the plug into her. Once it was fully inserted, he used his thumb to vibrate the base to add to the sensations of the small butterfly. He began to pull the plug almost out and push it back in. Sophia began rising as much as her unstable footing would allow to meet the thrusts of the plug. Bryan began timing his in and out movements with Sophia's raise and lower movements, picking up speed along with her until their combined movements took her over the edge of orgasm.

Sophia had felt the orgasm building from deep inside her, and when it finally rolled through her, it was like a runaway locomotive barreling at top speed. It completely derailed her thought process. As her brain started to clear, she realized that Bryan had untied her arms and was lifting her into a different position. She ended up straddling his lap on the motorcycle. Somewhere during her brief departure from reality, Bryan had removed the rest of his clothing and put on a condom. She really was enjoying being able to see his body in this bright light. Hopefully she would have more time to view and enjoy all of his amazing skin. She was lifted so that she could slide down onto his cock, and once he was fully inside her, she felt him lean forward and start the ignition of the motorcycle. That brought a whole new meaning to the word vibrator. The rumble of the bike caused his body to vibrate with a delicious hum inside of her. She had never felt anything quite this amazing in her life.

Bryan placed a hand on each side of Sophia's hips and began to slowly slide her up and down his hard cock. Sophia's hands were no longer bound to the handlebars, but they were now tied together. She lifted her hands and placed them behind Bryan's head so that she had something to hold on to. Bryan increased the speed and soon Sophia was helping to set the rhythm. Since she was able to use her arms and feet to help control her ride, Bryan's hands were free to do other things. He took one clamp in between the thumb and forefinger of each hand and tugged on them. The increase in stimulation made Sophia even more intent on her movements.

Bryan was about ready to explode; the vibrations of the motor and the rapid lap movements of Sophia were making him crazy. It was time for this round to be over, so he tugged hard enough on the right clamp that it came off. He immediately soothed the tender flesh with his warm wet mouth. That was all that it took for Sophia to grind down on him hard with her orgasm. His followed right behind hers, and he quickly removed the other clamp and soothed that nipple too as they both rode out the spasms of their bodies. They collapsed against each other holding tightly . Bryan leaned forward to kill the engine on the bike and then wrapped Sophia's legs around his waist before he stood and got off the bike. It wasn't a hard maneuver; she was so petite compared to him and the stand really was holding the motorcycle completely upright. He removed the plug and tossed it on the bench as he walked past it.

He carried her over to the stairs and killed the shop lights on his way up. There was a bedroom up there. He would really prefer to take her home to his house for the rest of the night, but that was a long drive out to the country, which would mean they would have to get dressed again and it would also mean taking Sophia out into the world again. He wanted to avoid that last part as much as possible. Anytime they were outside, it was an opportunity for Larry or someone who knew Larry to be able to see them. He was limiting her exposure as much as humanly possible. Besides, getting dressed meant less time with her naked, and a long drive meant less time holding her closely, so neither of those had any appeal. He wrapped one arm around her while she held him in her arms and her legs. Normally, he wouldn't use the handrail, but he wasn't taking any chances with Sophia in his arms.

The studio apartment upstairs had never been anyone's "fuck pad" or whatever; it legitimately had been created as a space any of them could use to crash if they had worked too late on a bike. There was a decent-sized bed and a kitchen and bathroom. It wasn't a place anyone would want to live for the long haul, but it was a decent place to crash for a night or two. They always kept the refrigerator stocked with beverages and things for a quick easy meal. All of them had nights where they just got so engrossed in a job that they didn't want to take the time to go home or they were too tired to drive safely. Bryan just hoped that the sheets were clean. They usually did a good job of cleaning up after themselves, but every so often, Riley or Trevor would crash there for a few nights and not remember to clean up.

As he deposited Sophia on the bed, he saw the note on the nightstand. "Hey, slobs, I stopped up to grab a beer and noticed the place was trashed. Pick up after yourselves, I'm not your maid." It was signed by his sister, Summer. He would have to thank her for saving him the embarrassment of taking Sophia to whatever mess his brothers had left behind.

Summer owned the tattoo parlor that was directly south of their garage. When the building next to theirs had gone on the market, they had grabbed it up quickly. The price had been right, so they helped their little sister set up shop. None of them admitted that they had done it so that they could be close by in case she ever got any unwanted attention, but that was totally why they had done it. She had a pretty good business going there now. She had started out small, but over the years, she had added two other artists to the shop as well as someone who did piercings.

The building just north of theirs had been for sale at the same time as the garage had been listed. They'd purchased both and opened up one of the walls between the two buildings. That part of the property had been made into a small shop where they sold clothing and other biker gear. He would run down in the morning and find a pair of pants and a shirt for Sophia so that she wouldn't have to put on the dress that she had worn to the party. He could just imagine how she would look in a tight pair of leather pants and a Harley shirt. She could wear his jacket if it was chilly in the morning. He liked the thought of that—her in his jacket. Of course it would be like a huge dress on her, but it would work okay for warmth until she got to her own clothing.

He looked down at Sophia and she had fallen fast asleep on the top of the blankets. He might as well go downstairs and get the clothes now. He could pick up the clothing and toys that they had left around down there too. He knew his brothers wouldn't be stopping by, since they were all on duty at Walt's house, but he could never predict what Summer would do or what her hours at the tattoo shop were. He didn't need little sis popping in and seeing the evidence of his night with Sophia. Bryan removed Sophia's shoes and then rolled her body enough that he could pull down the blankets and then rolled her back so that she could be covered up. She stirred a little but didn't really seem to wake up. Just in case, though, he kissed her gently and told her he was going downstairs to get their clothes and he would be right back. He thought she made a sound of agreement, but that could have just been a sleep noise of some sort.

As he headed downstairs, he pulled out his phone and sent a group text to Riley and Trevor letting them know that they were secure for the night and would head over in the morning in time to get ready for the reception. Before he tucked his phone back in his pocket, he pulled up the picture he had taken of Sophia draped on his motorcycle. Hell, that was going to be the thing he stared at every night before he fell asleep after she left for Colorado.

He found a pair of black leather pants and a Harley Davidson T-shirt in Sophia's size. It had green roses on it entwined with the symbol of the motorcycle brand. She would definitely look like his bad ass biker chick in this outfit. He cleaned up the toys and put them back in his kit and grabbed Sophia's dress. He headed back upstairs and felt the vibration of a text from Trevor.

All's quiet here, take care of yourself, and your girl.

He thought about texting back that she wasn't his girl, but really, if it weren't for that whole eleven hundred mile gap, she just might be his girl. So he left it alone and headed to bed with Sophia.

He tried to crawl in quietly beside her, but as soon as he was in the bed, she rolled toward him and snuggled softly at his side. He wrapped an arm around her and held her tightly to himself. Damn but this woman hit all of his buttons. She could be incredibly submissive, she could be a royal brat, and she could be the soft and tender girl who needed his protection and his strength. It was going to be a long time before he forgot about Sophia Hallowell.

Chapter Six

Sophie was starting to become aware of a few things. First, her bladder was in serious need of attention. Second, she was in a bed that she didn't remember ever seeing before. And third, there was a firm muscular nude male body next to hers, and she was pretty much plastered to the side of it with her leg across his. She tried to extricate herself from the bed, but there seemed to be a huge muscular arm pinning her against said nude body. She got herself free, although she had no delusions of having done so without Bryan knowing it. She had felt him tense up to hold her, and then relax so that she could move away from him.

She looked around the space she was in. It seemed to be a rather large, open floor plan apartment. The bedroom area that she was in was set apart with a partial wall, and there was a door across from the bed that was sure to be the bathroom.

After finishing her business, Sophie looked at herself in the mirror and oh lord, what a sight that was. Her hair and makeup had both suffered a fatal blow. She didn't look quite as bad as she had suspected she might, but she definitely didn't look attractive. She looked in the cupboards for a washcloth. She was just starting to let the water get warm when she heard a voice from the other room.

"What are you doing, Sophia? Come back to bed; it's five in the morning," Bryan rumbled.

"I was just going to clean up a little," she stated.

"Worry about that later. We can have a shower in a few hours. Now is the time for sleep."

Sophie really wanted to try to make herself look more presentable for Bryan, but it seemed that wasn't in his plan. She would just have to hope that the lights were still off, and she could get to the shower before the sun lit up the room too much in the morning. Sophie scurried with her head down back into bed and put her face against Bryan's chest, hoping he wouldn't see her with no makeup and her 'desperate for a brush' hair.

"What's wrong, Sophia? Did something scare you? You seem tense all of a sudden," Bryan asked.

"No, everything is fine." Sophie assured him. She was pretty sure she didn't sound convincing though.

Bryan rolled to his side so that he could look Sophia in the face directly. He kept her body pinned to his, though. "What is it, Sophia? Did you have a bad dream?" He was searching her eyes for an answer. He could usually read people fairly well. If she had woken with a bad dream or if she was afraid of what would be happening throughout the day, he needed to know that.

Sophie realized that he just wasn't going to let this go. If she didn't say something he would likely put her in a chair with a bright light in her face and interrogate her to get his answers. She had to say something, but if there was one thing she had learned during her time with Larry, the best answer was always to make herself sound like she was the one lacking, but to always do it in a way that sounded more like a joke than anything serious. "Uh, yeah, I thought I saw something scary in the bathroom, but turned out it was just me without makeup." She laughed.

Bryan rolled until he had Sophia fully pinned to the bed under his massive body. He didn't place his full weight on her, but she definitely wasn't moving out from under him anytime soon. "Are you saying that you think you aren't beautiful just as you are, my sweet Sophia? Because trust me, makeup or no makeup, you are the most beautiful woman I have ever seen. I happen to like your hair mussed from our sexual escapades. You don't need makeup and a fine hairstyle to be beautiful, Sophia." With that, he leaned down and took her mouth fully in a deep kiss. He pressed in for more, fully invading when her mouth opened for him. How could this woman think that she was anything less than absolutely stunning? She honestly was the most gorgeous woman on the planet.

How could this man think that she was beautiful, especially like she was right now? Her hair was in shambles, her face basically bare except for the few smudges that remained of her makeup where it hadn't been fully wiped away by sweat and tears. Sophie definitely couldn't understand it, but she wasn't going to argue with him. Especially not when he was kissing her so deeply that it almost took her breath away by the sheer passion that lay within that kiss.

After several minutes of deep passionate kisses, Bryan pulled away enough to be able to lock his eyes with Sophia's. He stared into them deep and long. He was starting to feel something with this woman that he had never felt with any woman before. He wasn't sure exactly what it was. It obviously wasn't love; he didn't believe in love at first sight, or even love within the first weeks of a relationship. But he did feel a connection with Sophia that he had never felt with anyone before.

Slowly he repositioned himself so that he could enter her pussy slowly. Once he was as deep as he could possibly go, he held himself there and continued staring into her eyes. Finally, the strength of it got to be too much for him. He continued to hold himself still inside her as he said, "You're fucking amazing, Sophia. You are beautiful and strong. You are a fighter and you are a conqueror. You are sexy beyond what words can describe. Hear me, Sophia: you are fucking amazing." Bryan began strong, hard thrusts inside of her. With each thrust, as he entered, he said one word and then withdrew, only to thrust again with another word. "You. Are. The. Most. Beautiful. Woman. On. This. Planet. Don't. Ever. Doubt. That. Sophia. Don't. Ever. Let. Anyone. Tell. You. Differently." When he had finished with his one word at a time thrusting, he let himself go and pounded her deep and hard and fast until they were both at the point of orgasm. As he let himself go over that edge, he reiterated, "Fucking amazing." What he didn't say, but his brain definitely thought was, *Stay with me, Sophia. I will keep you safe forever, just stay with me and give me a chance.*

Sophia had heard the words, and the emotion of everything Bryan had said and done. Her last conscious thought as she succumbed to the depth of the orgasm and of his words was, *Please, ask me to stay. I trust you to keep me safe forever, just please, ask me to stay.* She didn't say those words, but they were a thought that she just couldn't shake.

Bryan collapsed onto Sophia and then rolled them both so that she lay primarily on top of him. He kept his arm tight as they both drifted off to sleep.

Chapter Seven

The alarm on Bryan's phone went off at 7:30 a.m. Usually he was awake before then, but the great sex the night before and the really great sex earlier that morning had apparently taken its toll on his sleep patterns, and he hadn't woken up early. He lay there for a long while just looking down at the gorgeous woman that was currently using his left pectoral as her pillow. She had her arm and her leg draped across his body. Damn, she was gorgeous. She had so many qualities that he had always loved in a woman. She was everything he usually looked for in someone to date—actually, she was more. She was such a strong woman. Many wouldn't have made the trip to Michigan for her brother's marriage celebration, and those that made the trip would likely cut it short when it became obvious that their stalker hadn't given up and was still pursuing them. But not his Sophia; no, she wasn't going to go down without a fight, and he was going to make sure she didn't go down at all. He did realize that he was thinking of her as 'his,' but his mind was able to justify that with the fact that she was his, for the next few days anyway. She was his client, his responsibility, and his play partner. He wasn't going down the rabbit hole of just how wrong it was that he was playing with his client. He realized that it was now almost eight o'clock, and the morning was getting away from them. They needed to be at Walt's in a couple of hours.

He tried to extricate himself from Sophia's body so he could grab a quick shower. She stirred a little but snuggled up to his pillow and never actually woke up. Bryan jumped in the shower for a quick scrub. If there was one thing the military had taught him, it was to shower quickly and efficiently. The whole platoon was usually required to be ready to move in what seemed like minutes from the time they were roused out of bed.

When he finished he dressed in his usual biker gear, jeans, T-shirt, and boots. His suit for the reception was already hanging in the closet at Walt's house. "Sophia, sweetheart, it's time to wake up," he said as he walked back into the room.

Sophie started to stir and looked up at definitely just what a delicious badass biker would look like. In the time that she had been with Bryan, he had been in professional mode. Dress slacks, jackets, that type of thing, but this was definitely what he would most likely look like on a daily basis when not on a bodyguarding job that included country club visits and spa appointments. She had to admit she really liked what she saw. She could get used to waking up to this view regularly. Of course, she really liked how he looked naked too, but that was another thing altogether. When she met Bryan's eyes, there was definitely the same heat and desire that she felt being sent right back to her. She smiled at him and asked, "Why don't you come back to bed?"

"As much as I would love to do that, we don't have time" Bryan said regretfully. "We have less than two hours to be at Walt's house and I am sure you want a shower. I'm going to run down to the bakery on the corner and at least grab some coffee and a small breakfast. I know they are having a brunch at Walt's, but after last night, I am starving, and I don't want your blood sugar dropping when you are on the back of my bike for the ride over. I brought up your clothes from last night, but I wasn't sure you would be comfortable putting them back on, so I also grabbed you an outfit from our apparel shop downstairs. Either one is fine with me." He started to walk away but turned back to add "And no, you don't get the panties back, so choose wisely, little one." He turned to leave just in time to feel the pillow that Sophia had thrown hit him in the back.

"You're a brute, do you know that?" Sophie said indignantly. She heard Bryan chuckling as he continued to walk away. She got out of bed and walked into the bathroom. Her dress was hanging on a hook on the door, as was a really sexy looking pair of leather jeans and a black Harley Davidson T-shirt. Even though the dress was on a hanger, it was still somewhat wrinkled. So biker chick attire it was. This was definitely going to inspire some questions when they got back to Walt's, most especially from her bother and the other women. Oh well, it wasn't like she wasn't an adult who could do as she pleased. Sophie stepped into the steaming hot water and wished that Bryan was in here with her. She was adding that to her list of things to accomplish before going to back to Colorado: steamy shower sex with a hot biker. She could think of a list of things she would like to do with him that would take her way past her Monday deadline. And she knew that she would be on that plane on Monday; she had to be. Larry wasn't going to give up, so back into hiding it was.

When Sophie got out of the shower, she walked to the kitchen area of the apartment and sat down. Bryan handed her a large cup of coffee and pointed to the box of blueberry scones on the table. He got out a couple of small plates and sat down across from her. "Do you have any cream for the coffee?" Sophie asked.

"It's already in there, Sophia. I ordered it the way you like it. Extra sweet with just a dash of milk."

"How do you know how I take my coffee?" she asked.

"I'm observant, Sophia; in my line of work I have to be. I've watched you prepare your coffee for two days now. It's not a hard thing to remember." With that, he took a long drink of his extra strong coffee. It was hot and almost burned his tongue, but he didn't care; it was a good distraction from the sight of Sophia in those tight pants. She didn't have anything with her, so her face was clean and bare of any makeup, and that just added to her beauty. So many women thought they needed to be all dolled up to look good, but in his opinion, this woman in her biker outfit was everything any red-blooded male would want in their life. He ate his scones quickly before heading back to the bathroom. He found the drawer that Summer always kept a few things in and found a hair tie. He handed it to Sophia and said, "You might want to pull your hair back before we get on the bike. The wind is likely to turn it into a mess if it's down and still damp."

Sophie was stunned at the way Bryan's mind worked. Most men wouldn't think about a woman's hair getting mussed up like that, or if they did, they wouldn't care enough to go in search of a band to hold it back with. He knew how she took her coffee, but there was no way that he could possibly know that blueberry scones were her absolute favorite sweet breakfast treat. That one had just been pure luck, it had to be; Sophie didn't believe in psychic abilities. But there were things that Bryan said or did the almost made her wonder. It was most likely that he was just extremely observant and it came across as almost creepy with the things he could remember.

"Now, Sophia, just to double check, you remember the protocols for today, right?" Bryan asked.

"Yes. I stay attached to you at all times at the club. If I need something I send a waiter for it. If I need to go to the bathroom, you will escort me there and back. If I hear anyone yell gun, I hit the ground immediately." Sophia checked off the rules like she was reciting something in school. After a pause she added, "God, I hope I don't hear anyone yell gun."

Bryan reached across the table and picked up her hand. He brought it to his lips and kissed it gently. "So do I, Sophia, so do I. But you need to remember what to do if you do hear that. That's our best chance at keeping you safe." He continued to hold her hand and look into her eyes. God, he hoped he didn't hear anyone yell gun.

"I will, I promise," Sophie said after several minutes of Bryan's eyes boring into hers. That seemed to pull him out of wherever he was at in his mind and he let go of her hand.

"We should probably head out," Bryan said while cleaning up the garbage and putting the plates in the dishwasher. That was one appliance they had all realized they needed really quickly when they had first moved in. Most of the time they only used a plate or a cup here and there, and no one took the time to wash just one dish so they piled up in the sink. Then they had to fight it out as too who was doing the dishes. They all tried to count who had the most and claim that person needed to wash them all. They had also tried to tell Summer that was 'woman's work' so she should do them. That had not gone over well at all with little sis. They had agreed that the dishwasher was a necessity and everyone had to agree to run it if it got very full or whoever got to the shop first on Monday morning started it up so that they would start fresh for the week.

Sophie went back to the bathroom to use the hairbrush to pull her hair back into a ponytail and grabbed the rest of her things. That was pretty easy since she didn't have much there. She put her high heels from the night before back on and headed downstairs to find Bryan. He was pulling his motorcycle off of the rack thing that he had put it on last night to brace it in position. Realizing that they would be riding the same bike that they'd had amazing sex on did something to Sophie. It made her girl parts get all tingly again. She must have been pretty obvious about what she was thinking because Bryan came over and took both of her hands and looked down at her eyes.

"Me too, Sophia, me too," he assured her. "I don't know if I will ever be able to ride this bike again without thinking about you and about last night." He let go of one hand and reached into his pocket for his phone. "Speaking of last night, I have something I have to show you." He pulled up his photos and turned the phone toward Sophia. "I took this last night. If you want me to delete it, I will, but I really hope you won't ask me to do that. I would like to keep this memory of our time together. I promise that no one will see it other than me—well, Trevor might spot it when he goes through the cloud or whatever because we all have pictures from investigations on the cloud. But if he so much as tries to open it and look at it, I promise I will pluck his eyeballs out with a very sharp object."

Sophie took the phone from his hand so she could see the photo better. In all reality, no one could ever be able to tell it was her. Most of her face was hidden. She wasn't in some sort of Hustler magazine pose. It was almost artistic. Maybe she could use this as a reason to get a really hot picture of him to take home with her too. Besides, he probably had dozens of pictures of women in a similar pose. "It's fine, you can keep it. No one could really tell it's me, and I am sure you have others similar to it already on your cloud."

"Actually, no, Sophia, you're the only person I have ever done anything like that with. But I appreciate you not making me delete it." Bryan took his phone back and took another long look at the photo, then put the phone in his pocket. "Right, we should get you over there before your brother sends out a search party." He helped Sophia onto his motorcycle and put on the helmet he had grabbed from the store. It would fit her much better than the one she had worn of Riley's. Which automatically made it safer for her. He wouldn't tell her he had picked out the helmet for her. When she went back to Colorado he would put it into storage in case he ever got another chance to see her, or maybe in the far, far distant future, when his memories of her faded, he would find another woman that could wear it when she rode with him. Damn, but he wanted another picture, so he stepped back and took one. Sophia in leather sitting on his Harley was yet another sight to behold.

"You know, I'm going to need to take a few pictures of you at some point too. Turnabout is fair play and all that," Sophia said with a smile.

"I am sure we can work that out," Bryan said, then he put on his own helmet and got on his motorcycle. He pulled up the security app on his phone and looked to make sure that he didn't see anyone outside the shop. He texted Trevor and asked for a status update on the security feed for the previous night. When Trevor told him that all had been quiet, he started up the engine and opened the small bay door. He eased his way to the entrance and took a longer time than normal observing the road in either direction from their driveway before pulling onto the road and heading toward East Grand Rapids.

Sophie had her arms firmly around his waist and had scooted herself as close to his body as she could. Not because she was cold, but because she wanted to be pressed against him. In reality, they didn't have many more hours together, and almost all of those would be spent with a lot of other people around them. They might be able to sneak away again after the party for another amazing night, and possibly even the night after that, but the days were full of being with family and friends, and then she was going back to Colorado. Somehow, she was pretty sure that after this amazing time with Bryan the nights in her small home in the mountains would seem even longer and lonelier than they ever had before. She might be able to talk Bryan into coming to visit on occasion, or they could possibly meet somewhere in the middle of their two homes at times, but that wasn't really much of a relationship to have. She wished she could have so much more. But she had resolved herself to the fact that this would be all she would allow herself. Meeting him for clandestine weekends away would only serve to prolong her agony. Sure it would be wonderful when they met, but she would always be going home to her same isolated existence, and it would only serve to make her crave him more and more. No, this weekend was her one chance with him, and then she needed to go home and allow him to only live in her dreams. She wouldn't call him or text him, she wouldn't answer his calls if he made them. It would need to be a clean break when she got on that plane on Monday. She couldn't ever look back because that would only make her heart hurt worse. She felt the tears slowly falling down her face, and she pressed it to Bryan's back so he couldn't see her in the mirror.

Bryan could feel the warm tears as they soaked into his shirt. She wasn't crying openly, just a tear here and there. But she had hidden her face so he wouldn't see them, so he couldn't force the issue and ask about them. He could only assume that she was still thinking about what could happen to her if things went horribly wrong at the party today.

Chapter Eight

As soon as they walked in the doors at Walt's house, Sophie felt lots of pairs of eyes on her. Almost immediately, Pete said, "Sophie, I need to speak with you," and he led her up the stairs to her room at the end of the hall.

"What the hell, Pete?" Sophie asked indignantly.

"That's what I would like to know. You disappear with your bodyguard and don't come back for twelve hours. What the hell, Soph?"

"We had things we needed to discuss; he had to go over the protocols for being in the crowd today. And he took me to a safe location to be sure we weren't interrupted," Sophie said, her glare daring Pete to challenge her on that statement.

"I'm sure that could have been done in much less time and it could have been done right here," Pete argued.

"You're right, it might have been able to be done here, little brother." Those last two words were definitely said in a way to be a reminder of the fact that he was indeed the younger of the two. "But there were lots of other things that we did that couldn't have been done here, at least I don't think you would have wanted to hear all of that."

"Sophie, that's just TMI. I don't—God, I don't need to hear that," Pete said with disdain.

"Well, then stay out of it, little brother," Sophie stated. "Look, you hired them because you trust this team, right? Then trust them with me. I promise you that Bryan has done nothing to me that I wasn't one hundred percent okay with. He has kept me safe and has provided a bit of a distraction for me during this crazy visit." It was then that there was a soft knock at the door.

"Come in," Sophie snapped. Was everyone going to interrogate her on what she had been doing with Bryan? But actually, she wasn't surprised when Bryan himself walked in the door.

"Look, Pete," he began to explain. "I know that you don't think I'm very professional right now, and the fact is, you're right. What I have been doing hasn't been professional. If you want to fire me right now, that would totally be within your right. I have crossed lines that no one should ever cross in my position, and I apologize."

"Oh, hell no!" Sophie shouted. So what if everyone in the house heard her? "I am an adult, and Bryan has not asked me to do anything that I was not completely fine with. If you fire him now, I'm afraid I won't be going to your party after all, Pete. The Lawson brothers have taken great care with my safety and if they aren't going to be there to guard me, I don't feel safe going." She looked at her brother like she wanted to add *Put that in your pipe and smoke it*, but she didn't.

"Look, I wasn't trying to—Aw, hell, I'm just trying to make sure you don't get hurt, Sophie. I worry about you," Pete explained.

"And I appreciate that, but I promise you, nothing is being done to me that I haven't wanted done. At least not by Bryan or any of his team. Larry, on the other hand, has been nothing but a pain since I got here basically," Sophie explained.

"I know, and I really would understand if you stayed here. In fact, I would feel better if you did. Riley explained to us what a security nightmare this party is going to be for them. I just want you safe."

"I know little brother, and I believe that Bryan will do everything he can to make that happen. He has promised that he won't leave my side. But I am going today. I can't let Larry win by keeping me away from the one wedding celebration you have." She leaned in and gave Pete a tight hug. "Trust me, I trust them, it will be okay."

"Okay, okay," Pete agreed, hugging Sophie tightly. He pulled away and started back out the door. He turned around and gave her a smirk. "I like the new look, Soph. Not something I would have ever pictured you in, but it works." Then he walked out the door and headed for the brunch in progress downstairs.

"Look, Sophia, your brother is right: I have been totally unprofessional. I know better than to act the way I have with you over the last few days. If I had any sense of honor left at all, I would have one of my brothers guard you today, and I would take their position on the sidelines of it all watching for Larry," Bryan stated.

Sophia walked over and inserted herself firmly in Bryan's face. "Look, you haven't done anything that I haven't completely enjoyed, and I am honestly hoping that you will continue to do the same for the rest of my visit. But honestly, for today, as much as I am sure your brothers are great at what they do, you are the one that has earned my trust. You're the one that I connect with and that I already sense. So, no, I don't want to stay home like my brother suggested, and I don't want someone else doing the up close and personal guarding. I want more of what we have had so far, and I want you to be the one by my side." She raised up on her tiptoes, put her arms around his neck, and leaned in for a kiss.

Bryan wanted nothing more than to push Sophia backward onto the bed and completely forget that they had plans for the day—possibly dangerous plans. When he finally got his wits about him, he pulled his face away and told Sophia, "Your brother is totally right about the outfit, though. It looks great on you." He leaned in for one brief kiss and then pulled fully away.

"I kind of like it myself," Sophia agreed. "Although I'm not sure biker chick fits in where I live, but I will always love this outfit. Thank you for picking it out for me. How much do I owe you by the way?"

"Don't worry about it. I'll bill it to the case," Bryan said with a wink. He totally wouldn't; he liked the idea of Sophia having an outfit that he had bought and chosen for her. He didn't know how often she would be wearing it, but even if it hung in her closet and she thought of him fondly whenever she looked at it, it was well worth the money. With that, they headed down to the breakfast buffet that was set up similar to the day before. They were all going to eat before the women headed to the basement that had been set up as a changing station fully equipped with makeup and hair staff from the spa they had visited the day before.

Bryan noticed that this time, Sophia made a very healthy plate for herself. She had already had the sweet carbs that she had needed to fuel her energy to start the day, but now she had chosen good healthy proteins that would be needed to sustain her for the long day ahead. When she looked up at him from across the dining area, he gave her a brilliant smile and a brief nod. He was hoping she took that as the "good girl" praise it was intended to be. When she saw this, she beamed her own amazing smile right back and him. She had been able to feel and understand his praise and pleasure without having to say a word. Damn but this woman was everything he wanted in his life.

After she had finished eating, Sophie went upstairs to grab her outfit for the day. It was elegant, yet simple. It was a light mint flowy gown that came to mid-calf. There were embellishments along the empire waist, but otherwise it remained fairly subdued. She had chosen it because of how great it looked against her skin tone and her eyes. As she was walking back to the landing at the top of the stairs, Bryan caught her. "I was wondering what you were wearing today. I figure that since we are a couple, I should at least try to fit in. I think I have a tie that will complement that dress nicely. I'll see you in a bit, Sophia." With that, he leaned in and gave her a brief kiss on her cheek and headed to his own room to prepare for the day.

As Sophia made her way down the two flights of stairs, she was trying to sort out just what that statement had meant. He hadn't said 'since we need to appear to be a couple'; he had said 'since we are a couple.' Could he really be wanting to be a couple with her as much as she wanted that with him? She put those thoughts aside. Wishing and wanting would get her nowhere. The simple fact of the matter was that they would appear as a couple for the time being and then go their separate ways when the time came for this to all be over.

The ladies were all getting set up to have their hair and makeup done in the basement. As Sophia walked into the big open TV room, Rayne looked at her and said, "I have to say that outfit is totally hot on you."

"Thanks; it feels amazing too. I would have thought leather pants wouldn't be comfortable, but these are so soft they're like butter," Sophie admitted.

"So out all night with the sexy biker bodyguard, huh?" Autumn kind of teased. "Was it as amazing as we have all been thinking it was?"

"It was pretty amazing," Sophie said, blushing.

"Oh, wow, that blush says it all." Skye laughed. "It must have been really good."

"Let's just say he tied me to his Harley and had his wicked way with me, and by wicked, I mean totally deliciously hot." Sophie sighed.

"Girl, I can only imagine," Rayne said. "I mean, I totally love Walt, but you would have to be blind to not see that those three brothers are panty meltingly gorgeous. Those muscles and then the tats. Every girl's bad boy fantasy right there."

"Well, us old married ladies can still look, we just can't sample the goods." Autumn chuckled.

"I can sample the goods," Sunni said rather somberly. Sophie had noticed that on Thursday night it had kind of seemed like Sunni and Jason were at the barbeque together, but then at the dinner Friday night, they sat next to each other, but they really didn't seem to be together. It was pretty obvious something had changed in their relationship.

The ladies went on with their girl talk while the stylists worked to make them pretty.

Bryan was in his room getting ready when someone knocked on his door. He was still wearing his jeans, so he was decent and said "Come in."

Pete walked through the door. "Look, I'm not trying to be an ass about my sister, but you have to realize that I am very protective of her after what has happened."

"I totally get it, and you're absolutely right, I wasn't professional when I started things with her." Bryan was pacing the floor, trying to weigh his words carefully. "I can't say that what I have with your sister is a relationship, because we all know it has an expiration date of Monday. If she lived here or I could move there, maybe there would be more. For now, I guess what it is for both of us is a chance to have some fun in a way that is safe for her. I have not and will not promise her anything that I can't keep my word on. She and I both know that this is a distraction for her and enjoyable for both of us. I promise you I will not hurt your sister in any way, physically or emotionally. If you really aren't okay with that, I will step back and let one of my brothers do the one-on-one stuff with her."

"No, I have a feeling that my big sister would skin me alive if I tried that," Pete said. "And honestly I think I knew deep inside that you wouldn't hurt her. It's probably partially guilt that I didn't see things before and now we find ourselves right back in the middle of Larry's sick obsession with my sister. I had to say something and give her the chance to take an out if she needed it." He put out his hand for a handshake and questioned, "No hard feelings?"

He shook Pete's hand and said, "Nah, I totally get where you're coming from. My little sister thinks the three of us are pretty much overbearing jerks when it comes to her social life. We don't let many men get close to her, and trust me, we run every kind of check we can on anyone she does go out with. I get how it is to feel protective of a sister."

"Thanks for understanding, and to be honest, I actually appreciate the fact that you are distracting her from all of this as much as possible. I know she will never forget what happened, but if she gets a few hours of not thinking about it, that's a good thing for her, I'm sure," Pete said. He headed back out the door, saying, "Well, I'll get out of your way so you can get ready."

Bryan was in the process of changing into his dress slacks when someone else knocked on his door. He went to open it and saw Riley standing there. He opened the door so his brother could enter. "What's up, Rye?"

"Well, I just wanted to give you a heads up that Summer's going to be there today," Riley stated. At Bryan's raised eyebrow, he continued. "She got Jeremy to agree to bring her as his plus one. It won't hurt to have an extra set of eyes out there."

"True, and yeah, if she's with one of the brewery guys it's not like we have to worry about who she's dating," Bryan agreed. "Tell her thanks for being willing to help out today."

Riley nodded his agreement and left.

This time, Bryan actually got to finish dressing with no more interruptions. He was wearing black dress slacks, which were pretty much his standard work attire. He put on a light mint shirt with a deep green patterned tie. He figured that was as close as it was going to get for him to match Sophia's outfit.

He went downstairs to talk to Trevor and Riley about the set-up for the day. He really didn't like that it was a warm, sunny day. That meant that the party would be outdoors for the most part. They had been given the layout. The food would be set up on the veranda at the back of the country club. There were canopies with tables and chairs under them positioned around the yard and one large tent that had been set up to be a dance floor. Bryan had really hoped for a dreary rainy day; then all of the activities would have been forced inside. It would still be a logistical nightmare even in the club with the number of people that would be attending, but outdoors was virtually impossible to completely secure.

He met them in the bedroom downstairs and asked if they were all set up with their equipment. Trevor spoke first. "I am still tapped into the security feed. I have my computer set up to run facial recognition at all times. It will send an alert to my phone if the software thinks it hits on a match. It's not the perfect situation, eyes on the screen are preferred, but we don't have that luxury since we all need to have eyes on Sophie."

"I've actually gotten a little help for us in that area," Riley chimed in. "Summer is going to be there, and when I was talking with Jeremy, I found out that some of the guests are police officers. Makes sense with the connection to the legal system, but we have gotten them a copy of the picture of Larry and they know to alert one of us if they think they see him."

"Well, it's not perfect, but I guess it's the best we can do under the circumstances. God I hate outdoor assignments," Bryan said, shaking his head. They walked back out to the main part of the house just in time to see the ladies coming up the stairs. Sophia once again took his breath away. She had left most of her hair down, but the part surrounding her face had been pulled up and away so that her beautiful eyes and her high cheekbones were the center of focus when looking at her face. But then she smiled, and the whole room lit up, so he couldn't say it was any one feature of her face that made her beautiful; it was the whole package.

Sophie realized that with the fact that everyone knew she and Bryan were having some sort of fling, she didn't have to keep things strictly professional between them anymore in the group. She approached him slowly, giving him every opportunity to back up or to stop her progress in some way. When he put out both hands to take hers and pulled her to him, she was glad everyone knew. He pulled her to him and kissed her gently on the cheek.

"You look beautiful, Sophia," he said softly in her ear.

"You clean up pretty good yourself, Sir," Sophia replied. "Although I think you might want a jacket unless you're trying to make a statement with that shoulder holster and the one I'm sure is tucked into the back of your pants."

"Ha, ha. My jacket is right over there, little one," Bryan stated. "Although having them in plain sight might be a deterrent to this asshole." Bryan paused for a minute and then asked, "Have you ever fired a gun, Sophia?"

"I have. Shortly after the"—she paused briefly before continuing—"the incident, I took self defense lessons and shooting lessons. Why?"

"If you have any reason to need a gun, reach inside my jacket and take whichever one is easiest. Do anything you have to to defend yourself, Sophia. I hope it doesn't come to that, but if it does, do not hesitate to shoot." Bryan's face was so serious when he added, "Do whatever you need to, Sophia."

Sophie wanted to change the topic. She didn't like guns for the most part. She had learned to shoot out of necessity, but that didn't mean she owned a gun or that she was comfortable with them. But she also knew that Bryan wouldn't be happy unless she agreed. And in all honesty, she would use the gun if it became absolutely necessary. "As much as I really don't like the idea of shooting anyone, if it becomes necessary, I promise I will grab for one of your guns and use it."

"Thank you, Sophia. I hope you never have to, but we have to have our bases covered. I was hoping for a rainy day. Crowds are so much easier when indoors," Bryan grumbled.

Sophia smiled. "Well, I think you are the only one that's going to complain about the weather today. It's gorgeous outside. Maybe after the reception you can take me for another motorcycle ride."

"Hmm, I know just the place, a nice ride out to the country. I'll show you my home." Bryan's eyes heated up. He leaned in closer and added, "I would also love to show you my play room."

Sophie felt the heat in the room go up at least forty degrees. He had a home in the country, with a play room. Could a girl ask for anything more? Not likely. "I am definitely on board with that plan."

"We could just ditch the party all together and go to my place. I promise you the full tour," Bryan whispered. He knew Sophia absolutely would not go along with that plan, but it would make his life so much easier if she would.

"As tempting as that does sound, I have to ask that we wait until after the party. You know I can't ditch on my little brother." Sophia pouted.

"I know. You can't blame a guy for trying, though." Bryan leaned in and kissed her forehead. "And yes, I knew you wouldn't take me up on it. But it would make my job so much easier if you didn't even go to the party," he teased.

Chapter Nine

When they arrived at the country club, the limo dropped them off in the circular drive out front. Bryan guided Sophia into the entrance and off to the side of the large open lobby area. He wanted to get the lay of the land on where things were and how large the crowd was. There were just so many people. Autumn came from a large family, and Pete was from a very affluent and well-known family. It appeared half of Grand Rapids had shown up to this event. He leaned in and spoke softly to Sophia. "Little one, I don't want to keep you from having fun and doing as you choose at this party, but please keep in mind that the more you are out in the open, the easier it is for Larry to see you if he is here looking. Staying indoors or in one of the tents is preferable, especially if the tent is somewhat crowded. The dance floor is fine if there are already several couples there. I guess what I am saying is that most often, there is safety in numbers."

"Well, that is something I don't think I would have guessed about you," Sophia said with a small chuckle.

"What is that, Sophia?" Bryan was puzzled.

"That you know how to dance. At least I am assuming you do since you told me I have to be attached to you at the hip and you just said I could dance." She smiled.

"There are so many things you don't know about me, Sophia," Bryan said cryptically, "but yes, I do know how to dance. At least in a social setting. I wouldn't say I could win any competitions."

"I will definitely have to take you up on that." Sophia grinned. "As far as the rest, I understand what you are saying, but I refuse to stay inside all day when the party is outside. But I do understand the safety in numbers thing."

Another couple walked up to them as they were talking. Sophie knew Jeremy; she had known him pretty much his whole life. The young woman he was with was new, though. She was a gorgeous woman. She was dressed in khaki slacks and a pale peach blouse. Sophie could see the tattoos peeking out from the collar and sleeve. This wasn't the type of woman that Sophie would normally expect to see with Jeremy. She was even more stunned when Bryan reached out a hand to her and pulled her closer for a peck on her cheek, which she returned. Who the heck was this woman and what was she doing with Sophie's man?

Bryan looked at Sophia. Was that a bit of jealousy he saw in her eyes? He was pretty sure it was, at least a small bit. He reached out his free hand and shook Jeremy's hand. "Jeremy, good to see you."

Jeremey leaned in and kissed Sophia on the cheek and said, "Sophie, I'm so glad you could be here for Pete. I know it means a lot to him."

Okay, so Bryan got the whole jealousy thing. Even though he knew Jeremy and Sophia had been friends forever, and honestly she was probably more like a big sister to the man than anything, seeing another man lean in to kiss her, even on the cheek, caused a bit of jealousy to arise. If she had felt a similar feeling, he needed to explain who Summer was right away. "Sophia, this is my little sister, Summer Lawson. Summer, this is Sophia Hallowell." He didn't clarify who Sophia was. She was his client, yes. But she was a lot more than that to him now too. Summer would have to read into that however she wanted to.

Summer put out her hand to Sophia. "It's great to meet you. I don't do any of the 'heavy lifting' with the guys' business, but I'm always glad to be an extra set of eyes or ears when they have a case. When Jeremy was looking for a plus one, I figured this would be a way that I could help out my brothers and Jeremy's friends." She turned to Bryan and added, "If you need the bathroom checked out or need someone to go in there with her, just give me the high sign. Otherwise, I'm going to go and enjoy this party and keep my eyes and ears open."

"I appreciate that, Summer. I'll let you know." That was actually probably a much better solution. Bryan couldn't exactly go in the bathroom with Sophia, at least not until he knew it was empty, and entering to make sure it was empty could have some high society country club members screaming bloody murder. No, if Sophia did need the restroom, Summer going in first to make sure it was clear was their best plan. Before Summer walked away, he looked at Sophia and asked, "Do you need the bathroom right now, Sophia, before we go and mingle?"

"No, I'm fine," Sophia assured him. She turned to Summer. "Try to enjoy the party. I appreciate you being here to help keep me safe, but try to enjoy it anyway."

"I'm sure we will," Summer said, and she gave a small smile in Jeremy's direction. Sophia was pretty sure that neither of the men had even noticed, but it was pretty obvious that Summer had a thing for Jeremy. They seemed like an odd combination to her, but who was she to say?

As they walked away, Sophie noticed another person approaching. This one Sophie wasn't as happy to see. Mrs. Livingston had always been a huge busybody. If she was headed Sophie's way there was sure to be a long conversation about where Sophie had been and what she had been doing, and of course she would want all the details of who Sophia just happened to be standing so closely with. Bryan did have his arm around her waist. It probably wasn't a good idea to reach into his jacket to pull out one of his guns, though. Shooting Mrs. Livingston wouldn't be worth it, but just barely.

"Sophia," the older woman sort of sang out as she approached, holding out both hands for Sophie to take. She drew Sophie closer for a kiss on each cheek like she was some European diplomat. Sophia allowed it briefly but pulled back to Bryan's protective arm as quickly as possible.

"She prefers to be called Sophie," Bryan stated, holding out his hand to greet the woman. "I'm Bryan Lawson, Sophia's boyfriend. And you are?" It was pretty obvious that the woman was confused as to why he called her Sophia after just stating that she preferred to be called Sophie, but she had the grace to not say anything.

She shook Bryan's hand and said, "I'm Alice Livingston, I have known Sophia—" She paused at the stern look on the man's face and said, "I mean Sophie's family forever. Her mother and I are great friends."

"I am pleased to meet you, Alice," Bryan stated. Sophie could see the indignation in the woman's eyes that he had the audacity to call her by her first name. That just wasn't done in her circles, and Sophie was pretty sure that Bryan knew that. He just didn't care. Of course, that would also make the woman feel that he was not an appropriate boyfriend for Sophie, but that didn't matter since he really wasn't hers.

Alice turned back to Sophia and said, "Your mother tells me that you have been living out west somewhere. How have you been? What have you been doing these last several years? I haven't seen you visit in forever. You never come to visit."

"I know, Mrs. Livingston. Life has just been so busy for me lately. I always intend to come more often, but something always comes up."

"Well, I am sure that your family is happy that you are here for this wonderous occasion," the old woman stated.

"Yes, I'm so happy that I could be here to celebrate with my brother and his wife."

"But really, eloping like they did. That was the odd thing in my opinion. Couldn't they have waited a couple more months? I am sure your parents would have loved to have had a big wedding here for them."

"I am sure my parents are fine with the way things happened. We are having this party to celebrate. Sometimes people are just so much in love that they just can't wait," Sophie stated. She was not going to let this old biddy be derogatory about her brother and his new wife. Sophia knew why they had eloped, and that was absolutely no one's business except theirs.

"Well, yes, I suppose this is the next best thing," she hesitantly agreed.

Bryan got the impression that this woman would be very willing to stand here and monopolize Sophia's time for as long as they would let her. She likely didn't have very many people that would just let her go on and on without being rude. He was going to try not to be rude, but he also wasn't going to stand her and listen to this woman babble on and on, and he wasn't willing to allow Sophia to have to hear what he was sure would be this woman's toxic opinion of everything. He started to guide Sophia away, saying, "Please excuse us, Alice. I see someone that I need to talk to." And with that, they were free of the woman.

"Do you really need to see someone, or was that just a way to get away from her?" Sophia asked quietly.

"Oh, no, I would never be so rude, Sophia," Bryan said with a smirk. "I really do need to speak to someone." With that, he led her toward Trevor, who was standing just outside the doors leading onto the veranda.

As they approached, Trevor put down the phone he had been staring at. "Sophie, you look lovely," he said.

Bryan sort of growled at his brother but asked, "Anything yet?"

"No, it's quiet so far. Guests are still arriving, and my guess is that if he is going to do anything, it's not going to be until after the party is in full swing and people have partaken in the food and alcohol that is so readily available."

"Most likely," Bryan agreed. "He probably figures he can slip in unnoticed once the party is in full force. Let me know if you even think you see anything or if you get a ping on your facial recognition program."

"Will do, big brother," Trevor agreed. He was mostly keeping a position near the doors into the country club, at least until the actual speeches and things started. It was a raised veranda and offered him a better position to see out over the crowd that was quickly forming on the main lawn.

"Are you hungry, Sophia, or would you rather mingle some more before you eat?" Bryan asked.

"I'm not hungry. Honestly, I am not sure that I will be able to eat today," Sophia admitted.

"I understand, little one, but keep in mind that if you intend to have alcohol or toast with champagne, you need food in your stomach. I really need you to stay at the top of your game today," Bryan directed.

"I know, but honestly, I'm thinking that I might drink the non-alcoholic stuff they got for Autumn. I can't afford to let my guard down today," Sophia said somberly.

Bryan wished that he could take that away from her. He would prefer if he could take all of her worry and stress about the day away from her, but if he were being honest with himself, he couldn't, and he did need her to be as aware and alert as possible. She was being very sensible about keeping herself safe. "I agree, non-alcoholic for both of us." He pulled her closer to him by the arm he had around her waist and asked, "Do you see anyone you want to go and greet or talk to, Sophia?"

Just then an energetic young woman came up to them rather

quickly. Bryan was braced for an assault. Just because this wasn't Larry didn't mean this woman couldn't have been doing his bidding.

"Sophie, Sophie Hallowell, is that really you?" the woman exclaimed. "I haven't seen you in eons." She held out her arms for a hug.

Sophie hesitated for a moment. She was supposed to stay attached to Bryan at all times, but this had been her best friend for years when she had been in school. She felt Bryan drop his arm slightly, and she took that as his approval of her stepping in to the hug of her friend. "Oh my God, Betsy, it's been forever! How have you been?" Sophie hugged the woman briefly and then stepped back into Bryan's protective arm.

"I've been good, but obviously not as good as you," Betsy gushed, looking directly at Bryan. "You have apparently found a gorgeous man." Betsy held out her hand and Bryan shook it.

"Bryan Lawson, meet my best friend all though my school years, Betsy McClain. Betsy, this is my boyfriend, Bryan."

"It's a pleasure to meet you, ma'am," Bryan said in his best military voice.

Sophie heard the intake of breath from Betsy at being called ma'am, and she was pretty sure that Bryan had done that just to irritate the woman. She was okay with that, though. When she had first come back to Michigan after her relationship with Larry ended, Betsy had kept her distance. Sophie knew it was most likely out of not knowing what to say or how to react to Sophie losing her baby and having been treated so horribly. But still, it hurt when the person that had been her best friend forever didn't come to visit or spend time with Sophie. Betsy had called a few times, but even then the conversation had seemed stilted and tense.

"Oh, I've been living out west. I do graphic design mostly. I dabble a little bit in photography, but mostly nature pictures to use in my graphics," Sophie said.

"That's really cool. Have you done any ads or anything that I might have seen?" Betsy asked.

"No, I'm not in advertising, more like graphics for publishing and that type of thing," Sophia hedged.

Bryan knew exactly what Sophia wasn't saying. He knew exactly what type of graphic arts she did. She designed book covers and marketing materials for authors. Mostly authors of romance and erotica.

That would most likely be something that some people would take offense to. He hadn't seen much of her work, but if she designed covers like the ones that had been on the books he had seen his sister read, he could just imagine that it might be something she would be careful with letting just anyone know.

"Oh, yeah, I get ya," Betsy stated. "I've mostly been just taking classes and working at a boutique. Good thing Daddy is rich," she laughed. "I buy more than I sell some days."

"Hmm, that's great." Sophia didn't sound overly excited about that news to Bryan, but then again, even though she had grown up in a wealthy family, Sophia was not living the life of a spoiled little rich girl. She was doing her best just to stay alive some days. So far, no one thought Larry knew where she was living and what she was doing, but they also knew that it could just be a matter of time before he figured it out somehow. Bryan knew he could keep her safe here in Michigan; he wasn't so sure she would be safe forever in Colorado.

Apparently, Betsy got the message that Sophia wasn't going to gush over her like she obviously seemed to need because rather quickly she said, "Oh, look, there's Clint. I better go say hi. Some day I'll catch that man's attention, I swear I will." And with that, Betsy was off and trailing after a man that had to be at least a decade her senior.

"Isn't she about the same age as you?" Bryan asked when she was out of ear shot.

"Mm-hmm," Sophia agreed.

"And she still lives off her father's money?"

"She does. She was an only child, and her parents always spoiled her rotten. They haven't stopped even though they really should. I think they are hoping that she will find a rich man to marry who take her off their hands," Sophia declared.

"Well, maybe Clint will help her with that," Bryan said.

"Not likely. Clint doesn't come from money; he made his own and he sees right through Betsy. I think being self-made he's not crazy about the idea of a wife who just wants to be a sponge," Sophia stated. "Besides, I think Clint is too young for her. She's looking for a sugar daddy that is likely to die in the next few years and leave her all his money."

"She sounds like a wonderful human being," Bryan said derisively.

"Yeah, she's a real peach."

Bryan and Sophia made their way over to the bar at the side of the veranda. There were waiters carrying around trays of champagne, but if they wanted non-alcoholic they were better off asking for it at the bar. As they approached, Sophia's father stepped up to them.

He shook hands with Bryan and said, "I know who you are, and what you are doing here, and I just wanted to say thank you. My wife is unaware that you are anything other than Sophie's date, and I would like to keep it that way. She is unaware that this person may still be a danger, and I would like to keep her in the dark if possible. But I appreciate you and your family being here to watch out for my daughter."

"It's my pleasure, Sir," Bryan assured him. "We all take every assignment with complete devotion to keeping the client's best interest foremost in our actions."

Sophia could feel her cheeks heat a little at that statement. Bryan had definitely taken care of her interests last night at his garage and again early this morning. She had kind of zoned out on the conversation taking place between her bodyguard and her father. Thoughts of all the wonderful things Bryan had done to her were on replay in her brain.

Bryan leaned in to speak in Sophia's ear. "I bet I know what you are thinking about. That sweet blush says it all."

Sophie could not believe Bryan would refer to their lovemaking right in front of her father, but when she actually looked up, her father was nowhere in the area anymore. She had obviously fallen down the rabbit hole of memories and ignored her father altogether. He was currently talking to some of his partners from the law firm several yards away. She glanced at Bryan and felt the heat rise more in her face.

"Oh, you are a delight, little one," Bryan said with a heated smile. "I promise to give you more memories that will cause that heated look to show up on your face." He guided her to the bar so that they could get their drinks.

They spent the next hour or so mingling around the area. They remained closer to the building than the outlying areas. Bryan wanted to keep her as far from those woods as possible. Every time they came near one of his siblings, Bryan asked if they had seen anything, but no one had. Bryan couldn't really believe that Larry wouldn't take the opportunity to cause trouble in such an open public forum; the problem was that he wasn't sure what he would try to do. There was no way he was getting close enough to Sophia to try to touch her or take her. Bryan couldn't be sure that he wouldn't try or that he at least wouldn't attempt contact to be able to speak to Sophia. Actually, Bryan was hoping that was his plan. If he tried to get up close and personal, he would be taken down in a minute. No, it was the more ranged attack possibilities that had Bryan the most concerned. A gun from a distance would be much harder to control than a person who tried to grab her.

When it came time for the meal to be served, Sophie once again was seated at what would be considered the family table, which pretty much put her front and center. They were seated directly in front of the raised dais where the couple and their closest friends were seated. If there had been an actual wedding, these would have been their bridesmaids and groomsmen. The meal was served in a very formal fashion. Sophie was pretty sure if the reception had been the bride's family's responsibility it would have been much more fun. Probably a block party with all the tacos and enchiladas you could eat. Autumn's family seemed very down to earth and much more casual than Sophie's. She was pretty sure she would have enjoyed the block party more than this, but then again, she wasn't sure how Bryan would have felt about that. It was difficult enough trying to watch the crowd at a private club with a fence around it. Monitoring everyone that came and went at a block party would probably be far more difficult. Sophie looked around, and as she had suspected, Trevor was positioned at one back corner of the large tent and Riley was at the other. There wouldn't be a part of the large crowd that they couldn't see, and if anyone approached from outside the tent, they would likely be taken down before they got close enough that the crowd even knew they were there.

After the meal had been mostly consumed, it was time for speeches and toasts. The things that Autumn's father said made Sophie cry. It was very obvious how much this man loved his little girl. Sophie had never doubted that her parents loved her, but it was obviously very different than the way this family was able to openly express their feelings. She had vowed years ago that if she ever got to the point of having her own husband and children, she wouldn't be the kind of distant socialite mother that she had been raised by. Her children would know every day that Mom was there and that she loved them completely. Her parents had always shown their love in ways that didn't include a lot of their time.

The group moved to the large dance floor area for all of the traditional dances: bride and groom, father of the bride, mother of the groom, and finally all of the family shared one dance. Sophie was surprised that Bryan had not been exaggerating when he had said that he could dance. He wasn't doing anything overly fancy, but he was also not a stiff board that didn't know how to move.

After all of the family dances, they lined up for a dollar dance. While many couples did this to have extra money to spend on their honeymoon and such, Sophie was pretty sure that this was done as more of a tradition of the bride's family than it was the actual need for money. Her suspicion was confirmed when pretty much every member of Autumn's family from the oldest to the youngest lined up with a dollar bill or more in their hand. Sophie watched as one person after another danced with Pete. She wanted to get in line but she wasn't sure if Bryan was going to allow that. It couldn't hurt to ask though. "Would it be possible for me to dance with my brother? I know it's not like I haven't gotten to spend time with him in the last couple of days. I know that, but when he leaves here today, I don't know when I will see him again. I understand if it puts me at too much of a risk, and I can't, though. I'll do whatever you feel is best."

"Look at the line, Sophia," Bryan stated.

"Oh, I know, it's really long, it's probably not safe for me to stand there is it?" Sophie said. "I get it. Like I said, it's okay."

"Not what I meant, Sophia." Bryan stood and held out a hand to help her from her chair. He walked her over toward the front of the long line that awaited their dance with the groom. As they stepped closer, Sophie realized that Bryan's sister was approaching the front of the line; she would be next. Bryan pulled a dollar bill from his pocket and handed it to the person collecting money for Pete's dances.

When it was Summer's turn, she stepped aside, and Bryan guided Sophia to Pete. He told Pete, "Just keep her right here in the middle of the crowd. Don't go closer to the edge."

Pete nodded his agreement as Sophie stepped into his arms for their dance. As they moved, Pete was very careful to remain in the middle. Sophie realized that Bryan, Trevor, Summer, and Riley had all kind of closed in to form a loose circle around the dancing couple. They weren't in such a tight formation that it would be obvious, they just seemed like spectators to most, but Sophie was not just a casual observer. She knew what it had taken for Bryan to be willing to let her dance with her brother. She could see the worry on his face as he kept his eyes firmly on her. The other three Lawsons had eyes that were constantly moving to guard against any threat or to observe if anyone approached.

"So, little brother, you finally tied the knot," Sophie joked.

"Um, I did that a couple of months ago, Soph," Pete said.

"I know, but that's what I would be saying if we were dancing right after your wedding. I figured it was appropriate now too."

"Just keep in mind that I am the younger of the two of us. You should be an old married woman by now," Pete teased.

For a brief moment, Pete's comment stung, but she knew that he hadn't meant it to be hurtful. "Yeah, you know what they say about best laid plans," Sophia remarked.

"Look, Sophie, I'm sorry. I shouldn't have said that," Pete apologized.

"It's okay, I know you didn't mean anything bad by it. And, honestly, if I hadn't made such a poor choice, I probably would be married by now," Sophia assured him. "Just do me a couple of favors, okay? Don't be like Mom and Dad, don't love your family from a distance. Make time for them, make them a priority."

"Done. Autumn will never have a reason to wonder why I am always at work or if I care about her," Pete promised.

"And when you have your kids, bring them to see Aunt Sophie often. I can live vicariously through you." Sophie realized just what it would mean when Pete had kids. They would mostly grow up not knowing her other than maybe a yearly vacation to Colorado. She couldn't come back to Michigan to see them any time she wanted.

"I will, Sophie, I promise." Pete knew as well as she did what the limitations would be as long as Larry was out there somewhere still holding a grudge or whatever it was that he wouldn't let go of.

"I should probably let you get to your next partner; you have quite a long line with all of Autumn's family. Have a great honeymoon, Pete. And be happy." Sophie kissed him on the cheek and then stepped away. She hadn't made two steps before Bryan was at her side and ushering her back to their table. Trevor and Riley resumed their positions on the corners of the tent, and Summer made her way back to Jeremy.

"Why did Summer do that?" Sophie asked, although she was fairly certain she knew the answer.

"Oh, I just texted her and asked her to get in line as soon as it started to form. I knew you would want to dance and have a chance to talk to your brother, but I also didn't want you standing in that long line with no real protection," Bryan explained.

"You really do think of everything, don't you?" Sophie asked.

"I always try to anticipate the needs of a client, yes," Bryan replied.

"I don't think that's all of it though," Sophie began. "I think it's part of being a good Dominant too. You understand what your partner at the time needs and you do your best to give it."

"You could be right," Bryan said with a shrug.

Sophie figured this was as good a time as any to get to know Bryan a little better. They were sitting with their chairs touching—if she moved slightly she would be sitting on his lap—and she was leaned in to him with his arm around the back of her chair. She knew it was mostly about protection, but it also felt very intimate. She could keep her voice low and no one else would hear anything they said. "So how long have you been in the lifestyle?" she asked.

"I don't know that I've ever been in the lifestyle so much as it's always been my life. I was the oldest of four kids. So I was always given more responsibility and felt protective of my siblings. It's how my dad raised me: men treated women a certain way. Men were the head of the household but not in a way that was ever lorded over the females. When our parents died, I was only nineteen. I fought like hell to be able to have custody. I think if Riley had been any younger, they wouldn't have gone along with it. But Trevor was seventeen, so he was able to step up and help a lot too. When Trevor turned nineteen, Summer and Riley were both old enough to take care of themselves really. So I joined the Marine Corps. I think I've just always had a take charge kind of personality."

"I can see that," Sophie agreed.

"It was in the Corps that I learned about what people refer to as the lifestyle and started to learn more about what it actually meant to be 'a Dominant,' not just dominant. In Europe there are clubs and things that are far more open than we as Americans tend to be. My buddies and I used to hang out in those clubs. We liked the fact that they weren't like a seedy strip club or bar. The alcohol was either minimal or not present at all. We could see that it was more about discipline and structure than just getting your rocks off so to speak, and we wanted in. We found ourselves being welcomed into some of the private clubs because of our attitudes and personalities." Bryan paused. "That's pretty much the Bryan Lawson cliff notes. What about you? Tell me all about the young Sophia," Bryan asked.

"I grew up in a very different type of family than you did, obviously. My parents being wealthy meant that they could pay others to do anything that they didn't have the time for or felt was beneath them. I'm not saying they left us to nannies and cooks all the time, but my dad probably worked seventy or eighty hours a week when I was little. He was trying to build the firm into what it is today. My mom was there; she just wasn't super emotionally attached. And she was trying to enter the higher society that being the wife of an up-and-coming law partner was accustomed to. We knew she loved us, but she didn't say it a lot. Pete and I were pretty close, despite the fact that he was the annoying little brother. All of the sloth guys grew up together, so I knew all of them since they were little." Sophia paused for a bit, and when she went on, Bryan could tell what was coming was the part of her life that wasn't easy to talk about. "I went to school for graphic design, not because I thought it would be a lucrative career as much as I thought it sounded fun. That's where I got my first exposure to the idea of dominance and submission. For me, it was more about private play parties that some of the students threw. It was nowhere nearly as structured as what you described. Anyway, my parents helped me get all the state-of-the-art equipment when I graduated, and I started my business. Of course, I didn't make much money to begin with because no one knew who I was, but I was doing something that I loved. I went to a play party that someone I had known on campus was throwing at this big house out in Grandville. It was basically just a bunch of people who thought they knew what they were doing but really had no clue. That's where I met Larry. Which is really ironic because after we started dating, he was the one who kept telling me that my wants and desires were wrong and that sane people didn't do those things." Sophia took another long pause. "Anyway, at the time, he seemed to really be dominant and he was attractive and so attentive to me that I got hooked pretty quickly. By the time I realized that he wasn't what I thought he was, I was pretty much trapped in the relationship. He alienated me from my friends and family. It started out with seeming like he just loved me so much that he didn't want me to go hang out with others. And he always had excuses why he couldn't go with me to see friends. He did go to my parents' house a few times, but for the most part, he would whine about me leaving him alone all the time, so I didn't go. It was just easier that way. When the physical abuse started, I stayed away because I was afraid someone would see a bruise and say something or somehow they would figure it out and I was scared to death of what would happen if anyone ever confronted him about it all. He decided that we needed to move to Oregon and I was pretty much dependent on him by then, so I went along." Sophia seemed to draw in on herself, and Bryan knew why. This was where the story took a very bad turn, and Sophia didn't need to tell him those details. He knew what the outcome had been and he didn't want to have her going that deeply into the story in a crowd of people. "You don't need to say anymore, Sophia." Bryan pulled her tighter to himself. "I know the basics of the rest of the story. It's why Pete hired us to track down Larry."

Sophie was relieved to not have to say the rest of it. She wouldn't be able to do so without crying, and this was a place for making happy memories, not dragging out sad ones. She leaned into Bryan and gathered the strength that he offered. She realized that while they had been talking, the dollar dance had ended, and now couples were dancing on the hardwood dance floor and others were mingling and visiting around the large yard. "Would you dance with me?" she asked.

Bryan wanted nothing more than to hold her in his arms and pull her body tight to his. "I would love to dance with you, Sophia." He stood and again offered his hand. They made their way closer to the center of the group of people dancing, it would be better cover for them to not be on the edge. Bryan pulled her in close, and she tucked her head onto his shoulder. He offered her his strength without having to say a word.

Sophie let herself just close her eyes and be in the moment with Bryan. The past needed to be put out of her mind for the rest of the time they had together. Thoughts of the future needed to be set aside too. Sophie needed to just live in this moment. She would be all in for whatever she could have with Bryan for the next thirty-six hours or so before she had to go to the airport for her flight back home. She was going to do her level best to not think about Larry other than knowing that he could be out there so she had to be cautious. She wasn't going to dwell on what a mistake it had been to get involved with him. She was going to forgive herself for her poor choices back then and try to remain relevant and present in every moment she had left here in Michigan. They danced through a couple of songs before they heard the DJ announce that the bride and groom would be cutting the cake soon and that would be followed by the tossing of the bouquet and garter. Sophie knew that soon after that, Pete and Autumn would be heading out for the airport and to whatever destination Pete had decided on for a honeymoon. It was a surprise to Autumn, so no one was allowed to know except a friend of hers that had packed her luggage.

Bryan walked with her to the front of the crowd, preparing for the cutting of the cake. The massive cake that had been on the table earlier had been removed by staff and cut into pieces to be served by the waiters. All that remained was the top two layers. Pete and Autumn cut into the second layer and served each other a piece. Autumn went first and did what everyone hoped brides did: she smashed it into Pete's face. Pete was far more gracious, he didn't want to get the frosting in Autumn's beautiful hair or on her dress. They returned to their table to find that pieces of cake had already been placed at each seat. This staff was efficient. Unfortunately, they were a little too efficient for Bryan's liking. Sophie was just lifting her fork to dig in for a juicy bite when Bryan stopped her. He pulled the plate away and waved down a server.

"What, I don't get to eat cake?" Sophie muttered. "Some people would say that's an affront to the bride and groom you know." She was very indignant. How dare the brute take her cake? Taking her underwear had been bad enough. This was worse by far.

When the server approached, he asked, "Is there a problem, Sir?"

"Yes. As we were walking back to our table, I noticed a rather large bug on my girlfriend's cake. Would you kindly get her another?" Bryan was very smooth and polite.

Sophia was having none of it. "I didn't see a bug. What bug?"

"I saw it, Sophia, and I don't want you eating that piece of cake. This kind gentleman will gladly get you another, won't you"—Bryan glanced down at the nametag—"Brad?" He looked at Sophia and dared her to challenge him on this one.

"Of course, Sir, right away," the young man said while taking the plate from Bryan.

"There was no bug on my cake. Why did you send it back?" Sophie asked.

"Because I don't trust coming back to find it on the table, Sophia," he said with a very serious tone. "I have no idea what could be on or in that slice of cake."

"Oh," Sophia said as the reason dawned on her.

"Yes, oh," Bryan repeated. The server returned with a fresh piece of cake.

"I got you one with a rose this time, ma'am, to make up for the bug," Brad stated. If Bryan was guessing correctly, the young man found Sophia attractive and was trying to impress her.

"That's very kind of you Brad," Sophie said with a smile. "Thank you so much." The young man nodded and sort of stumbled away from the table.

They enjoyed their cake and then prepared to join the crowd waiting for the bouquet to be thrown. All of the single women gathered around. Sophie would have been content to just watch, but Bryan gently pushed her toward the crowd. "You don't want to break tradition now, do you, Sophia?" he challenged.

"I just thought you didn't want me to leave your side," she whispered.

"Normally, I wouldn't, but I think the crowd is enough to keep you safe. Give it your best try, Sophia."

With a command like that, the submissive part of Sophie could do nothing less, although she wasn't really sure why she was trying. The point was supposed to be that whoever caught the bouquet was the next to be married, and Sophie had no prospects of that happening anytime soon. Still, the command given in that deep, dominant voice made her have to try, and sure enough, she caught the bouquet.

When the men began to gather to catch the garter, Sophie tried to get Bryan to join in. "You made me go. Why won't you?" she pouted.

"Because you were in the crowd, Sophia. If I am in the crowd, where does that leave you?" he asked.

"Outside of the crowd, right, I get it now," Sophie stated. Still, there was something in her that wanted Bryan to catch the garter. Maybe kismet would make them have to stay together if they were the couple that caught the bouquet and garter.

As Sophie had expected, it was then announced that the couple would be making their way to their limo to leave for the evening. The guests could pick up pouches of birdseed if they wanted to toss it as the couple made their way out. Bryan made sure that he and Sophia were close to the center line where Pete and Autumn would be making their escape. He wanted people around them as much as possible. Sophie was just getting ready to throw her handful of birdseed when she heard voices both masculine and feminine shout the word "GUN!"

She dropped to the ground as quickly as she could, which was aided greatly when a solid body of pure muscle tucked her to him and took her down under him. Going down so fast with a large man on top of her winded her and made her feel like she was going to pass out.

When Bryan had heard the word "Gun" his natural instincts had taken over, and he had wrapped himself around Sophia and taken her to the ground under cover of his body. Within what seemed like less than a second after hearing that word, he had felt the sharp pain that pierced his flesh just below his left pectoral muscle toward the outside of his body. He knew then that he had been hit by the shot; what he didn't know was whether or not Sophia had been hit too. The last thing he remembered before passing out from the pain was looking down and seeing Sophia with her eyes closed, her pale green dress starting to change to a deep red. He was praying with all that was in him that it was his blood and not hers. And then everything went black.

Riley, Trevor, and Summer had all yelled out the word gun at the same time. It wasn't difficult to figure out why. Apparently, their suspect had gotten tired of the waiting game and he had stepped out of the shadows and stood right in front of the limo with a gun pointed into the crowd.

Summer headed toward Bryan and Sophie to check their status while Trevor and Riley went in pursuit of the man who was currently running toward the woods surrounding the country club. Trevor fired a shot at the man's leg, and it hit solidly in his thigh. He tried to continue to run, but he was impaired by the bullet. Trevor called out for him to stop. Larry turned to take aim on Trevor, but before he could pull the trigger, Riley took aim and shot the man dead center of his forehead. His second shot hit the man squarely in the heart, although it was highly contestable as to whether or not he actually had one. Sirens were heard in the distance as both men made their way back to the limo to see how their brother and their client were.

Summer cautioned everyone not to touch Bryan. She didn't know exactly where the bullet was in his body, but moving him could prove fatal if it were close to a vital organ. Sophie started to stir, and Summer spoke to her quickly. "Sophie, I need you to stay still. I know that's really difficult right now. But we don't know where the bullet is. Moving Bryan could cause the bullet to move and that could be fatal. Please, just stay still, the ambulance is almost here." Summer had tears streaming down her face.

"Bullet?" Sophie asked. There had been a bullet, and now she couldn't move. Bryan was on top of her. Oh, God, Bryan had been shot. She felt her head start to swim again before she fainted once more.

Chapter Ten

Sophie came to in a dimly lit hospital room. She started to sit up, but she heard her mother say "Hold on, Sophia, let me call the nurse."

"Nurse? Why am I in the hospital?" Sophie asked, but as soon as the question was out of her mouth, memory started to return. "Oh, God, Bryan was shot. Is he okay? Where is he?" Sophie was madly tearing the blankets off of herself, trying to get out of the bed, but she seemed to be in a tangle and couldn't extricate herself.

"He's in surgery, Sophia, but they think he will be fine. Please, just let the nurse come and make sure it's okay for you to get up. You blacked out and I just want to be sure you're okay," her mother pleaded.

Her father was there also trying to keep her in bed. "Listen to your mother, Sophia."

Fortunately, a nurse came in and said, "I see you're awake, Ms. Hallowell. Let me check a couple of things and then I will help you get out of that bed. We don't want you up and walking around until we make sure your vitals are stabilized. Then we will get you up and you can get dressed."

Sophie lay back against the raised bed and let the nurse make her assessment. "I don't think I have clothes," she said. "I think my dress was ruined."

"One of Peter's friends brought you clothes from Walt's house. You have a bag and I can help you whenever you can get dressed," her mother offered.

"Okay. I just need to see Bryan," Sophie stated.

"Your friend is in surgery at the moment," the nurse said. "As soon as I'm done here, we'll get you dressed, and you can follow me to the waiting room where his friends are."

Pete and Autumn walked in the door. "Oh, God, Sophie, you're awake. I'm so glad you're okay," Pete enthused.

"Aren't you supposed to be on your honeymoon?" she asked.

"We are, but we couldn't leave until we knew you were okay," Autumn said.

"I'm fine. I think I just passed out from shock or something." She looked at the nurse and the nurse nodded her agreement. "It's Bryan I'm worried about. He was shot, but that's all I know. I remember Summer asking me to stay still because Bryan was shot."

"He was, but they are sure he's going to be fine. The bullet didn't hit any major arteries or organs. It did crack one of his ribs, and there was quite a lot of blood loss, but they are sure he will be fine," Pete assured her.

"Okay, good, that's good." Sophie was babbling a bit because she was relieved to hear that Bryan would be okay, but until she saw him for herself, she wouldn't be okay.

"Your vitals look great. Can we please clear the room, so I can help the patient get dressed," the nurse commanded.

Everyone walked out of the room to wait in the hallway. The nurse brought the bag to the bed and started to pull things out of it. She was pretty sure it had been one of the women that had packed the bag. Instead of the practical clothing her mother or one of the men would have packed, the bag contained her leather pants and the Harley shirt that Bryan had given her just that morning. That seemed like a lifetime ago, but it hadn't even been twelve hours since they had sat and had breakfast together. Now Bryan was in surgery with a bullet wound that was intended for her.

After she was dressed, the nurse said, "I'd prefer to take you to your friend in a wheelchair. It's not that I think you couldn't walk, but you still may be a little unsteady and I don't want to take any chances, and it's quite a distance." Sophie nodded her agreement, and the nurse smiled and said, "Good. I have one right outside."

They exited the room, and Sophie sat in the chair. The nurse began pushing her down the hall, and her family followed along behind.

When they got to the surgical waiting room, Summer rushed over to Sophie and gave her a hug. "I'm so glad you're okay. Thank you for not moving. I wasn't sure where the bullet was." She wasn't outright crying, but Sophie could tell that she had been.

"It's okay, I would have done anything. Is he going to be okay?"

"He is," Trevor said, stepping to her side. "They are just finishing up in the operating room, then he'll be in recovery. As soon as they transfer him to a regular room, we can go see him."

Sophie noticed that Riley was sort of standing off to the side and seemed a little quiet, more so than normal. Riley was always the more silent one. "Riley, are you okay? They said Bryan is going to be fine," Sophie asked.

"He's just a little quiet right now," Summer said softly. "He's never killed anyone outside of the military."

"Killed?" At first Sophie was confused. But the facts didn't take long to compute in her brain. She stood from her chair and walked over to Riley. She wrapped her arms around him and was sobbing tears of relief as she said, "Thank you, oh God, thank you Riley. I never have to be afraid of him again. Thank you so much."

It took a moment, but Riley wrapped his arms around Sophie and started to try to calm her tears. "It's all right, Sophie. He will never hurt anyone again."

"And don't for a minute think that it wasn't a righteous kill, Riley. You did it by the book. He was going to shoot me if you hadn't taken him down," Trevor said. "Even the police said it was justifiable."

"Oh, Riley, you're my hero, thank you so much," Sophie cried.

Sophie's entire family came forward to shake Riley's hand and thank him for making her safe. A person in scrubs came in and asked, "Are you the Lawson family?"

"We are," Trevor and Summer said while stepping forward. As Riley stepped forward, he put his arm around Sophie's waist and took her with him to the front of the group.

"I'm Dr. Veldt. I removed the bullet and repaired the internal damage. There is one rib that is pretty severely cracked, that will be the most painful part of this whole ordeal. He had quite a bit of blood loss, but the places the blood was coming from are all repaired. He may be out of it for a while. We plan to keep him sedated for at least a day or two because his body just needs the time to rest and restore. They should be taking him up to a room shortly. The nurse at the desk can tell you which one. But please limit the amount of visitors until he is out of sedation. He really does need rest. Do you have any questions for me?"

They all looked back and forth with each other, and Trevor said, "No, Doctor, I think we are all set. Thank you so much for taking care of our brother." He held out his hand and shook with the doctor then he turned and walked out the door.

Sophie looked at Pete and said, "See, we're all set here. I'm going to be fine, Bryan's going to be fine, and Riley took out the big bad wolf. Please go on your honeymoon now."

Pete stepped forward and hugged his sister. "Okay, you convinced me, but just because we're going doesn't mean I won't be in touch. Family is important to Autumn and me." He looked at his beautiful wife, and she smiled her agreement.

Sophie hugged Autumn and said, "I'm so glad you're a part of this family and I can't wait to know you more. Enjoy your honeymoon." With that, the newlyweds took their leave. Sophie's parents were the next to go, although they tried to get her to go with them, insisting that she needed her rest. "It's okay, Mom and Dad, I really do feel fine and I want to stay here for Bryan. But I promise we will spend some time together soon." That was the first moment when it dawned on her that she had no reason to need to go back to Colorado anytime soon. She could stay in Michigan for a long visit, maybe even permanently. They reluctantly left.

Riley came back to the group and said, "The nurse said he will be in room 847 as soon as he is released from the recovery room." They all headed for the elevator down the hall.

While they waited for the elevator, Sophie realized that she should probably make sure that the family was okay with her staying. She had just assumed it was okay for her to wait with them for Bryan, but they hadn't invited her. "Look, if you guys want this to just be a family thing, I'm sure I can catch my parents."

"No, Sophie, please don't feel like you need to go. I'm sure Bryan will want to see you when he wakes up. At least if you haven't left by then," Trevor said.

"Actually, I was just thinking that thanks to you guys, I don't have a timeline for leaving. I think I'm going to stay in Michigan, at least for a while." Sophie smiled. The elevator doors opened, and they all stepped inside.

When they arrived at the eighth floor, they walked down the hall to the room. As they stepped inside, they realized that Bryan had been given one of the large private rooms that were usually reserved for the wealthy or the famous. "This can't be right. We don't have insurance that would cover a room like this. Let me go speak to the nurses' desk," Trevor said.

As he started to walk out of the room, the same nurse that had helped Sophie came in. "I just wanted to let you know that recovery estimates that your family member will be up here in the next half hour or so."

"Um, yeah, about that. Would it be possible to transfer him to a regular room?" Trevor didn't want to make a big issue of it, but there was no way they could afford the bills that would come from a room like this.

"This room was assigned based on what your father requested," she said, looking at Sophie. "All bills are to go directly to him. He requested the best room and the best of everything we have to offer. He has also taken care of any meals any of you have during the stay."

Well, you couldn't say that Peter Hallowell Sr. was a cheapskate when it came to thanking someone for saving his daughter's life. The nurse walked back out of the room.

"He really didn't need to do that," Riley said.

"Yes, he did," Sophie replied. "Trust me, it's a small thing in his mind, and it's his way of thanking Bryan and all of you really for saving my life."

The room was large enough and had enough chairs that they could all sit and wait comfortably. There was also a sofa that could be made into a bed. Sophie was hoping that the family wouldn't mind her staying for however long it took for Bryan to at least wake up so she could thank him personally. "You guys don't mind me sticking around, do you?" she asked. "I know I'm not family, but I would really like to see for myself that Bryan is okay."

"No, Sophie, we don't mind you staying," Trevor said. "I don't know exactly what all is going on between you and my brother, but I do know that he's never done this before."

"What, taken a bullet for a client? Don't remind me that I'm the one that could have gotten him killed," Sophie said remorsefully.

"No, um, dated a client," Riley said. "We've never seen him be anything less than professional. And I don't know exactly how you feel about him, but I do know that from what I see he does care about you as more than a client." The others added their agreement.

"Oh," Sophie said quietly. So this wasn't a normal, casual thing for Bryan either. She really did need to see where things stood when he woke up. Although she wouldn't blame him at all if he didn't want to see her again to be reminded of getting shot for a client.

A short while later they wheeled the bed in with a sleeping Bryan attached to all sorts of tubes and wires. The nurse and the transport person worked to get him all connected to the oxygen and other things, and then all but the nurse left the room. She leaned over toward Bryan and said, "You rest, Mr. Lawson, we'll take good care of you." She adjusted his pillows to try to make him comfortable and then turned to the rest of them. "Hospital policy for this room is that there can be as many visitors as you want. However, keep in mind that Mr. Lawson will be sedated for at least 24-48 hours. You can speak to him and talk amongst yourselves. But try to keep this a restful environment for him. The best chance he has for healing quickly is for his body to be able to do the work it needs to do, and that will mostly be accomplished by his body not having to focus on anything else."

"Will he know what we are saying?" Sophie asked.

"Well, there are different theories on that. Many believe that he does hear you. Some say it's not possible. I believe he can. Anything that you can say that is encouraging or uplifting definitely can't hurt," she said with a smile. She showed them where the call button was for the nurses' station and told them to call her if they needed anything. She told them how to order food from the cafeteria and how they could charge food to the room if they did go downstairs. "I have been instructed that all of you are to be taken care of one hundred percent while you are here. Let me know if you want sheets, blankets or pillows." With that, she headed out the door.

"That's very generous of your father," Summer said. "Please be sure to thank him for us."

"I will, but like I said, it's his way of thanking you."

Summer stepped up to Bryan's bedside. "Hey, big brother. You get better quick. We all need you here."

"We should probably plan to take shifts while he is sleeping. He doesn't need us all here watching him sleep. If he wasn't going to be sedated, I could see the point of us all being here. But until they make the decision to let him wake up, there isn't much we can do. And we'll be more benefit to him when he wakes up if we are rested and on top of our game," Trevor said.

"I would like to stay," Sophie said. "But I need clothes. I don't know, maybe I should run and get them. I can call someone for a ride to Walt's house."

"Don't worry about it. We have to go get our surveillance equipment and stuff anyway. We'll have Rayne pack your things and I'll bring them in the morning," Riley said.

"Thank you," Sophie replied.

"Unless you need something for tonight. I can run and get a bag for you and come back," Trevor offered.

"No, I'll be fine," she said.

"I'll run down to the gift shop before they close. I am sure they'll have a toothbrush and things to get you through the night," Summer offered.

"Thanks. I don't know what happened to my purse, so I'll have to pay you back," Sophie offered.

"I'm not worried about it. We'll figure it out," Summer responded.

"We'll just add it to the expense report when we bill," Riley joked.

"Trust me, you really should pad that bill with anything you can think of. I can't believe that he was so vindictive that he brought a gun. Did we ever figure out why?" Sophie asked.

"When Riley and I approached him, he kept saying something about you ruining his life and that he needed to make sure you didn't ruin anyone else's," Trevor said. "I pretty much think that was the other way around."

"Well, he'll never hurt anyone else again," Summer said. "Thanks to you, Rye. You really did do society a great service today."

Sophie could tell that Riley didn't necessarily feel comfortable with having taken the man's life, but from what she had been told there really hadn't been any other choice. It was Larry or Trevor, and Riley had definitely made the right move. She would do her best to help him see that. She was sure that Bryan would have nothing but praise for his brother's actions when he woke up and heard the details too. Summer headed down to the gift shop, and Trevor and Riley each took a turn talking to their brother and assuring him that they would be here taking care of business until he was awake and fully back up to speed. Sophie could easily see the bond between these siblings. They had grown up in a close-knit family, and when they had lost their parents, they had stuck together and gotten each other through. They had come out on the other side of it as a cohesive unit that always had each other's backs.

When Summer returned, she had everything Sophie could possibly need to be able to spend the night in the hospital with Bryan. She had thought of everything, including a set of scrubs that would be comfortable to sleep in. "They were limited on brands and fragrances, but I just got the basic stuff. I'm sure Rayne will pack a bag with your preferred stuff, and one of the guys will bring it in the morning."

"I'm sure it will be fine. Thank you," Sophie said. "How much do I owe you?"

"Oh, don't worry about it. Apparently the gift shop was given the same carte blanche for expenses for this room as the cafeteria was. This was all billed to the room," Summer assured her.

"Why don't you order some food, Sophie? I know you haven't eaten since the dinner at the reception, and that was hours ago," Trevor said.

"I'm not really thinking about food at the moment," she replied.

"I understand that, but my brother will have my hide if I don't get you to eat something. Even soup or something light. You need to keep your strength up if you're going to be spending a lot of time here waiting for him to wake up," Trevor stated.

"Okay, I'll look at the menu." Sophie agreed.

"You know what, Mom always made us grilled cheese and tomato soup when we were kids. 'It's comfort food,' she always used to say. How about I go down and see if I can find you something like that?" Riley offered.

"Sure, comfort food sounds good," Sophie agreed. Riley headed down to the cafeteria to see what he could find for her to eat. After he had left the room, Sophie told the other two siblings, "I'm really sorry about all of this. I am so sorry Bryan got shot protecting me, and I'm sorry Riley has to deal with having killed a man on my behalf."

"Don't be. It's all a part of what we accept as necessary risk in our line of work. Rye will be okay; he just has some ghosts from his time in Iraq, and any time there is gunfire involved, it's something that takes him longer to process. Deep down, he knows what he did was necessary. He just has to process it in his own way," Trevor assured her.

"Yeah, Rye is the only one of the guys that was injured in the military. We don't even know the whole story of how, but he came home with something haunting him. He doesn't talk about it, but we all know it's there," Summer said.

Sophie could relate. She hadn't wanted to tell anyone all of what had happened to her when she was with Larry. So she could understand that Riley might not want to talk about his experiences in the Middle East. She didn't know if it would do any good, but she was going to try to get a chance to talk to him alone.

When Riley came back, he had a tray loaded with way more than enough food to feed Sophie. "I wasn't sure what you liked, so I grabbed a lot of stuff," he explained.

"I'm sure I'll find something I like." Sophie smiled.

"Do you want us to stay while you eat?" Summer asked.

"No, you don't all need to hang around. Maybe Riley can help me eat some of this food and keep me company for a while," she said, looking at the young man hopefully.

"Sure, I can do that," Riley agreed softly.

Trevor and Summer each took a turn leaning in to say their good nights and well wishes to Bryan. He only had one side that was easily accessible because of all the machines and wires on the other side. Trevor again assured his brother that they would take care of things while he focused on getting well. Summer told him that he needed to heal quickly, or she just might find herself a new boyfriend to hang out with. She leaned in and kissed her brother's cheek, and Sophie noticed a few tears in her eyes. Most likely they had all looked up to him as the strong one, and to see him taken down by a bullet wasn't easy for any of them. Sophie could totally relate to that concept.

When the two had walked out of the room, Sophie went to the tray that Riley had set on the table. There was a lot of food, including a grilled cheese sandwich and tomato soup. Sophie decided to choose other options for herself. There was a ham and cheese sandwich and a small garden salad. There was also a large order of French fries. Sophie took the ham sandwich and salad along with a portion of the fries and pushed the rest of the tray toward Riley's side of the table. He picked up a fry and started munching.

"I was hoping you would stay," Sophie began. "I really want to thank you, Riley. I know what you did today couldn't have been easy. But you saved me and gave me my life back. I won't give you a literal blow-by-blow detail of what happened, but the last time I saw Larry, I ended up hospitalized for a week with internal injuries. I also lost my baby from what he did to me. I don't know if he's ever done anything like that to any other women, but I wouldn't doubt that he has. You literally gave me my life and my freedom back today, Riley. And I don't take that lightly. You and Bryan are both heroes in my book."

Riley didn't respond; he just nodded his understanding. He picked up the grilled cheese sandwich and dipped it into the tomato soup and took a large bite. They ate the rest of their food in silence except when the nurse came in to check on Bryan's vitals. She asked if either of them were planning to spend the night and if they needed any blankets.

"I was planning to stay," Sophie said. "If that's okay with you," she asked, looking at Riley.

"That's fine with me. I'm sure Bryan will be glad knowing you are here. Do you want me to stay too?" Riley asked.

"No, you go home and try to rest," Sophie assured him. "He'll be out for a while anyway." She asked the nurse for a blanket and a pillow for the couch.

Before he left, Riley offered to help her set up the sofa bed, but she said she would just sleep on the couch as is. Finally, it was Sophie's turn to say all the things she wanted to say to Bryan but didn't want anyone else to hear. She lay on her side next to Bryan on the bed, facing him so that she could speak into his ear. She was sure he was so heavily sedated that he wouldn't wake up, but she still wanted to speak softly just in case. "I just really want you to know how grateful I am for you and your siblings and what you all did for me today. I haven't felt this alive and this free in years. I realized tonight that I can go or stay or do whatever I want now. I don't have to live in fear. If it's okay with you, I'm planning to stick around here for a while. I can finally spend time with my parents and catch up with old friends. I can even be here to help Autumn with the baby. Lord knows my mom won't be much help. Not that she won't love the baby, but babysitting and diaper duty just aren't her thing." Sophie laughed a little at that thought. "But if you're up for it, I thought maybe you and I could, I don't know, maybe date a little. You did promise me a motorcycle ride in the country. I want to cash in on that as soon as you are cleared to ride your bike again. I'm not expecting some great romance. I'm open to whatever you are okay with. Even if it's just being play partners. I just want to see where this could go. Like I said, it's the first time in a long time I've felt free to do something just for myself without having to be afraid." Sophie lay her head on his shoulder. She was on the uninjured side, but she was still cautious to not do anything that might cause him pain. After just soaking his presence for a while, she began speaking again. "I don't know what happened to Riley when he was in Iraq. From what Trevor and Summer say, none of you know either. But I hope he can banish those demons. He's a really sweet kid, and he deserves to be happy. I like him a lot. I like your whole family a lot. Them accepting me as easily as they have today and being okay with me being here means a lot."

The nurse came in again to check on Bryan, and she saw Sophie lying next to him. "You're fine to stay where you are while you are awake, but it would really be better if you not try to sleep there, miss. We wouldn't want to take a chance on you bumping something in the night."

"Of course. I'll go to the sofa in a few minutes," Sophie offered. "I just wanted to be close to him."

"I understand," the nurse said. "I'm just being overly cautious."

After the nurse had checked all the machines and Bryan's vitals, Sophie asked, "He really is going to be okay, isn't he?"

"Oh, yes, miss," the nurse assured her. "He's fine. The doctor just wants to keep him sedated for a few days to give his body some quiet time to heal. He doesn't strike me as the type that would lie quietly in bed in order to heal."

"No, that wouldn't be him. I'm sure this is for the best," Sophie agreed. After the nurse left, she kissed Bryan on the cheek gently and went to get ready for bed. She decided to take a shower. They had cleaned most of Bryan's blood off of her, but she still didn't feel clean. As suspected, the water was tinged slightly pink. The fact that she was seeing the evidence of Bryan's blood and what she had almost lost was more than she could stand. She crumpled to the floor and let the water wash away her tears along with the blood and the fear and stress the day had piled onto her. She wasn't sure how long she lay there; it could have been minutes or an hour. She was so lost in thought. She remembered every minute of the last few days. Since she had gotten off of the plane she had experienced so much, almost too much to fully process it all. When she lay down on the couch, she feared that sleep would be elusive, but the long cry in the shower and the long hours of the day helped her to fall asleep almost immediately.

Chapter Eleven

Sunday morning dawned late for Sophie. Apparently sometime during the night or early morning hours, the nurse had closed the room-darkening shades so the room remained dimly lit. She thought she heard someone in the room moving around, so she sat up. Summer was quietly placing a duffel bag into the closet.

"Oh, sorry, I was trying not to wake you," Summer said when she turned and saw Sophie sitting up.

"It's okay. Apparently I slept really well; it's almost noon," she said, looking at the clock on the wall. Apparently, her cell phone had died and was currently sitting on the end table next to her. "Please tell me someone packed my phone charger in there."

"It is," Summer said, reaching back into the closet to pull the charging cord out of a side pocket on the bag. "Here you go." She handed the cord to Sophie and went to her brother's bedside. Sophie plugged in her phone immediately. "How's he been?"

"Well, he's slept heavily, but every time they check his vitals, they say everything is looking good," Sophie offered.

"That's good, that's really good," Summer said. "I don't know what I would do without him. I don't know how much he has told you about our family history. But he's been the best big brother anyone could have."

"He told me that your parents died when you were all quite young and that he fought to keep you all together," Sophie offered.

"He did," Summer agreed. "We had people from the courts dropping by all the time to make sure we were being taken care of, and they never found one thing that they could complain about. When Momma and Daddy died, Bryan sat us all down and told us that we needed to step up and be responsible or we were going to lose each other. He got a job that would let him work around what he needed to do for us. That's where he learned how to ride and how to repair motorcycles. We each had chores to do to keep the house running smoothly. If one of us slacked off, he never got mad; he just sat us down and talked to us about how Momma and Daddy would want us together and how they had taught us all to be responsible. It was time for us to step up and be a family and carry our share." Summer had never taken her eyes off of Bryan while she had said all of that, and the respect was abundantly clear. She continued with a smile on her face. "Oh, there were times when I would have told you he was a horrible human being. Most of those were the times when he caught me trying to sneak out or hanging out with the wrong crowd. But still, he never got angry. He always sat me down and explained to me how he was trying to take care of us and how the courts were just looking for a reason to separate us. If I got into trouble, they might think that he wasn't doing a good job and might put us in foster care. He and Trev would have stayed together regardless; they were both old enough the courts didn't really have much say. But me and Riley would have been a different story if anything had gone wrong."

"He sounds like an amazing big brother," Sophie said.

"Oh, he is. I didn't always see it, but he always has been," Summer added. "Why don't you go down to the cafeteria and grab something to eat? I'll stay here with him. It's not like he's going to wake up and realize you aren't here. I'll have them page you if anything does happen."

"That sounds like a really good idea. I might even try to find a place to eat outside. It looks like it's a beautiful day," Sophie said as she opened the heavy, dark blinds.

"Oh, that it is. It's gorgeous out there," Summer assured her.

Sophie brushed her teeth and ran a comb through her hair. She was going to stay in the scrubs for now and worry about clothing later. It wasn't like she wouldn't fit in at a hospital. Sophie literally ran into Walt and Rayne as she stepped out of the room. Walt caught her arm to keep her from falling. "Oh, hi!" she said, a little thrown off.

"Hi Sophie," Walt said, making sure she was steady and upright. "Pete asked all of us guys to keep an eye on you since he can't, so we just wanted to stop by and see if you needed anything."

"Uh, actually, I was just headed down to get something to eat. If you want to join me that would be great."

"Sure," Walt said. "We'd love to."

They walked toward the elevator, and Rayne asked, "How is Bryan?"

"Well, the prognosis is great. They are sure he will be fine. The bullet cracked one of his ribs pretty badly, though, so the pain of that will be pretty intense. They want to keep him sedated for a couple of days just to let his body rest and focus on healing. They aren't convinced that Bryan would be the type of guy that would sit quietly and let things heal. I have to say I agree with them on that."

"Oh, yeah, for sure," Rayne agreed. "I'm not a bodybuilder or whatever, but as a dancer, just sitting didn't feel right to me. But it's the best thing for him."

Sophie didn't know every detail, but she did know that Rayne had had a tragic accident, and that was how she and Walt had met.

As they stepped off of the elevator, Walt asked, "Are you going to need a ride to the airport tomorrow, or are your parents taking you?"

"Actually, I realized that thanks to the Lawson family, I can be anywhere I want to be, and right now, that's here in Michigan. I want time to catch up with my parents. I will probably stick around for a while. Maybe even stay until Pete and Autumn have the baby. I haven't decided for sure yet, but it's amazing having those options."

"Stick around and see where things go with the hot bodyguard?" Rayne asked, raising her eyebrows. Walt quickly looked at Rayne. "What? I'm married, I'm not dead. I can see that he's attractive, and I know he and Sophie have something going." Walt looked at Sophie for confirmation.

"Well, sort of, I guess. I'm not really sure. I mean, yeah, we had some fun. But that was when both of us thought it was a short-term thing with an end date. So I don't really know if or what happens from here. But, yeah, that's part of why I want to stay too. I want to make sure Bryan heals and is taken care of, even if that means I have to help him, and I want to see if there's anything between us more than just a few hot sweaty nights. You know." Walt looked like he really did not want to know, but Rayne was nodding in total understanding.

When they got to the cafeteria, Walt started to pull out his wallet, but Sophie stepped up and told them to charge it all to room 847. They took their food to one of the tables out on the patio area and enjoyed the warm spring day.

"It's amazing how this feels," Sophie said. "Just sitting out here in the sun, not having to wonder if or when it all might come crashing down on me. Even in Colorado, I was extremely cautious. I went to the grocery store and things when needed, but for the most part, I stayed locked up in my house."

Walt and Rayne decided there wasn't really any point in going back up to Bryan's room after they had eaten and visited with Sophie for a while. Bryan was sleeping, and they had seen both Trevor and Riley that morning when they had stopped by to clean up the gear. So they said their goodbyes and made Sophie promise to keep them in the loop after offering for her to stay at their home as long as she wanted if staying with her parents would be awkward. She thanked them and then headed back upstairs.

When she got there, she realized her phone was charged enough that it would turn on. She had about a hundred texts from everyone: her parents, Pete, Autumn, even Betsy. She was "so shocked by what had happened" and "couldn't believe it" and wanted Sophie to call her soon so she could find out what was going on. Yeah, Sophie would get right on that last one. She did text her parents, though, to let them know that she was fine and was planning on staying at the hospital at least until Bryan was out of sedation. To the message to her father she added her profound thanks for all he was doing to take care of the expenses of Bryan being in the hospital.

Her father replied with, **"It's the least I can do, cupcake, he took care of my little girl."**

Summer was still there sitting by the bed, and she appeared to be reading something out loud to Bryan. Sophie went to the closet to see what clothes had been packed for her. She found two more outfits that had obviously been purchased at Triskelion hanging in the closet. She didn't want to interrupt Summer, so she just went into the bathroom to clean up and change.

When she emerged, Trevor was there also. "Thank you to whoever got me the clothes."

"No problem," Trevor said. "Bryan made a comment yesterday before the wedding about how much he had liked giving you those clothes, so I figured you could use more of them."

Riley arrived a short time later, and the siblings spent the afternoon and early evening sharing stories of their childhood and of the years after their parents had died. They talked about how Bryan had always been there for them. Some of the stories they shared were happy ones and some were sad, but Sophie heard the love in every single one. She had offered to leave if they wanted to reminisce without her present, but they had assured her that they wanted her to stay.

Late in the afternoon, the doctor stopped by to check on Bryan and his injuries. He said that he would be back the next day and if all continued to go well, they would begin to reduce the sedation level and see how Bryan did without the medication keeping him asleep.

Zak and Skye stopped by and asked if Sophie would join them for dinner. She had no doubt that her brother had asked them to do so, but she was happy to have people that cared. She told them she would go, but they needed to stay close by the hospital, just in case. She took her cell phone with her and made the Lawsons promise to call if anything changed. They went to a restaurant a few blocks away, and Sophie was glad for the time to get to catch up with Zak and get to know Skye better.

When Sophie got back to the hospital, Summer had left. "She had a client scheduled," Trevor explained.

"I'd love to see some of her work. I bet she is very artistic," Sophie stated.

"Well, everything we have was done by her, although we stick with the pretty bland stuff. But yeah, she does some amazing work. I'm sure she'd love to show you her photos or even give you some ink," Riley offered.

"I'll keep that in mind," Sophie replied.

"Not afraid of needles, are we?" Trevor joked.

"No, not afraid, just something I've never really thought about, and if I'm getting a permanent mark on my body, I want it to be something I've contemplated over time," Sophie defended.

"Okay, I get that," Trevor said.

"But, seriously, Summer's good," Riley stated. He stood up and pulled his shirt over his head. He turned so that Sophie could see his back. It was a beautiful design. She was impressed with Summer's work.

"That is really good," Sophie said.

"Look closer," Riley commanded.

As Sophie looked closer, she could see that the skin wasn't smooth beneath the ink. It looked mottled and distorted. She let out a small gasp.

"Yeah, it pretty much looked like hamburger when it happened," Riley said. "But when it healed enough that she could work on it, Summer gave me that. You can still see the scars if you look close, but from a distance no one can tell."

Sophie had no idea what had happened to Riley, and she wasn't about to ask. He or Bryan would tell her if and when they felt it was right. But it made her heart hurt for whatever he had gone through to make his back look like that. Summer had done an amazing job of camouflaging the scars. It was true, you had to get fairly close before you could see what was really on the surface.

Shortly after that, Riley and Trevor headed out. They planned to go to Five Sloths and grab a couple of microbrews. They promised Sophie they would be back before the doctor returned the next day. Again, Sophie got ready for bed and then lay beside Bryan to talk to him. She told him how amazing his family was and how she was learning that was mostly because of him. She told him that she missed talking to him already and she missed being in his arms. She told him that she hoped he was okay with her staying and she hoped he wanted to try with her as much as she wanted to try with him. Again, she got out of his bed before she fell asleep, but she lay there for a long while before she got too tired just listening to the strong beat of his heart and reassuring herself that he was just resting, and he would be back with her soon.

The night before she had been so tired she didn't remember dreaming, but this night, she had dreams of spending time with Bryan, and she had dreams of the little girl Pete and Autumn would have. Her dreams were the happiest they had been in a long time.

Chapter Twelve

Late Monday afternoon, the doctor came in and checked Bryan again and said that they would remove the sedation drugs from his IV. He cautioned them that that didn't mean that Bryan would wake up immediately. It would likely take several hours for the medication to begin to purge itself from his system. He also cautioned that when Bryan did wake up, they needed to remind him that his body still had a long road ahead of it to heal fully, and the best way to do that was to rest and follow doctor's orders.

Sophie's parents arrived at 5:00 p.m. and asked her to join them for dinner. Since it would be hours before Bryan was awake, she agreed but only to go as far as the hospital cafeteria. She took her cell phone with her and asked Trevor or Riley to text her if Bryan did start to wake up. Her parents had a hundred questions about what her plans were. Was she moving back to Michigan permanently? She didn't know. Would she stay at their house for the time being? Again, she didn't know. Question after question was asked, and for the most part, the answers were the same. She didn't know what her plans were. She hoped to sit down and have a long talk with Bryan to see where his feelings were. She knew that he would likely be out of the hospital in a few days if everything went well, and then he would be going back to his house he had talked about in the country. She just wasn't sure where or if she fit into that plan, and until she did, she couldn't answer her parents' questions.

Bryan felt like he was in a fog that he just couldn't clear from his head. And his left side hurt like hell. Why did his left side hurt like hell? He was trying desperately to swim to the surface of his clouded brain. He remembered being at the wedding reception with Sophia.

They had flirted and danced. They were having a good time, sending off the happy couple on their honeymoon. It was a beautiful day. The country club was crowded with well-wishers. There had been an old busybody talking to Sophia, and then some younger woman who seemed to be looking for a man. Both had been rather snobbish to Sophia. They had been drinking and toasting, but he knew that had been non-alcoholic champagne. He never drank the real stuff while he was on a job. So the fog in his brain wasn't from liquor. Why the hell was his left side so painful and what was that humming and beeping that he was hearing? It was annoying. It wasn't loud, but it was just incessant. Humming and beeping, and he thought he heard voices. He wasn't sure whose voices they were at first, but as he concentrated on them, he recognized Trev and Rye. His brothers were here, wherever here was. The bed didn't feel like his bed at home or the bed in the apartment above the bike shop. He couldn't figure out where he was. And what had happened to Sophia? He needed to remember the celebration and what had happened to Sophia. They'd had cake, and she had gotten bratty when he took her cake away and asked for a new piece. The young kid had rushed to get Sophia a new piece. He obviously thought she was pretty, and he was trying to impress her. Sophia had danced with her brother during the dollar dance. That had been a bit nerve wracking for him because she wasn't right at his side. But it hadn't lasted for a long time, and she was safe. It had all gone smoothly. He remembered talking to Summer and Jeremy. He wasn't sure he was getting these things all in order because they kept jumping back and forth from being inside and outside. It was likely that the events were still muddled in his brain from whatever it was that seemed to make him feel like he was trudging through swampland in his head. Sophia had caught the bouquet; he remembered that too. A part of him had thought that maybe that was a sign that they could have something real someday. But the larger part of him knew that Sophia was going to back to Colorado on Monday, and catching the bouquet really didn't mean anything. It was just a nonsense tradition that people still insisted on doing. They had been given small bags of birdseed to throw at the couple when they ran to the limousine. He hadn't taken any. He'd needed to keep his eyes ears and hands ready for anything that might happen. Sophia had been right beside him. He'd had his arm around her waist. She had a handful of birdseed, ready to toss it. He heard someone yelling something. He couldn't remember what they were yelling. Why were people yelling? He needed to remember. This was important. He knew it was; he just couldn't remember why it was important. Someone was yelling. It was more than one person too. He remembered distinctly hearing both a masculine and feminine voice. Maybe more than one. They were yelling a single word. He knew it was a single word. He just couldn't remember what it was. It had been Summer; he was sure of that now. Summer and Trevor and Riley maybe. Why were his siblings yelling? What were his siblings yelling? This was important; he needed to remember what they were yelling. Why wouldn't his brain let him remember? What was the word that they were yelling?

As soon as his brain finally remembered the word they had yelled, the rest of the memory came flooding back like a raging tide. The word they had yelled had been "Gun!" He had tackled Sophia to the ground, although she had already started to go down on her own. He was on top of her. He looked down and just before the pain took him under, he had seen her pale green dress begin to bloom red with blood. Sophia had been shot. He sat up in bed quickly and yelled "Sophia!" The pain in his left side about took him back under again, but he had to fight it. The pain couldn't take him down. He had to know what had happened to Sophia; he had to know where she was.

"Whoa, Bry," Trevor said, rushing to his side. Riley was there too, right next to Trevor. "It's okay, man, you're in the hospital. The doctor needs you to take it easy. You were shot. You need to calm down before you rip something open."

Bryan didn't care if he ripped something open. In fact, he was looking forward to ripping something open. He was looking forward to ripping Larry's chest open and removing his internal organs one by one. The man would pay with a long and tortuous death if Sophia had been harmed. He looked from Riley to Trevor and asked, "Sophia. She was shot?"

"No man, only you were shot. You took the bullet he intended for her," Riley stated.

"But I saw the blood on her dress."

"That was yours. You were on top of her so your blood was soaking her dress. She wasn't hit, she's fine," Trevor assured him.

"And Larry, you guys caught him, right? He's rotting in a jail cell somewhere? Please tell me he's rotting in a jail cell somewhere," Bryan pleaded.

"Nope, not rotting anywhere except maybe the city morgue. Riley took him down when he turned his gun on me and started to pull the trigger," Trevor said with pride.

"He's dead?" Bryan couldn't believe it. "Sophia's free of him forever?"

Riley and Trevor both nodded.

"What day is it?" Bryan asked.

"It's Monday night," Riley said.

"So you got Sophia safely to the airport, right? Just because the scumbag was taken out, our job didn't end until we knew she was safely at the airport." Bryan, always the boss and big brother stated.

"Actually," a feminine voice said from the doorway, "I decided not to go to the airport."

Bryan turned toward the door, and there was his beautiful Sophia. He had never seen a more beautiful sight. She was wearing jeans and a Harley shirt. Not the one he had gotten her, so apparently someone had gone to the shop and gotten her more clothing. But was she ever a sight for sore eyes, as his daddy used to say. "Sophia. Oh, God, it's so good to see you. I thought you took a bullet."

Sophie walked over to the side of the bed, and Trevor and Riley stepped back so she could get closer. She looked at them and said, "What part of keep him calm and resting did you guys not get from the doctor's speech earlier?"

They both just looked at her. She knew it wouldn't have been easy to keep Bryan down, but she needed to try. "Well, you need to lie back and take it easy. The doctor said the only way you are going to heal is if you get adequate rest. So rest."

Bryan lay back against the bed, but said, "I'll stay like this as long as you sit here beside me. I need to know that you're okay. I was positive you were shot."

Sophia said, "Deal" and climbed into the bed beside him. He put his good arm around her, and she began to recount the details that he had missed. "I didn't get shot. Although a perfectly good dress did get ruined. I would have you take the cost of it out of Larry's hide if it weren't for the fact that he's dead."

"I'm so glad you're okay." He pulled her to him, and she saw him wince a little.

"Okay, if you can't be still and quit causing yourself pain, I'm not going to stay here on the bed," Sophie warned.

"Damn but you got bossy in the last couple of days," Bryan teased. But he did let up on the tightness and readjusted himself so his left side was back against the pillows more.

"Well, someone has to make sure you take care of yourself. You have a whole list of promises to keep," she teased. "You promised me a ride on the Harley out in the country. And I'm guessing it will be a while before the doctor clears you to ride a motorcycle. You promised me a tour of your house."

"I believe those were the only two," Bryan replied.

"Maybe, but I'm holding you to those," she said. "That is, if you still want to do them."

"Oh, yeah, definitely," Bryan said. He knew Sophia would have none of him pulling her in for a kiss or of leaning toward her for one, so he just puckered his lips and hoped she would take the bait. And she did. She leaned in to him gently and kissed him.

Somewhere along the line, Riley and Trevor had found the good sense to leave the two alone and had left the room. "So you decided to stay so I can give you a ride and show you my house?" he asked.

"I decided to stay in Michigan at least for a while. I don't have any reason to have to run and hide anymore, thanks to you and your siblings. I want to reconnect with my parents. I want to be here for the baby this fall." She lowered her eyes a little because she wasn't exactly sure how he would feel about the next part. "And if you're game, I was hoping maybe we could see where things go between us or at the very least be play partners for a while."

He lifted his left arm, a movement that hurt like all holy hell, but it was necessary; he wasn't moving his right arm away from being around her. He tilted her chin up so she looked him in the eye. "I'd like that very much, Sophia, and no, I don't want to just be play partners. I'm all in for us being boyfriend and girlfriend—to start, anyway. We can see where it goes from there."

He leaned in for another kiss, but she heard the sharp gasp from the pain, so she kept the kiss brief. "Then you need to listen to me. I know you're not one to take orders, but I need you to listen to the doctors and relax and rest. If we want to give this a real shot, you have to take it easy and let your body heal."

Bryan again lay back and relaxed. If that was what it took to get back to full health and to be ready to make love to her again, he would do his best to follow every order the doctor made. The nurse walked in, and Sophia started to get up, but Bryan just held his arm tighter. His left side might be a mess, but his right arm worked just fine. He wasn't about to let a nurse make him lose his hold on his girl.

"I heard you were awake, Mr. Lawson." If she had a problem with Sophia's location, she had the good sense to not say anything. "I'm here to check your bandages and answer any questions you may have." She smiled at Sophia. "I will need you to move briefly, dear, so I can get the bandages taken care of, but otherwise, as long as you promise to not jostle him and be careful, I don't have a problem with you sitting with him."

Sophia got off the bed, and Bryan reluctantly let her go, but this nurse better hurry up. The woman laid his bed back in a flat position, which caused a stab of pain to shoot through him. "You took a bullet to your left side. It cracked one of your ribs and caused quite a bit of blood loss. The doctor felt you would heal best if he kept you sedated for forty-eight hours. He turned off the sedation medication a few hours ago," she said.

So that was why his brain had felt like pea soup. "How long will I be here?" Bryan asked. He knew there would be restrictions, but he wanted nothing more than to take Sophia on that tour of his home and maybe get her beneath him again—or maybe on top of him. That might be easier with the whole cracked rib thing.

"Well, that depends on you really, dear," the kindly nurse said. "The more you rest and heal, the sooner the doctor will feel you can go. If he sees you not trying to get better, he's more likely to force the issue of you staying here and getting your rest." All the while she was talking, she had been working at removing the bandage over the incision in his side. "Your incision is healing nicely. The rib will be a different story. Those take a long time, and moving, sometimes even breathing deeply can cause extreme pain." She didn't have to tell him that. When he had yelled out for Sophia he had gotten an introduction to cracked rib pain 101. It hurt like nothing he had ever experienced in his life. Still, he would bet it had been nothing compared to what had happened to Riley. Riley didn't talk about it, ever, but the files had laid out a painful story.

When the nurse was finished changing his bandages, she asked "Are you hungry, dear? I can order a tray for you."

Was he hungry? He was starving now that she mentioned food. "I'm starving actually."

"I'll call down and order something, or your girlfriend can do it. Keep in mind when you order that you will mostly be eating one-handed because the left one won't want to cooperate if the rib pain kicks in, so I wouldn't suggest anything that needs two hands like a large sandwich. Otherwise, you have no dietary restrictions and you have no limit on amounts. I'm sure a strapping young man like yourself can put away some food. Everything is included in the room, dear. Your girlfriend is welcome to order too. Do you have any other questions for me?" she asked. Bryan said he didn't, so she left the room after helping him sit back up in a more comfortable position.

Sophia brought the menu to him, telling him she had just eaten downstairs in the cafeteria with her parents so she wasn't hungry, but he should order whatever he wanted. After the order was placed, Sophia again climbed on the bed and sat at his side. "This room is huge," Bryan stated.

"Yeah, it's one of the private suites," Sophia agreed.

"I don't think I have the insurance for this," Bryan objected.

"It's all on my dad. He's pretty much made it so that your whole family and I are taken care of for food or anything we need while you are here. He says it's the least he can do for the man who saved his little girl's life," Sophie said, settling in closer.

"It was the least that I could do. I was just doing my job." Bryan sounded like he didn't really see himself as the hero she and her family saw him as.

"Well, you may say that, but I and my family will be eternally thankful for what you and your siblings did, part of your job or not," Sophia assured him.

Bryan held her as close as he dared without causing himself too much pain. If she needed him to heal so he could get out of here, he would try to refrain from making things worse for himself. He didn't realize he had drifted off to sleep until he heard Sophia telling the cafeteria worker to put the tray on the table and she would get it when he woke up.

Sophie realized that the talking had woken Bryan back up, so she went and grabbed the tray and put it on the hospital table that could be moved right up to the side of the bed. She positioned it to make it easy for him to do it all with his right hand. Since he needed his hand for eating, she sat in the chair beside his bed and offered assistance if he needed anything opened or whatever.

It was a challenge to eat completely right-handed, but Bryan was starving, so he worked at it as fast as he could. When he had completed most of the plate, he asked Sophia to remove the table and come and sit at his side again. Just as she was snuggling in beside him, his hospital door opened, and Summer came rushing in.

"Oh, yay! It's so good to see you awake," Summer enthused. "You had me really worried."

"It takes more than a bullet to take me out," Bryan stated. "Come here. I can't really hug you, but you can hug me."

Summer approached his injured side and carefully leaned in and gave him a hug. He removed his arm from behind Sophia long enough to give his little sister a long embrace. As soon as she pulled away, his arm was right back around Sophia. If he had his way that's where it would stay for a long, long time, like maybe years. Summer stayed for about a half hour before she stated that he needed his rest, and she would be back to see him again tomorrow.

When she left, he turned to Sophia. "You are going to stay with me tonight, aren't you?" he asked.

"I've been here the last two nights; I don't see why tonight would be different," she said, smiling.

"You've been here the whole time?" he asked.

"Yeah, well, other than running down to the cafeteria for food. And Zak and Skye dragged me a couple of blocks away for dinner last night, but otherwise, yeah, I've been right here. That couch actually isn't too uncomfortable," she stated.

"Tonight you're sleeping right here," he said, drawing her to his body even more.

"That will be up to the nurses," Sophia debated.

"Oh, no, trust me, Sophia, either they let you sleep right here or I'm signing myself out of this place and they can just try and stop me." Sophia settled in against him and soon, they both drifted off to sleep.

Sophie woke a couple of hours later when the nurse came in to check on Bryan. "He wanted me to stay here. If that's not okay, I'll sleep on the couch," she said softly.

"I'm fine with you sleeping there, as long as that's all that you two do. And you do your best to keep his ribs and incision from getting bumped," the nurse stated. Sophie promised to do her best, and the nurse picked up the tray and walked out the door. She turned off the big overhead light on her way out so the room was only lit softly by the small lamp on the table and the light that shined upward over the bed so that the nurses could see to get around.

She pried herself from Bryan's arm. He started to protest, but she said, "I'm just going to the bathroom and changing into my sleeping clothes. I promise I'll be right back." That seemed to satisfy him, so she quickly went into the bathroom to brush her teeth and change into her scrubs. On her way back to the bed, she picked up her phone to check for messages. There was a text from Trevor asking her to text him when Bryan was up and more alert the next day. They hadn't had a chance to fill him in completely on the facts of the operation.

She turned off the lamp on the table, pulled the room darkening shade, and climbed back into bed beside Bryan. He didn't seem to really wake up at all—most likely he still had a lot of sedation medicine in his system—but he did put his arm around her and pull her to him like it was the natural way things needed to be.

Sophie slept off and on. She was worried she would move wrong and hurt Bryan in some way, so she never really let herself go deeply asleep. But if that was what it took for him to remain in bed and content, she was happy to oblige. It wasn't like it was a hardship for her.

Bryan woke up once during the night and realized two things. Sophia was still nestled beside him, which was a very good thing, and he had a catheter, which was a very bad thing. Yeah, that needed to be gone first thing in the morning.

Chapter Thirteen

Tuesday morning, Trevor, Summer, and Riley came to see Bryan and give him a full debrief on the details of what had happened in the woods that day. To Sophie, it sounded a lot like the police dramas she sometimes watched on TV. It was a very professional process. Trevor began "You and Sophie were by the limo getting ready to see the couple off on their honeymoon. Larry came walking out of the edge of the woods with his eyes focused directly on Sophie. He lifted his hand, and that was when all three of us realized that the guy had a gun. He pulled the trigger at almost the exact time we yelled gun. Riley and I both ran directly toward him, and Summer ran to you and Sophie. When he spotted us coming at him, he turned and ran back into the woods. As Riley and I closed in on him, I fired one shot into his thigh to impede his progress. Larry turned and aimed his gun directly at me. He kept repeating things about 'If I can't have her no one will,' 'She ruined my life,' and 'That tattooed meathead doesn't deserve her.' Anyway, he was spewing bullshit. Then he got more serious with the gun. It had been pointed at me, but not with any real focus. All of a sudden, he lifted it and aimed it directly at my head. That's when Rye fired his gun."

Riley took over with the debrief. "I hit him in the head with my first shot. I didn't know if it was muscle reflex or if he was still with it enough to be consciously aware, but he pivoted and the gun was pointing at me. I fired one more shot into his chest. He fell to the ground and was dead when we checked him." Riley seemed to be reciting things with no emotion, but his eyes showed the disdain he had for his own actions. "We waited for the police to come so we could give our statements. They agree it's pretty much an open and shut case, but they would like to talk to you and Sophie as soon as you're up to it. We totally took advantage of Sophie's dad being a big shot in a law firm to make them back off on questioning either of you until you were holding your own."

"Thanks for that," Bryan said, turning to see what Summer had to add to the accounting of that day.

"Right, so as they said, we had all spotted the gun. When they gave chase to Larry, I came over to check on you and Sophie. You were on top of her, and I believe she sort of passed out from the lack of oxygen when you landed on top of her. She came to briefly and I begged her not to move. We had no idea where the bullet was lodged, and I didn't want her to jostle you and cause it to move. When her brain registered that you had been shot, she passed out again. This time from shock most likely." Summer was not without emotion while telling her tale. Hers was personal, not professional. "I remained beside the two of you until the paramedics took you. I wasn't sure exactly what was going on with Larry at that point. We had all heard the gunshots in the woods, but I didn't know who had been shot or how badly. When they got you into the ambulance, I stayed with Sophie while they checked her and put her in the second ambulance. I rode with her to the hospital."

Sophie was surprised at that last part. She would have assumed that Summer would want to be in the ambulance with Bryan. At her puzzled expression, Summer responded, "I knew that Bryan would want you protected at all cost. I didn't think there would be any danger for you on the trip to the hospital, but there was no guarantee. If Larry had eluded my brothers, there would be a possibility that he could follow you."

"Thank you for that," Sophie said. She knew she had tears in her eyes. This family blew her away with the care and concern. To some it may be written off as part of the job, but Sophie realized that even though it was a job, they cared about their client, and they cared about her.

"I wasn't trained by the military like my brothers. Although they have taught me to use a gun and I'm pretty decent at hand-to-hand." Summer smiled. "But client or not, I think we could all see pretty clearly that Bryan considered you special. It was the least I could do."

"You did very well, Summer. I am proud of you and I appreciate you taking care of Sophia when I couldn't," Bryan said. "I'm proud of all of you," he declared, looking at each of his siblings. "You handled this operation in exactly the way you should have. Everything was by the book. Thank you all for a job well done."

They were all murmuring about it all being okay, and that it was what they did when the nurse came in. "I just wanted to let you all know that the doctor will be doing his rounds shortly. I knew you were all here, and I knew you would probably want to talk to him and be here to hear his prognosis." She smiled. "I think if he knows that Mr. Lawson has this much support, he will be more likely to release him earlier rather than later. Is there anything I can get for any of you?"

They all smiled and thanked her for the offer but said they could handle it. When she left, Trevor and Riley offered to go downstairs and get everyone some coffee and a small bite to eat. They came back a short time later with a tray of muffins and bagels and coffee for everyone. Sophie didn't tell them that a small bite didn't usually mean a couple of dozen muffins and a dozen bagels. Who was she to control their eating habits?

The doctor arrived about an hour later, and the first question out of Bryan's mouth was, "When can I go home?"

"Well, considering the fact that less than twenty-four hours ago you were heavily sedated, it won't be today," the doctor began. "Let me check your incision and injuries, and we'll see. I will have the nurse remove the catheter and work with you to begin to sit up and then stand up. If that goes well, we'll let you walk to the bathroom with assistance. It's a progression, Mr. Lawson, not a race. I'll be back tomorrow morning to see where things are. I promise you, I will get a report from the nurse, and it won't be to see how much you can accomplish in how little time. It will be about whether or not you can pace yourself to progress without overtaxing your body. I have no doubt in my mind that if I let you go home you would push things further than you will here, so your job is to prove to me that you can still let your body heal even if you are at home. Is that understood?"

Bryan nodded, and the doctor proceeded with his examination. He said that the incision was beginning to heal well and that Bryan needed to not put too much strain on it when he began moving around. He replaced the dressing on the wound and asked if there were any other questions. When there were none, he exited the room.

A few minutes later, the nurse arrived to shoo the family out so that she could remove the IV and catheter and give Bryan a sponge bath.

Before she left the room, Sophie remarked, "You must have long hours. You're the only nurse I've seen here taking care of him."

"Oh, I'm his only nurse, dear," the woman explained. "Your father hired me to be Mr. Lawson's private nurse while he is here and after he goes home if it's needed."

"My father can be very pushy. Don't let him overwork you," Sophie remarked.

The middle-aged woman just chuckled and said, "Oh, you have no idea how persuasive your father can be. But that has little to do with why I was willing to take this job. Your father represented me in a wrongful death suit for my husband several years ago. As they say, he took on the big pharma and he won. He was tenacious. He not only made them pay, but he got them in so much trouble with the FDA. It was a sight to see. No, this job has little to do with your father's persistence in asking or about the pay he offered, although both were strong incentives. It's about repaying a man who saved everything I owned."

Sophie had always known that her father was a well-respected attorney, but she had never met someone who regarded him so highly for a personal reason.

The group walked down the hall to a waiting area until the nurse said they could come back. "So, we should probably discuss Bryan's release and the plan for that," Summer said. "I can't imagine him not doing everything in his power to be out of here tomorrow."

"And as nice as that nurse is, Bryan's not going to want her around twenty-four seven," Riley stated.

"We'll work out a schedule. We can take shifts at the garage depending on what bikes are in and rotate. Summer, you can let us know what you can work out after you check your appointment schedule. We may have to tell some of the customers that their jobs are delayed, but that can't be helped," Trevor said.

"Or you can let the girl who has absolutely no commitments other than things that can be done on a computer stay with him," Sophie suggested.

"What do you need for a computer?" Trevor asked. This was his department all the way.

"Well, I do graphic design. So something with a good Internet connection. Decent RAM and hard drive. Pretty much what you would guess a person would need for doing lots of complicated graphics."

"Oh, I am on that. Bryan has great Internet. I've made sure we all do, but I can make sure that his computer is tweaked for what you need until we get you one of your own." Trevor was a little geeked that he got to upgrade Bryan's computer. Bryan had always wanted just the basics. Pretty much email and the occasional Amazon purchase was all Bryan had needed.

"I can go check his grocery supply and stock up on the things he likes," Summer offered. "Is there anything special you want, Sophie?"

"I'm pretty flexible. I like fruits and vegetables. I prefer fresh over canned if it's available." Sophie thought for a minute. "I enjoy making my own spaghetti sauce if I have decent tomatoes."

"You got it. If you think of anything else just text me." She asked Sophie for her number and sent a text right away so they would have each other's numbers.

Sophie heard her phone go off two more times, signaling text messages. While she had been paying attention to Summer, apparently Trevor and Riley had been texting her too so that she had contact information on all of them.

"Look, we really appreciate you being willing to stay with Bry, but don't feel like you're trapped there. If you need to get out and do something, one of us will gladly come and stay with him," Riley said. "I know you and he started some kind of relationship while he was guarding you, but if it gets to be too much, we can always step in."

"I appreciate that," Sophie said. "And I promise to let you know if I can't handle something or if I need a break."

The nurse came and told them they could go back to Bryan's room. When they walked in, he was sitting up in the padded recliner chair that had been in the corner. He looked more like the healthy man he had been just a few days ago than he had since taking a bullet three days before. "He is allowed to use the restroom, but only if someone goes with him. We don't want to take any chances of him getting weak or dizzy and falling. That would be catastrophic for his ribs. Any of you can go with him, but if you would feel safer with me helping, just press the red button. I'm right down the hall."

"You look good," Trevor said.

"I feel so much better being up and out of that bed, and not hooked to all the crap. Now if I could just have some actual clothes," Bryan said.

"I was planning to run over to your place and see how well you are stocked for groceries. I'll pack a bag to bring so that you have something to wear. I'm pretty sure what you had on Saturday went into the biohazard waste bin," Summer said with a wrinkled nose.

"Actually, when we moved out of Walt's house, we packed you up too. Your bag is in my truck," Trevor offered. "I can run out and grab that if you want me to."

"What about my cell?" Bryan asked.

"That was pretty much toast," Trevor replied. "Something about getting soaked with blood makes them tend to not work. I can pick up a new one tomorrow if you want me to."

"Damn, I hope that cloud thing works like they say it does," Bryan stated remorsefully.

"I can make sure everything loads back up on it," Trevor offered. "Your emails and all that stay in the folders."

"It's not the emails I'm worried about, it's the photos," Bryan said. Sophie started to blush. She knew exactly what photos he was hoping he hadn't lost.

"I can double check those too," Trevor offered.

"NO! You leave the photos alone," Bryan stated adamantly.

"Got it, man. You don't have to have a heart attack. I won't touch your photos," Trevor replied. "It's probably because you have dick pics that you send to girls. I'll bet that's it."

Riley and Summer just laughed. Bryan was not finding any of this funny.

Bryan asked Riley to run and grab a couple of pizzas. He was hungry, and while the hospital food was nowhere near as bad as some hospitals were, he was hungry for some of the good stuff. He told him to sneak in some beer too, but Riley did not agree to that plan.

Sophie's cell phone rang and it was Pete. She answered it with, "Hello little brother, what part of go enjoy your honeymoon did you not understand?"

"Yeah, I know, I just couldn't stop wondering how Bryan is, so I thought I'd check on him," Pete stated.

"He happens to be sitting right here beside me. I'll put him on,"

Sophie said and handed the phone to Bryan.

"Hey, Pete. Your sister is right. Enjoy your honeymoon, I'm going to be fine," Bryan assured him.

"Great, I just needed to check in and well, thank you for saving my sister's life," Pete said.

"Hey, it's no problem. That's what you hired me to do," Bryan replied.

"Well, I'm reasonably certain that taking a bullet for someone makes you a hero in any book," Pete said sincerely.

"I hope to never have to do it again, but for Sophia, I would do it all the same way all over every time," Bryan replied.

"Well, thanks for taking care of my sister. I'll stop by and see you when we get back." And with that, Pete ended the call. Bryan handed the phone back to Sophia.

When they were done enjoying the pizza, Bryan asked Trevor if he would help him walk to the bathroom and then get back in bed. "You'd never think just sitting up in a chair for a couple of hours could wear you out, but I'm beat."

"Well, you just got shot, had major surgery, and were drugged for a few days. I'm pretty sure being worn out is normal," Summer said, rolling her eyes. "And with that, I'm out. I'll go get your place stocked with food. Hopefully you get to go home tomorrow." She gave him a quick hug as he walked toward the bathroom leaning against Trevor and left the room.

When Bryan was back in bed, Trevor ran out to get his duffel bag, and when he got back, the two brothers left.

"Come sit with me, Sophia," Bryan commanded.

"I think you just wanted back in bed so I could be next to you," Sophia teased.

"Well, it's not the full reason, but it's definitely an added benefit," Bryan said.

"So what's this about dick pics on your phone?" Sophia asked.

"I don't have dick pics on my phone, Sophia. That was just Trevor giving me a hard time. No, the only sexy picture on my phone is one of a very gorgeous naked woman tied to my Harley," he said as he pulled her closer.

"Oh, and here I was hoping for a dick pic," Sophia said, settling against him.

"Hush little one," Bryan commanded. "I need sleep and I just want to hold you while I do."

"Yes, Sir," Sophie agreed. She wasn't really tired, but if being there could offer Bryan any level of comfort, she was all in.

Bryan slept solidly for a few hours. When he woke up, he asked Sophia to hit the call button for the nurse. "Is it something I can help you with?" Sophia asked.

"No, sweetheart, I need to go to the bathroom, so please call the nurse," Bryan said.

"I'm stronger than I look. I can walk with you," Sophie offered.

"I have no doubt that you could walk me to the bathroom and back," Bryan began. "It's in the bathroom that I am concerned about. I don't really think the hospital is the place to have you help me with the bathroom."

"Oh, right," Sophie agreed, jumping up to get the button.

After Bryan returned from the bathroom, he sat in the chair again. He needed to try to stay awake at least a little bit. He couldn't imagine it was fun for Sophia to sit beside him and watch him sleep for so many hours. He looked at the menu and had Sophia order their dinner. While they waited for the food, he suggested they play a game to get to know each other better. Sort of a twenty questions type of thing. "I'll start," Bryan said. "Favorite flower?"

"Yellow rose," Sophia said. "Favorite color? Mine is purple."

"Emerald green," Bryan said, looking into her eyes. "Just like your eyes. Favorite type of food?"

"To cook, Italian; to eat, Mexican," Sophia said. "What's your favorite food?"

"I mostly like the good old American home cooking," Bryan said. "I love a good pot roast with potatoes and gravy. That type of thing."

"Just like Momma used to make?" Sophia asked.

"Oh yeah, just like my momma used to make," Bryan agreed. "We didn't grow up fancy, but my mom sure could turn a simple meal into a feast. With us three boys, she had to make a big meal too. Summer didn't eat a lot, but we sure could put it away." Bryan was quiet for a minute, remembering all the great meals his mom used to make for them. Each and every one cooked and served with love. He pulled himself back to the present and asked Sophia, "Did your mom cook?"

"No, she hired people for that." Sophia laughed.

"Ah, lifestyles of the rich and famous." Bryan started to laugh, and quickly tried to stop, "Oh, God, that hurts," he said, holding his side.

After he stopped grimacing from the pain, Sophia stated, "We weren't famous, at least not the way most would think. My dad was making his way up through the ranks of the levels at the law firm. My mom came from money and had a lifestyle to maintain. We had a cook for as long as I could remember. We didn't have a nanny when we were little, but as we got older, we did have tutors and got lessons that were paid for. Tennis lessons, swim lessons, that type of thing. I honestly don't think my mom knows how to cook. She never had to."

"But you like to cook Italian food?" Bryan asked.

"Oh, yeah, I enjoy cooking. I'm not a gourmet or anything; I don't cook real fancy stuff. Growing up, I loved to hang out in the kitchen with our cook. As soon as I was able to safely do so, she had me helping peel something or stir something." Sophie was lost in thought for a minute. "Yeah, like I said, we didn't have nannies, but my mom wasn't super present either. Once Pete was out of diapers, she started going to the club more and more often. She had her bridge ladies over, was on committees, and always had parties for the higher-ups at the firm. So I hung out with the cook. Pete always followed the gardener around. The gardener wasn't full-time, but when he was there Pete was out there helping him. And like I said, we had tutors and coaches coming over all the time. We did always sit down to family dinner together, though. That was a priority for my parents. My dad worked long hours at the firm, but we all had to be home by six for family dinner. He went in early or worked weekends, but he was home by six every night. I don't know; I guess it is what it is, you know. I didn't know any different. Pretty much all of my friends were living the same type of lifestyle, so I thought that was what life was. Until I got older, I didn't know that kids weren't babysat by their cooks and their coaches."

The person came with their tray of food. Sophia pushed the table so that it was between them, and they shared their dinner. The conversation became more light-hearted than it had been. They talked more about the things that they liked, favorite this or that. It was a good way to get to know a little more about each other and see what they had in common.

When they were done eating, Sophia pushed the table to the side and told him, "I told your family that I would like to come and help you at your house when you get to leave here. If that's okay with you. I know they have businesses to run, and with you being out of commission for a while, the guys will need to put in extra duty at Triskelion. I don't really have a place to stay other than with my parents. Trevor assured me that he can tweak your computer so I can keep up with my graphic design business. And I can cook and clean..." Sophia stopped rambling when Bryan leaned forward enough to place a finger over her lips in a shh motion.

"You had me at 'I would like to come and help,' Sophia. I'd love to have you stay with me. You don't need to sell me on the idea," Bryan said. When Sophia just nodded, he used his finger to make a 'come here' motion. He was leaning about as far forward as he dared without causing himself excruciating pain. When she leaned in, he kissed her, and it wasn't just a quick peck. The more they kissed, the more Sophia leaned in to take more and more kisses from him. Finally he had to pull away because he was sure the doctor wasn't going to allow sexual activity for a while, and they definitely didn't allow it in a hospital room. "We need to stop now or I'm not going to be able to pretty soon," he said.

Sophie leaned back in her chair. She totally agreed: they needed to stop for now. The last thing she wanted was to have the nurse or some visitor walk in on them if things got any more heated.

When Bryan was ready to go back to bed, he once again had the nurse help him to the bathroom and then back to bed.

"I'm going to take a quick shower if that's okay with you," Sophia said.

"Of course, take your time, do whatever you need to. Even if you have to leave, you don't have to stay at my side every minute, although I like having you here," Bryan said.

"No, I have no way of leaving anyway." Sophia laughed. "My car is in Colorado."

"Right, I wasn't thinking. I'm sure if you need something one of my siblings would be glad to take you," he offered.

"Actually, they brought all of my stuff here, so I'm set. I'll just grab a quick shower and be right back."

Just before she closed the bathroom door, Bryan said, "Sophia, thanks for staying with me, and if I'm asleep when you get done, I'd really like to have you come to bed with me anyway. I sleep better when I know you are next to me and safe."

"Okay," Sophie said softly. How could she say no to this man? His brothers had told her that he had jolted awake yelling for her, and his first concern had been for her safety. He really was special. When she was done with her shower, sure enough, Bryan was out cold. She took a few minutes to organize her things; hopefully they would be leaving the hospital soon. She also texted her neighbor that was keeping an eye on her place letting her know that for now she was staying in Michigan for a while longer. She told her she would keep in touch. She put her phone in her pocket but kept it on silent and climbed into bed with Bryan. Her crawling in beside him made him stir enough to put his arm around her, but then he was back to deep sleep in no time. Sophie didn't sleep a lot that night. She realized she had probably had more sleep in the last three days than she usually had in a week. But she was content to lie with Bryan and daydream about her future. One that looked pretty good right now.

Chapter Fourteen

The following morning, all of the Lawsons were there waiting for the doctor's visit, hoping for Bryan to get the okay to be released. They all started reminiscing about their childhood and their parents and all the wonderful things they remembered about growing up. Sophie enjoyed listening to them. She'd had obviously had a very different childhood than the Lawsons. Many days growing up she had wished for something that more like the families she saw on television, but looking back, what she had grown up with had made her who she was today, and she was proud of who she had become—despite having had to walk away from her life for so long.

When the doctor arrived, he examined Bryan and then asked several questions as to who would be staying with him, what the plan was for care, and a layout of the house regarding stairs to climb and such. Apparently he felt satisfied with their answers because he agreed to discharge Bryan. He gave him a list of dos and do nots and said the nurse would be in shortly to give him the plan for wound care and follow up.

They had all agreed that the easiest mode of transportation for Bryan and Sophie would be Summer's SUV. It wasn't as high off the ground as the big pickup trucks that Riley and Trevor owned, so she went down to bring it closer to the exit while Riley and Trevor rounded up what luggage was there. They left behind the clothes that Bryan wanted to wear home and loaded up the rest in Summer's vehicle.

By the time the nurse came with the discharge papers and instructions, Bryan was dressed and ready to go. The nurse explained to Sophia when and how to change the dressing on the incision and what signs to look for as far as infection and what was good and what was bad. She got a wheelchair and took Bryan down to the patient pickup area. She set up an appointment to come and see Bryan at home in a couple of days and made sure he had the information for follow-up appointments with his doctor. Summer was there waiting with her Jeep Grand Cherokee. Bryan sat in the front because the seat could be reclined so that his rib didn't have as much pressure on it. Sophie climbed in behind Summer so Bryan could lean as far back as he needed to.

Sophie realized that Bryan hadn't been exaggerating when he had said taking her to his house would be a ride in the country. It took them forty-five minutes, and they drove down several winding rural roads to get there. When they pulled up to the house, Sophie had to keep from letting her jaw drop to the ground. This house was built for far more than one person. It wasn't anything fancy, but it was large. It looked to be an old farmhouse that had been restored. She could see a more modern garage to the side of the house, and it looked like there was a rather large barn in the backyard. "Your house looks amazing. I had no idea it would be this big," Sophie said.

"Well, I'm not a person who likes to move much. I got way too much of that in the military. So when I looked for a house, I looked for one that I could be happy in for the rest of my life. I wanted one that would work for me and the family I always planned to have someday. A lot of the rooms are finished in a very basic way so that they could be made into children's bedrooms or whatever, depending on where life takes me," Bryan explained.

Riley and Trevor had followed behind in one of their two trucks. Sophie didn't know which since it seemed to her like all three brothers drove pretty much the same vehicle. Their motorcycles were a different story. Those showed their preferences and the variety of their taste, but apparently to them a truck was a truck. Sophie could understand that when someone's life and livelihood pretty much revolved around motorcycles, their personalities would be shown more in their bikes.

Apparently somewhere along the way, Trevor and Riley had stopped to pick up steaks for the barbeque grill. They all made their way out to the back deck, and Bryan sat in a comfortable lounger. Summer went inside to make a salad and some things to go with the meat, and Trevor started up the grill.

"I'll come help," Sophie offered.

"Actually," Riley began, "I could use your help out in the barn. I'm sure Summer can make a salad."

Uh, yeah, okay, sure." Sophie was confused. She looked at Bryan to see if he gave any sign of what was going on, but apparently the activities of the last hour or so had worn him out, and he was asleep. So she followed Riley down the path to the barn.

"I am hoping that you are willing to help with the horses," Riley began. "If not, we'll take care of it. I am sure one of us will drop by each day and we can take care of the food and water and all that. All you would really need to do is let them out of the barn so they have some time to run each day." He just kept walking as he talked, so Sophia just kept up.

When they finally got to the barn and Riley stopped to open the door, Sophie finally had her chance to speak. "Horses?" she asked.

"Yeah, they're all really friendly and everything so they shouldn't be a problem. I just know that if they don't get let out every morning, Bryan is going to try to do it, and I would hate to see him hurt his rib."

"Oh, yeah, of course," she agreed. "I just didn't know that he had horses."

"You aren't afraid of horses, are you? These ones are all gentle," Riley assured her.

"Oh, no. I haven't been around them in years, but I used to love to ride them," Sophie said.

"Hmm, I wouldn't have figured you for a horse riding type." Riley chuckled.

"Oh, come on now, Riley, what self-respecting rich family doesn't get horseback riding lessons for their kids?" Sophie laughed.

As they walked into the barn, the horses all perked up and began to come to the doors of their stalls. Riley made his way to the far end of the barn to open the large sliding door before coming back and opening each stall. As he opened a gate, he took a moment to pat the horse while it nuzzled him. He told Sophie the name of each horse. When they were all outside in the large paddock, Riley grabbed a bale of hay and took it out and broke it up for the horses. Closing the sliding door to the paddock, he directed Sophie back out and around to the side of the building. He showed her where the hose hooked up and how to put water in the trough. "If you can give them some hay and some water in the morning or whenever you let them out, one of us will stop by and get them back in for the evening and give them their oats."

"Sure, sounds easy enough," Sophie said.

"If you can't carry a whole bale of hay, that's okay. Just break one up in the barn and take about half of it outside," he offered. Then they went back up to the house to help with the meal. They let Bryan sleep until the food was ready.

Sophie woke Bryan by softly calling his name. He woke instantly. Military men tended to sleep lightly, although with the pain meds, he was in more of a fog than normal. It took a minute for everything to fully register. He was back home, on his back deck. The horses were out in the paddock, so one of his siblings must have taken care of them. The steaks smelled amazing. Everyone dug into the food.

"I showed Sophie how to let the horses out in the morning and where the hay and water are," Riley said. "For the time being she will let them out in the morning and one of us will stop by to make sure they get fed and put in for the night."

"Thanks for that, but I need to do something other than just sit," Bryan argued.

"Yeah, well, you can walk out and see them, but you can't lift a bale of hay," Trevor ordered. "Look, man, we aren't telling you to sit in a rocking chair on the front porch all day. We just want you to take it easy for a couple of weeks. I have seen you wince over taking a deep breath. Going out to the barn with all that dust and trying to lift a bale of hay is just asking for trouble. We'll bring you all the paperwork from the garage. You can keep up on invoicing and ordering. I'll make sure that everything we have on the computer for the PI jobs is up to date. I'm sure Sophie wouldn't mind going out to some of your favorite places. We just want you to take it easy and heal. We need you back on top of your game sooner rather than later."

"Yeah, you're the big brother, we can't have you hurt yourself worse," Summer said softly. "We have depended on you for so long, let us step up and take care of you for a while so you can just focus on healing." Riley nodded his agreement.

"Okay, okay. I get it," Bryan agreed. "But I'm not going to sit still for long."

"Just long enough to heal properly," Sophie stated. "And I'm going to be here to help make sure you do what the doctor tells you."

"Yes, Ma'am!" Bryan teased. Sophie just rolled her eyes.

After they ate and visited for a few hours, Bryan was starting to act tired again, so his siblings and Sophie cleaned up from the meal. Riley and Trevor went and took care of the horses for the night while Summer and Sophie went inside with Bryan to make sure the house was set up the way he needed it. When they got into the big open living room area, Sophie could definitely tell this was a man's place. There were pictures of family, but no other decorations. The sofa was a large leather sectional that had enough ottomans that it could be put together to form a bed of sorts. And of course, the TV was huge—that seemed to be a guy thing.

"Hey, Summer, can you show Sophia where the sheets and blankets and stuff are upstairs? I'm thinking I might crash down here for tonight at least so I don't have to climb up. Today kind of wiped me out," Bryan admitted.

"Sure, come on," Summer said to Sophie. She showed her a large linen closet and helped her pick out a big fluffy blanket and some flat sheets. When she got downstairs, she asked if Bryan wanted her to make up the couch, but he said he was sure he and Sophia could handle it. So Summer wished them a good night and headed home.

Sophie pushed the ottomans together and started to make the couch into a bed. "If you don't think this will be comfortable enough for you, I am sure I can make the climb. It might take me a while, but I can do it," Bryan offered.

"No, I'm fine with this. We can stay down here as long as you need to. It's got to be more comfortable than sharing a hospital bed." Sophie smiled.

"Come on, let me show you how to lock up and set the alarm," Bryan said.

"Is this a high crime area?" Sophie teased.

Bryan laughed a little but stopped as soon as he realized how much laughing hurt. "No, but honestly with the PI business we all figured it's not a bad idea to have alarms. You never know who we might piss off."

"Ah, yeah, I hadn't thought about that. I'm sure Larry would have tried something if he knew where you were. Especially since he apparently thought you were trying to steal me from him," Sophie said, shaking her head. "There is a part of me that still doesn't believe he's not out there somewhere waiting. I know he's dead, but it's not real somehow."

Bryan picked up his house phone and dialed Trevor. Sophie couldn't hear the other side of the conversation but from Bryan's response, she could guess what Trevor had said.

"Yeah, everything's fine," Bryan said then paused. "Yes, I know you just left. I need you to work some of your magic for me. I need to know where Ribinsky's body is. Find it and let me know in the morning. And get me that new cell." Then he hung up the phone and finished locking up the house.

Sophia offered to run upstairs and get anything that Bryan might need as far as toiletries or whatever, but he said that was all still in his suitcase from Walt's house, so she helped him get that set up and open so he could get what he needed. Currently, they were both living out of suitcases, so it made it easy to just stay on the first floor.

Chapter Fifteen

Bryan was already in bed when Sophie came to join him. She hadn't been sure how to dress for the night. She wasn't really comfortable with walking around the house naked. She knew it was out in the middle of the woods and in the middle of nowhere, but still it wasn't something she was comfortable with yet, so she had grabbed one of the T-shirts she had seen in Bryan's suitcase. It was pretty much a dress on her. When Bryan raised his eyebrows at her, she quickly explained. "I felt kind of odd walking around naked, with being new to the house and all. I was hoping you wouldn't mind me borrowing your shirt."

"Sweetheart, I don't mind at all. I understand you not being comfortable with the house yet, especially since we are sleeping in the living room. I think my shirt looks great on you. However, you are way overdressed for sleeping," Bryan stated.

Sophie made sure that all of the lights were off except the lamp that was on the end table beside the couch. She sat on the edge of the bed and pulled the T-shirt over her head, then lay down beside Bryan. She was on his right side, so he wrapped his arm around her and pulled her closer.

"I've missed your body, Sophia," he said heatedly before he began kissing her lips then moving to her neck and then lower to her breasts.

Sophie was all for what Bryan was starting, she just wasn't sure that they could finish it. "Maybe we should slow down a little," she suggested.

"Hell no, little one, I'm not waiting any longer. I agree that it's going to take some more consideration than it normally would in order to make sure I don't hurt my rib or my incision, but this is happening."

"Yes, Sir," Sophie agreed. What else could she say?

Bryan's kissing and caressing was definitely having the desired effect. When he put a hand between Sophia's legs, she was already quite wet. He fingered her to orgasm, wanting her ready for him. After her orgasm, he said, "Ride me, Sophia." Sophia hesitated, unsure how to do that without hurting him. "Sophia, you're a little bit of a thing compared to me. You won't hurt me or put pressure on my ribs. Trust me, you'll be sitting much lower," he said with a mischievous smile.

Sophie carefully got on her knees, straddling him, and lowered herself down onto his thick cock. She paused for a minute to make sure he wasn't in pain. "Are you sure this is okay?" she asked.

"Oh, hell, this is far more than okay. It feels like it's been forever since I've been inside of you," Bryan replied. "I can't do much of the work, though, so you're going to have to ride me well, Sophia." When Sophia began rotating her hips and rising up and down, Bryan placed his thumb directly on her clit and made firm circles. His actions caused her to become even more aroused, and she began moving faster and harder too. Soon she was moaning out her release and his followed soon after. She gently fell to his chest and then rolled to his good side. She fell asleep quickly with her head on his pectoral muscle. Sharing the hospital bed with him hadn't given her the most rested sleep she'd ever had, so she was really tired. Bryan, on the other hand, had taken that nap earlier in the afternoon, so he didn't fall asleep as quickly. He lay there and pondered just what the future could hold.

Bryan knew that Sophia could do her work anywhere; what he didn't know was how attached she was to her home in Colorado. Of course, with Larry out of the picture, she had no reason to have to race back because of safety concerns. He didn't know how long she could stay, though. He knew she had said that she wanted time to catch up with her parents. She had mentioned being able to see Autumn's baby. What he didn't know was if she was planning to stay until the baby came or if she intended to go home and come back again later. He hoped she would stay long term, like maybe forever. He hoped she would at least stay long enough for them to spend time together and see how compatible they were. It was obvious that sexually they were on point, but they really knew so little about each other. They hadn't even known each other a week, although he felt a connection to her like he had never felt with anyone before. He was hoping he could convince her to stay with him even beyond the healing process of his rib. Maybe if she stayed they would develop a routine together and would both realize that it was something they could enjoy long term. Eventually he fell asleep and had dreams of all the things he wanted to do with Sophia. Not just sexual things—he wanted to do those, but he wanted to take her horseback riding, he'd love to take her for a fall color drive on his Harley up north, and he had dreams of many other things he hoped he got a chance to do.

The following morning Bryan and Sophia were sitting down to a nice breakfast of cheese omelets and bacon when someone knocked on the door. Sophia started to get up to answer it, but Bryan stopped her and got up himself. He wasn't sure who would be at his door, but he didn't feel comfortable having Sophia answer it just yet. Besides, she was currently still wearing just his -shirt, and while that was a beautiful thing, it was his beautiful thing and he didn't want to share it with a stranger that might be at his door. He looked out the small peep hole and saw his brother Trevor standing there. That kind of surprised him because usually his siblings just came walking in. They all had keys to each other's homes and knew the security codes if they did happen to set off an alarm. "You knock now?" he asked Trevor.

"Well, with Sophie here I wasn't sure if you'd want me just barging in, and I didn't know if she was prepared for the fact that we all do that. So I knocked," Trevor explained.

"Yeah, I wasn't thinking about that, and I appreciate that you did think of it. I'll talk to her and see if she would prefer it one way or the other, but come on in. We're just finishing up breakfast," he offered, walking back to the small breakfast nook in his kitchen.

"Hey, Trevor," Sophie greeted him.

"Hi Sophie. I stopped by to drop off Bryan's new cell, and I have those business files for you to look over," he said, turning back to Bryan.

"Great, you can put them in my office. We're almost done," Bryan instructed.

Trevor carried a box down the hall and returned to the table. "The other information you asked about, the answer would be the city morgue. They are still waiting for a positive ID. I think they are checking dental records or something like that."

"Hmm, okay." Bryan let his mind sort through what the reasoning could be for there to not be someone to claim the body and ID it, but it must mean that Larry didn't have family, or at least not family in the area. He turned to Sophia and said, "This is totally your call, sweetheart, but you said it was hard to believe that Larry was out of your life for good. If you want to, we can take you to the morgue and you can identify the body. It might give you closure, but on the other hand, seeing a dead person is never pleasant. He will be cleaned up. The bullet holes will still be visible, but there won't be actual blood. We will most likely be in a separate room with a viewing window. You probably won't be in the actual room with the body. But we can take along some vapor rub just in case they don't have the viewing window. That combats any odor that might be present."

Trevor chimed in with, "It's definitely your call, but if you do want to go, I can take you both down there."

Sophie pondered that for a while. Did she want to see a dead body? No, not really. Did she think it would help her put the past behind her if she had confirmation that Larry was dead? Yeah, probably. She didn't think she could handle doing something like that alone, but if Bryan and Trevor were there maybe she could. If she passed out, Trevor would probably be able to pick her up and carry her out of the room. She knew Bryan could and even would, but with his broken rib, she didn't want him having to try. "I think I need to," she finally said quietly.

"Then we'll be right beside you the whole time, Sophia," Bryan assured her.

When they were finished eating, Trevor said, "I'll go let the horses out and give them water while you two get ready to go."

Sophie decided that she was going to wear the leather pants and Harley shirt that Bryan had picked out for her. It kind of felt like armor to her, and it definitely was a symbol of the new life she could have with Larry not out there anymore.

When they arrived at the morgue, it was apparent that Trevor had called ahead to tell them that he had found a person that could positively ID the body that they had assumed was Larry Ribinsky. The Lawsons had only based their identification on pictures used during their assignment as Sophia's bodyguards, but Sophia would know the man personally. Before stepping into the viewing room, Bryan turned Sophia toward him and put a hand on each upper arm. "If at any point this becomes too much, you turn around or you turn to me, and I will take you out of the room so you can't see him anymore." She nodded her understanding, and they walked into a small room with a window. The curtain on the other side of the window was closed. A person came in and pushed a button on the wall.

Someone on the other side opened the curtain and there in front of the window was a gurney with an obvious body covered by a white sheet. Bryan stood on one side of Sophia and Trevor stood on the other. When they pulled the sheet back, she was glad that she was on Bryan's good side because she sagged against him. Trevor started to reach for her, assuming that she was going to pass out and not sure that Bryan could support her if she did. But she wasn't going to pass out; she was sagging from the sheer relief that the man who had tormented her physically and mentally for so long would never have the chance to do so again. He was dead. There was a pallor about him, no life left there at all. She could see the two bullet holes, one in the head and one in the chest, but like Bryan had promised, the wounds were clean. Larry was gone forever, and she could move on with her life and not have to look over her shoulder ever again. She realized that everyone was kind of looking at her. "What?" she asked.

"They are wondering if you know who this person is, Sophie," Trevor began. "From our investigation during our case for your brother, we believe that this may be a man named Larry Ribinsky. Can you confirm if that is true or not?"

"Oh, sorry, yeah, that's definitely Larry," Sophie said with a sigh.

"May I ask how you know or I should say knew Mr. Ribinsky?" the medical examiner said.

"I dated him for two years and lived with him for over a year," Sophie stated. God, why had it taken her so long to see what he truly was? Even when she had, it had taken her almost a year before she'd found a way to walk away from him. If she hadn't ended up in the hospital, she wasn't sure when or if she ever would have gotten away from him.

"I see, well, yes, we can consider that a positive ID then," the man said. He signaled to the person beside the gurney and she pulled the sheet back up to cover the body. The curtain began to close.

Sophie still just stood there for a moment staring at that stark white sheet until the curtain was fully in place. It was over, truly and finally over. As they walked back out of the viewing room into the outer office, they were met by a police detective. "Mr. Lawson, Ms. Hallowell, I was told you were coming down here to see if you could positively ID the body. Could I ask you a few questions?"

"Umm, I guess so," Sophie said. She noticed a very familiar person walking their way. "Daddy, what are you doing here?"

The officer turned to see who 'Daddy' was. Recognition dawned immediately.

"Hey Sophia" her father said, stepping in to kiss her cheek. "Riley called me a bit ago and told me that he had received a text from Bryan asking that I meet you here. He said that you came to ID a body and that the police would likely want to question you. I'm here to make sure that questioning is done properly." He had a sort of daunting smile on his face as he looked toward that detective. "That's okay with you, I assume, Officer—?"

"Jiminez, and yes, Sir, Mr. Hallowell, that's fine," the detective replied, directing them to another side room.

Damn it was nice having one of the city's most prominent attorneys for a father. There was a small table. Sophie sat with Bryan on one side and her father on the other. Detective Jiminez sat in the remaining chair. Trevor stood by the door.

"So, Ms. Hallowell, may I ask how you know Larry Ribinsky?" he began.

"I dated him for a couple of years and lived with him for about a year," she replied after looking to her father for a nod to answer the question.

"I see, and when did that relationship end?"

"Three years ago," Sophia stated dryly.

"And why did that relationship end?" he asked nonchalantly.

"Because he ran away and hid when I ended up in the hospital from being beaten to the point that I miscarried my baby," Sophia said, looking him right in the eye. There were no tears; she was so beyond letting that man make her sad. She was wearing her biker armor, and she could handle anything this cop threw at her.

"I see." That one kind of threw his resolve off a little bit. "Have you seen him since that incident?" he asked.

"Not until five minutes ago," Sophia answered

He turned toward Bryan and said, "I have the report your brothers gave me for the events at the country club and your investigation leading up to that day. Is there anything you can add to that report?"

"Not really. I was standing next to Sophia, and I heard multiple people yell the word gun. I tried to block her and take her down to cover her. I felt a sharp pain to my side. I remember seeing Sophia with her eyes closed and blood soaking her dress. I wasn't sure if it was mine or hers and then I passed out. I woke up in the hospital," Bryan stated succinctly and matter-of-factly.

"Is that all?" Mr. Hallowell said pointedly, giving the officer his best *Don't bullshit me* look.

"I believe so for now," he said. "If I think of anything else I will call you and set up a time to talk to your daughter or Mr. Lawson."

With that, they all stood to leave. After the officer had left the building, Sophie thanked her father for coming. He told her it was his pleasure.

"Thank you for taking care of everything at the hospital," Bryan said, extending his hand to Sophia's father.

"It was the least I could do. If I had realized the situation, I would have hired you before my son got a chance," he stated. "But since he hired you, and you got shot protecting my girl, I wanted to make sure you were well taken care of."

"I was, thank you, Sir."

Mr. Hallowell hugged Sophie and said, "Your mother would have my hide if I didn't ask you to come to dinner soon, Sophia. And bring your gentleman friend." Sophie promised to call her mother and set up a day soon.

They all headed out, and when they got to Bryan's house, Trevor told them he had to get back to the garage; he had a repair job to finish.

"Walk with me, Sophia," Bryan said, holding out his hand. They started walking down the path toward the barn. Bryan had always found the horses calming. They were such big magnificent animals, yet they had such grace and dignity. When they got to the side of the paddock, Bryan sat on the bench he often sat on to watch the horses. Sophia sat beside him. "I was just wondering what your plan is. Do you have any idea how long you are planning to stay in Michigan?"

"I don't know that I have an end date in mind," Sophia said. "I know that I want to be here for a while, maybe permanently. I don't have any reason to have to go back to Colorado at this point. Other than to sell my house if I decide that I'm staying here permanently. I honestly have kind of kept to myself out there. I was always afraid if I got too well known around town that Larry might somehow find me. I have acquaintances but not friends really. I lived a pretty quiet life. I don't want to do that anymore. I want to live a life. I want to be near my parents. I want to be an aunt."

"I was hoping that was how you felt," Bryan said. "I would love it if you would stay here with me for however long that feels okay for you. If that's not comfortable for you, I still want to date you or whatever you want to call it. I think we have something here, and I think we could have something more."

Sophia thought for a minute, and Bryan was afraid she was trying to think of a way to let him down gently. "I'd like that," Sophia finally said. "I love your house and I love the horses. I would like to see where things go between us too. I'm here at least until you are fully healed. You have promises to keep." She smiled.

"I do?" Bryan asked.

"You promised me a ride in the country on your motorcycle and the doctor said no motorcycle riding for at least six weeks. So you're stuck with me that long at least," she teased. "And you promised to show me your playroom. I'm thinking you can't really do that room justice until you are fully healed either, so I'm waiting you out."

"Oh, you are on for both of those as soon as I am able?" Bryan said. He leaned toward Sophia and started with a simple kiss that turned into a deeper kiss. "God, I can't wait until this is healed. I want so badly to carry you up to my bed and welcome you fully to my home. But that too will have to wait," he said with regret.

"That's okay," Sophia assured him. "We have time, I'm in no rush. We can get to know each other in other ways too." She leaned in and kissed him but pulled away before things got out of hand. "In the meantime, I'm going to show you what an awesome cook I am. Summer picked up all the stuff I need to make my homemade spaghetti sauce." She stood up and reached out a hand to Bryan like she was helping him up.

He rose from the bench and followed her into the house. "I have a feeling that I am going to have a lot of exercising to do when I am able to take off the weight I'm going to put on while you cook for me."

"Yeah, like you have anything to worry about," Sophia scoffed. "But I do love to cook, so maybe."

A few hours later, Bryan and Sophia were seated at his dining room table eating the most amazing spaghetti he had ever tasted. "You have to make this for Trev and Rye sometime. This is delicious," he said, taking his second large helping.

"Apparently I will need a much bigger pot." Sophia laughed. "I'm not used to people that can put away as much food as you three can."

Just then the doorbell chimed. Bryan pulled up the app on his phone that let him see who was at the door. "Come on in, Rye," he said into the phone.

Riley walked in the door and found them at the table. He eyed the big pot. "Something smells great," he said.

"Might as well go grab a plate," Sophia said. Riley walked to the kitchen to get a plate and utensils.

"Damn, I was hoping for leftovers," Bryan said quietly. "No way that will happen now."

Sophia just giggled. "I'll make it again soon."

"I came by to put the horses in for the night. I wasn't planning on dinner, but thanks for inviting me," Riley said.

"Sure, no problem," Bryan said reluctantly. And he was proven right: by the time Riley was done, the pot was empty. "Look, Rye, I just wanted you to know that I really appreciate the way you handled this opp. You definitely saved Sophia, and you most likely saved Trevor too. If that asshole had pulled the trigger, I don't think Trevor would have stood a chance at that close range. You did exactly what needed to be done under pressure, and I just want you to know that I appreciate that and I'm proud of you."

Sophie had noticed that although the praise had obviously felt good to Riley, it wasn't until his brother said that he was proud of him that it had fully registered with the young man that he had done extremely well.

After dinner, Riley went out to settle the horses in for the night. Bryan invited him to stay for a while, so they settled in to watch a movie on the big TV. When the movie was over, Riley headed out, and they crashed on the sofa again. Sophie was curious where Bryan's play room was, but she also agreed that it needed to be off limits until he was completely healed. She knew he had a basement and an upstairs, but she wasn't sure which level the room was on.

Chapter Sixteen

The days continued much the same as each other. Sophie always cooked a nice dinner, and Bryan sometimes made breakfast, or they sometimes went out to a little local diner that Bryan loved. They usually threw together something easy for lunch like sandwiches and soup. Sophie had learned to always make a bigger portion of whatever was for dinner because inevitably, Trevor or Riley showed up to take care of the horses about the time they were eating. Sophie was pretty sure that was intentional. But she was okay with that; they were Bryan's family, and they would always be welcome at his home.

Bryan had a two-week check-up with his doctor, and the doctor released him for most light activities. He still couldn't ride his motorcycle or the horses. But he could take over feeding them with Sophia's help.

After the doctor appointment, they stopped by the Triskelion shop. Bryan needed to pick up his leather duffel bag that contained many of his toys and the things he had bought specifically for Sophia. He asked if Riley and Trevor would bring his bike to his place. "I can't ride yet, but I want it there when I can," he explained. They made arrangements for the whole family to come over for dinner that evening. Sophie stopped at the store and got enough to make a very large pot of spaghetti and the things to make a salad. She also bought garlic bread and a Boston cream pie. In one of their many conversations over the last few weeks, she had discovered that was a dessert that she and Bryan both loved. When they got home, she got all the vegetables ready to begin the pot of sauce. It would take time to simmer and blend, so she wanted to start it early.

After she had the pot on the stove, she went looking for Bryan. She hadn't heard him go outside, so she knew he must be in the house somewhere. She called down to the basement, but she didn't get any response, and she didn't hear any movement, so she headed upstairs.

She found Bryan in the large master bedroom. He had his suitcase and her suitcase both on the bed. When he heard her walk in the room he said, "Oh, hey, I was just moving us in up here. If you'd rather put your own things away so you know where they are, go for it."

Sophie had been in this room before but hadn't really spent any time here. Now she could explore. Bryan had the large walk-in closet open. She could see that it had two sides; one was full of his clothing, and the other was completely bare. Both sides had two long rods to hold clothing and a shoe rack that would hold more shoes than Sophie owned. The bottom two shelves were further apart so that boots could be placed on them and in the center directly in front of the door was a large full-length mirror. On his side of the closet there was a dresser and what Sophie thought was called a butler. She had seen them before; it had a few wooden hanger-like things. Her father had always put his suit for the next day on his. Bryan's held a couple of leather jackets. One was definitely his riding jacket with patches and things on it, and the other was a more dressy type coat. The other side of the closet held a dresser and a vanity that most women would die for. It was well lit and had several drawers and shelves so that makeup could be easily organized. Bryan truly had thought of everything when he'd had this house remodeled.

"So how long have you lived here?" she asked as she began hanging her clothes in the closet.

"Well, I bought the place shortly after I got home, but I still lived in the home I grew up in for a few years while I worked on this one," he replied.

"This is what, a four bedroom?" she asked.

"Yeah, it used to be five," he said. "I tore out the bedroom that was next to this one so I could make the master bath larger and have this walk-in closet."

"Well, you definitely have a closet most people would envy," she said. "Is there a place you want me to keep my toiletries and things?"

"There's space in the bathroom," Bryan said, pointing toward the other door.

Sophie walked in there and wondered what he had meant. It was a very small room, barely enough for a toilet and a pedestal sink. There wasn't room for her to put anything in here. But she also saw a door directly ahead of her. She opened that door and thought she had died and gone to heaven. There were two sinks. One was obviously where he kept his things but again, the other was completely bare, like he had been saving all this space for 'someday.' There was a large shower stall and also a huge bathtub. It was the perfect set-up, if someone was taking a shower or a bath, and the other needed to go to the bathroom, there was a door that would separate them. She put her things where she wanted them on her side. She took her makeup case and put it on the vanity in the closet. When she was completely unpacked, she laughed. "Wow, it barely looks like I moved in. All this space and so little stuff."

"Well, we can get you more," Bryan said like it was no big deal.

"I don't really need to buy a lot. I have it all back in Colorado," Sophie said. She noticed Bryan visibly tense when she said that. He must have thought that she was still planning to go back. "I am trying to decide how to handle all of that. I should probably just take a couple of days and go back there to pack up more clothes and stuff. But on the other hand, if I decide to move here permanently, I would have to go and pack up everything to put the house on the market."

Bryan seemed relieved. "No, there's really no point in making two trips," he said, pulling her into his arms. He still moved somewhat carefully because that rib pain wasn't gone, but he could hold her tighter. "You can wait until you decide and then if you are going to move, I'll fly out there with you and we can pack everything up. In the meantime, I have a washer and dryer in the basement. And you are always welcome to go pick out more things at the shop. I kind of like the biker chick look on you." He leaned down and gave her a long kiss. The kissing turned more and more passionate. "I don't want your dinner to burn, but baby, I want you really bad."

"We have time if we make it quick," Sophie agreed. "It's on a slow simmer so the flavors can blend."

Bryan backed up and let himself down onto the bed taking her with him. They had had sex in other positions, but her on top seemed to be the one that worked the best for now with his rib still being tender. She was obviously as into this as he was because she sat up and took off her shirt and bra immediately. He leaned up to take her luscious nipple in his mouth. She began tearing at his shirt to try to get him undressed too. Soon they were both naked, and Sophia was once again riding him. This woman was amazing; he needed to figure out how to make her want to stay forever.

At dinner that evening, Bryan spent a lot of time just observing. His siblings obviously got along with Sophia. They all were amazed at the dinner she had prepared for them. They sat and talked about everything and about nothing. They were all getting to know Sophia and were already accepting her as a part of him and a part of their family. He decided to go out on a limb and say something to that fact. "This is great, having a wonderful meal surrounded by family."

"Yeah it is, and Sophie is an amazing cook," Trevor chimed in.

"Well, it would be better if there was a dog," Sophia joked.

She wanted a dog? "What do you mean it would be better if there was a dog?" Bryan asked.

"Every family needs a dog," she explained. "Well, I mean every fun family needs a dog. I've never had one because, well, you've met my parents. And then I was with Larry and then I sort of went into hiding. So I haven't had a dog, but I've always wanted one someday."

"What kind of dog did you want, Sophie?" Riley asked.

"Oh, I don't know, not one of those little fru fru dogs, but not something huge either. Something fluffy and cuddly. Maybe a miniature labradoodle or a poodle," she said with a smile.

"We had a cockapoo when we were kids," Summer said. "Dad got him from some guy he worked with. They were selling all these puppies, and my parents didn't have money to spend to buy a puppy. With all of us kids things were always good, but there wasn't extra for an extravagance like a pedigreed dog. Anyway, the guy was going on vacation and he had one puppy left. He figured that it would cost more to board the puppy than he was going to make if he sold it. He came to work one day and asked our dad if he thought us kids would like a puppy. Dad thought he was trying to give him a sales pitch so he said we probably would, but he wasn't going to buy a puppy. The guy explained that he wanted to give us the puppy if Dad thought we would like it. He didn't want to board the puppy and he would rather see it go to a home where it would be loved." Summer was obviously remembering the dog; she got quiet and had a faraway look in her eyes.

"We had that dog forever," Trevor said fondly.

"I remember him. His name was Tinker," Riley added.

"A cockapoo would be cute too," Sophia agreed.

So some kind of "poodle" then. That's what he needed to find: a poodle, labradoodle, something. If Sophia wanted a dog to make this feel like family, then he was getting her a dog.

The weather was getting really nice, so they decided to take some beer out on the back deck and enjoy the Boston cream pie. Sophie thought Bryan seemed distracted; he was doing something on his phone. She wasn't sure what, but she wasn't going to let it bother her. He was probably getting cabin fever of sorts. Not that they hadn't gone out of the house, but he couldn't work out, he couldn't work on motorcycles, and he couldn't even ride. He was probably just trying to keep his mind busy.

Bryan found what he hoped was the perfect puppy from a local breeder. He texted the information to Trevor and asked him to double check the reputation of the breeder. He didn't want to get a puppy mill puppy. He wanted to be sure that this was a local family that had not been reported in any negative way. Trevor got the text and read it, then he looked at Bryan and just gave a slight knowing nod and smile and put his phone back away.

Bryan put his phone away and rejoined the conversation.

That night, it felt so right to finally have Sophia in his big bed in his bedroom in his home. After they made love again, he lay there awake while Sophia slept softly on his chest. He had always known that he wanted a wife and family someday. He just hadn't met the right woman before. He hadn't really known Sophia all that long, but every minute with her just felt right. He would have no problem asking her to marry him right away, but he also knew that her past experiences might make her feel a little hesitant to jump in that deeply this quick. But he was going to figure out a way to ask her to stay, for more than just a week or a month. His cell vibrated on the nightstand. He reached over and picked it up. There was a text from Trevor.

They check out. Never had any complaints filed. Definitely a family farm type set up. They have two girls and one boy currently available. I think you've got a great idea here. Get your girl a puppy, she'll love you even more.

Bryan texted back his thanks and then went to the breeder's page. He looked at the puppies that were available and messaged them that he would like the little blonde girl puppy and would be able to pick it up whenever the puppy was ready to go. He laid his phone back down and cuddled closer to Sophia. He had a plan, and he hoped it would work.

The following day, he took Sophia out to his favorite steakhouse for an early dinner. When they got back home, he said, "I realized you have been here for a while now, Sophia, and I have never actually given you a full tour of the house. I need to rectify that." He took her hand and led her upstairs. "As you know, this is the master bedroom; you've seen that." He led her to the next room down the hall. "This room is the biggest of the remaining bedrooms. I always figured it would make a good nursery if I ever get to that point. It's big enough for all of the furniture and paraphernalia a baby requires."

Sophia stepped into the room, and she could see what Bryan was talking about. It was finished in very neutral colors so it could easily be adapted into any sort of room if Bryan never married or if he and his wife didn't have children. But he was right: it was spacious enough that it could hold all of the furniture without feeling crowded. There was even a small bathroom attached.

They moved on down the hall, and Bryan showed her that there were two bedrooms across the hall from each other and the door directly at the end of the hall held a decent-sized bathroom. It would be a great layout for children. Rooms for the children with a bathroom in between. Some of this had obviously been part of the original layout, but Bryan had remodeled and finished each room. Every room was fine how it was but could easily be painted or decorated to be a child's bedroom or a guest room or whatever. It was very easily changeable. The man was definitely smart in how he had done things.

They went back down to the main floor. "You've seen most of this floor, but I don't think you have seen all of it," Bryan said. He walked to the first door down the short hallway.

This was his office. She hadn't been in the room, but she had seen it a few times when she went to tell him a meal was ready or to ask him about something she was thinking about cooking. The next door down the hallway was the small bathroom they had used while he had been staying on the main floor. The final door directly at the end of the hall had always been closed, and Sophie had never felt comfortable snooping so she had left the door alone She had often wondered if maybe this was his play room.

Bryan opened the door, and there was a fairly spacious room with a soft beige carpet. This room had windows almost completely covering the two exterior walls, and the remaining wall was covered with bookshelves. "I thought maybe you would want to set up this room as your office or workspace or whatever. I know you've been doing your graphics at the table or the breakfast nook. But we can get you a desk or whatever you need to make this a place you can set up in whatever way is convenient for you," Bryan offered.

"That would be amazing," Sophie said. "I definitely need to put thought into this. I have some stuff in Colorado that would really work in making this a good office for me. Maybe I can just set up a simple table for now and see how it goes."

Bryan could tell that there was a part of her that wanted to jump in with both feet and go to Colorado and pack up everything and move, but part of her was still hesitant. He got that; she didn't exactly have the best history with living with a man. He was going to keep working at making it feel okay for her.

They headed down to the basement. Sophia had been down here to do laundry but again, hadn't really explored. It was Bryan's home, and she didn't want to go in places she hadn't been given free access to. Bryan stepped up to a door and said, "This room is basically for storage. I don't have a lot of stuff in it, but there are shelves and stuff that can be filled up as life goes on and more stuff is accumulated. If you do move your things here, feel free to use any of this space for things you want to keep but don't need everyday access to." He stepped to the door on the other side of the basement. This looked to be about half of the basement. He pulled a key out of his pocket and unlocked the door. He opened it and stepped inside. Sophia followed behind him. She stepped in to what he had called his play room. With the fact that it was in the basement it could have easily taken on a dungeon feel, but Bryan had gone to long measures to make sure that wasn't the case. There were no windows, but it was a nicely modern place. It reminded her more of the playroom in the movies she had seen than it did of an actual dungeon. It wasn't red like the movie, but it had sturdy furniture that was a deep ebony color. The walls were a soothing deep blue color. He had racks with various implements hanging from them. He allowed Sophia several minutes to look around and acclimate herself to the space. When she turned back to face him, he could see the heat in her eyes. So it was time to begin.

"Today will be the first and only day you are allowed into this room with clothing on, Sophia. In the future, when you come into this room, you will leave your clothing on the bench just outside the door. Unless I instruct you to be wearing a specific item or outfit then of course you can leave that on. If I am not in the room when you enter, you have the automatic command to kneel on that mat by the door. All of these protocols are in place unless I give you a specific order that differs for one occasion. You will kneel in your submissive pose and wait for me. Today is going to be a learning process for both of us. I have no need to keep any of these implements if they are something that is a hard limit for you. You and I will walk around and you will consider each implement. You will be allowed to say one of four words. If you say 'no,' that implement will be removed. If you say 'maybe,' I will know that is an item that you may not be comfortable with right now, but it is something you would be willing to try at some point or work our way up to. If you say 'yes,' that item will stay where it is and I will know that you are fine with my using it whenever I see fit." He had kind of been looking around the room and gesturing as he had said all of that part. Now, he stood directly in front of Sophia looked her directly in the eye and said. "Your fourth word, little one, is 'please.' That will let me know that this would be a favorite of yours. Even possibly something you want me to use on you today. After today, I will come down here and rearrange everything so that it fits for our taste and our preferences. Is this all understood, Sophia?"

Damn this man knew how to make her weak in the knees. His voice and the way he used her name made her feel all gooey inside. He was definitely a dominant of the good kind. "Yes, Sir," she replied.

"Good girl, Sophia," he praised her. "Now let's begin our walk around the room."

They walked up to the first rack of toys, and he pointed to each one. Sophia almost never said no to any of them. If he had more severe things she would have, but he didn't have any of the things that would be used for blood play or the more extreme types of play.

When they walked up to the rack that had several different single tail whips on it, Bryan noticed Sophia tense noticeably. "You just got very tense, Sophia," he said gently in her ear. "Explain to me why whips frighten you."

"Um, well, I have been whipped before and it wasn't a pleasant experience," she said.

"Was this done by Larry?" he asked.

"Yes, Sir."

"Then I would ask that you give me a chance to show you that whips can be used in a variety of ways. I can promise you that I will never break skin, I do not do blood play. I can control the whip so as to give you a light little tap, something known as a whip kiss, or I can make it hit with enough pain to sting a bit, but nothing beyond what I have already seen you tolerate with a flogger. It's all in the level of control used by the person wielding it. Do you trust me to try, little one?"

Did she trust him to try? She thought about that for a second. Yes, she pretty much trusted him with anything. He had saved her life, after all. "Yes, Sir, I trust you."

"Very good girl, Sophia" he said with a beaming smile and leaned in to kiss her cheek.

They made their way around the rest of the room, and Sophia gave her input on everything in the space, even the table that held the butterfly and anal plug he had used on her before, as well as several other things still in their packages. He had explained that the more personal things he had always bought new if he had a play partner and given them to the person when their play sessions were not going to happen anymore. He opened a drawer that was completely empty and gave Sophia these instructions. "I don't plan to have another play partner, Sophia. It's time for this room to become our space. I would like you to take everything that is on that table that you are willing to use and unwrap it and place it neatly in the drawer. While you do that, I'm going to go upstairs and change into something more comfortable. If there is anything on there that you aren't sure of, you are allowed to leave it wrapped and on the table until we discuss it. Any questions, Sophia?"

"No, Sir."

"Very good. Now please step out of the room, remove all of your clothing, and place it on the bench. You may then return and put your things away. If you are done before I return, I expect to find you kneeling on the mat by the door." With his final instruction, he walked out of the room. Sophia hurried to do as she had been told. She removed all of her clothing and folded it neatly on the bench. She returned to inspect the things on the table. There were plugs in various sizes; those could stay. She trusted that Bryan would work her up to the larger ones and not just jump right to the largest. She placed those in the drawer lined up by size. There were a few different types of vibrators; those definitely could stay. Again, she tried to line them up in a fashion that made sense by size or style. The next thing to sort were the nipple clamps in various styles. There were the tweezer looking kind, the clover style, and another one that she had never seen before, but was willing to try. Nipple clamps had always been a turn-on for her. She placed those in the drawer in order of the way she liked them, with the unknown type last. Next to the table, she also noticed a large spool of bondage rope. It was a beautiful emerald green color. She thought it sort of matched her eyes. But all of the items were put away, so she needed to take her position. She got into her most submissive pose: on her knees with them spread, wide hands open palm up on her thighs, and eyes dropped to the floor. Spine straight. And she waited, but not for long. She soon saw Bryan's bare feet in front of her. She could tell that he was wearing a pair of leather pants, and from what she could see of them, they were something he had worn often. They looked soft.

"Very lovely, little one," Bryan praised her. "You may look at me."

Sophia looked up and Bryan's smile said that she had pleased him with her pose.

"Now, let's set the rest of the ground rules. When in this room, for the most part you won't speak unless it's to use your safe word or if you are asked a direct question. Today however, I will have some grace with that because everything between us is very new. As long as you do so in a respectful manner, you may tell me if something is softer than what you enjoy or if something is difficult for you because of past memories or any other reason. And, yes, I expect that as we start becoming more comfortable with what each other likes in this area, I will begin to see the brat that I know is just beneath the surface. But keep in mind, brats have consequences. I am sure that it goes without having to mention, but I am still not up to full speed. I am sure I will tire more easily or may have difficulty with certain actions because of this damn rib. But it is what it is, and I didn't want to wait any longer to have you down here with me."

He walked over to the drawer she had organized and opened it up. "The order of the anal plugs is obvious, and the vibrators is pretty self-explanatory. But tell me why the clamps are the way they are, little one."

"Um, well, I put them in the order that I like them, except for the last set. I've never used those before, so I am not sure how I feel about them," she explained.

"Makes sense," Bryan replied. He picked up the spool of rope and began unrolling a length of it. "This color is going to look lovely on your skin, Sophia." He kept unrolling absently as he spoke. "So many go with the obvious red or black for rope. But when I saw this, it made me think of your eyes, so I had it delivered right away. Tell me, Sophia, have you ever done any shibari?"

"No, Sir," she answered, but man was she willing to try.

"I'm no master of it by any means," Bryan explained, "but I do enjoy doing a rope corset or some interesting designs with my bondage." He cut the rope from the large spool into several long lengths and then turned to Sophia. "Please get onto that table there in the middle, Sophia, sitting on the edge for now."

Sophia did as she was told and sat at the edge of the table. When Bryan approached her, she realized that it had been put at the perfect height for him to be able to have sex with the person if he so chose. He began wrapping the rope around her stomach. He instructed her to put her hands on her head so that her arms would be out of the way for the time being. He laced the rope all the way up her torso to her breasts. When he got to them, he made an intricate diamond design around each one and formed it into a bra of sorts ending with a set of ropes that he tied off behind her neck. He stood back and admired his handiwork. "Absolutely lovely, Sophia," he praised. "Here, let me show you." He brought over a large full-length mirror that was obviously on a platform with wheels so he could place it anywhere in the room. He placed the mirror in front of her and then went to stand behind her. "You are so beautiful, Sophia."

"Thank you, Sir, you make me feel beautiful," Sophia said. "This really does match my eyes."

After he had admired her for a bit longer, he moved the mirror and said, "On your stomach, Sophia."

She lay down on her side and then rolled to her stomach. Having the use of her hands made it very easy to do. When she was in position, Bryan began winding another length of rope around her right wrist, and when he had it securely tied, he took the end of the rope over to the other side of the table and soon, both wrists were securely tied together behind her back. He then moved to tie her feet not only together but apparently to some ring or something at the end of the table. All the while he was tying her, words of praise flowed freely from his mouth. Between his voice and the attention he was lavishing on her, she was slowly becoming aroused.

When Bryan had Sophia tied the way he wanted her, he just stepped back and admired the beautiful woman. When looking at her had him fully aroused, he stepped to the end of the table and unbuttoned his pants. "Take me in your mouth, Sophia," he instructed. She turned her head and opened her mouth wide for him to enter. Bryan placed a hand on each side of her face and started with slow thrusts into her mouth. She lavished him with her tongue in between thrusts. Soon he was so aroused that he couldn't be slow and gentle anymore. "If you need your safe word, just raise your hands up, Sophia. I know they are tied together, but they aren't tied down. You should be able to lift them enough that I will see it." With that, he put one hand firmly in the hair at the back of her head and tilted her to the best angle possible. He started thrusting deeper and harder, watching her for any signs of distress. Not only did he not see any distress, her eyes rolled up in her head like she was enjoying this almost as much as he was. Eventually it became too much for him to take any longer. With one long deep thrust that hit the back of her throat, he commanded, "Swallow all of me, Sophia," and he came in long thick jets into her mouth. Sophia swallowed everything he had to give her.

When Bryan untied her feet and helped Sophia sit up at the edge of the table again, she got her first full look at the hot as sin man in front of her. His leather pants were still on, but the fly was open and they were dropped down enough that his magnificent cock, which was still half hard, was in full view. His upper body was completely naked. The incision was still very evident, but it barely marred the perfection of his sculpted torso.

With her arms still tied behind her back, Sophia was a little off balance, so Bryan kept a hand on her arm to make sure she didn't fall. He led her over to the hooks and carabiners that he had attached to a beam in the ceiling. He released the piece of rope holding her arms together so that her hands could go over her head. He tied them back together and used the slack that he had left between her hands to hook her to the carabiner. She wasn't dangling by her arms, her feet were on the ground, but she wouldn't have much stability to try to move.

Sophie couldn't see what Bryan was doing behind her, but she thought she heard him strike a match. The distinct smell of sulphur confirmed her suspicion. She just wasn't sure what he would be using a match for. She heard Bryan approaching from behind, and her heart was racing with excitement and anticipation of what he would do to her.

Bryan walked up to Sophia and, holding the candle at the perfect height, he tipped it so that a trickle of wax dripped over her gorgeous ass. She flinched a little, but he knew it wasn't out of pain; it was probably out of surprise. So he dripped more. After he had several long streams of wax cooling on her backside, he walked around to the front and drizzled it over her breasts and nipples. She had her eyes closed and was very obviously thoroughly enjoying the sensation. He was pretty sure she would enjoy the next step of the process too. From what he had seen of her so far, pain was definitely a turn-on for her.

After he had her bare areas mostly covered in wax, he asked, "Have you ever done wax play before, Sophia?"

"No, Sir, but it feels amazing," Sophia said. Her voice was a little floaty.

"Oh, I think you'll like the next part even better," he said. He walked back to where he had left the flogger and proceeded to flog the wax off of Sophia's body. It was reasonably painful to have it removed that way, and soon, Sophia was squirming and moaning out her pleasure. Yep, Sophia was definitely a masochist. "I thought you might like this. I love watching you squirm."

By the time Bryan had removed the majority of the wax with the flogger, Sophia wasn't even sure where she was anymore. She was floating somewhere in the clouds. She vaguely thought she heard Bryan instructing her to spread her legs wider. She did her best to oblige his command. When she did, she felt the flogger hit directly between her legs and that was it; she was flying and falling at the same time. Soaring high from the endorphins released in her body and falling over the precipice into a huge orgasm. That was the last thing she remembered.

Bryan could tell when Sophia had surrendered fully and that hit with the flogger made the orgasm rip through her with a scream. He knew this next part was going to be difficult for him because of his rib, but it couldn't be helped, and to be honest, he didn't really care if he endured a little pain to be able to finish his night with Sophia the only way he ever wanted to finish a night with her again. He wrapped her legs around his waist and wrapped one arm around her back to support her while his other hand released her from the carabiner. She was dead weight against him. Fortunately, the table wasn't very many steps away. He carried her to the table and laid her back. He pulled his pants the rest of the way off, put on the condom he had in his pocket, and buried himself in her. With him standing and her lying at the perfect height, it was an easy thing to accomplish. He held her legs around his waist and entered her with one long, hard thrust that immediately made her orgasm again. With the blow job she had given him earlier, he didn't come quite as quickly as he would have otherwise. This woman almost unmanned him with how quickly she could bring him to orgasm. He would get more used to that in time, and hopefully it would last longer in the future. For now he had to be content with sex not lasting as long as he would like it to as long as they both got their ultimate release. He bent over Sophia and softly kissed her face and lips, giving her praise for how amazingly well she had taken his torture.

Sophie kind of registered Bryan moving her, and she definitely felt the amazing sex; it was just that her brain was a little foggy. She loved that he could so easily take her to sub space. She slowly came out of the haze as he kissed her and talked to her. She felt like she could conquer the world when he told her how well she had done and how beautiful she was. She was falling for him more and more all the time. The consideration of him wanting her to have her own workspace. The way he never assumed that she was going to move in. The way that he could take her to places she had never been before sexually. He was consistently becoming more and more a man that she was sure she could love forever. She wasn't sure how he felt about a forever with her. He definitely seemed like he wanted the now and the near future for sure. Forever hadn't been discussed, and she really did understand that. Forever took time to be sure of. Forever required that both parties be on the same page. She felt like they were getting closer, but she wasn't sure they were there yet. That was okay. Forever lasted, well, forever, and it didn't have to start until and unless they were both ready.

As Sophie became more and more aware of her surroundings, she realized that Bryan must have carried her to the table. As a person who cared about him, she wanted to scold him for doing that with his rib, but as a submissive, she knew better. So she tried the gentler approach. "I hope carrying me didn't overtax your rib too much, Sir."

"It's fine, Sophia. There was a brief twinge, but nothing I can't handle. It really is getting much better," he declared. He walked over to a cabinet that held a small refrigerator and pulled out two bottles of water. He also opened a tall cabinet and pulled out a big fluffy robe. He brought them to Sophia and opened her bottle of water. He helped her into the robe and then took a long drink of his own water. "When you are steady on your feet, we'll head upstairs. Someday I will be back to full strength and I will gladly carry you up there, but for now, we can walk."

"I am fine to walk now, Sir," Sophie stated. Bryan helped her off the table and put his right arm around her waist. They walked up the two flights of stairs, and Bryan went into the big master bathroom. Sophie heard the bathtub start running and smelled something wonderful. It wasn't flowery or feminine, but it definitely wasn't totally masculine either, She couldn't place it, but it was a scent that either a man or a woman would enjoy. Bryan came back out of the bathroom and said, "You go get in the tub. I'm going to go back downstairs and clean up the things we used. I'll be back to join you shortly, so don't let the tub get overly full." He leaned in and kissed her gently and then left the room. Sophie walked into the bathroom and stepped into the tub. The hot water caused a few places on her body to sting and tingle a bit. Most likely those places would have small bruising in the morning, and that was a really awesome thing. Some people would never understand it, but to a masochist like her, having a little bruising that wasn't done in a mean way was sort of a badge of honor. She sank down into the tub but made sure that she didn't get it too full. It would be easy enough to add more if it wasn't full enough when Bryan got in, but she didn't want to cause water to overflow onto the floor.

Bryan returned several minutes later and stepped into the tub. He lay back against the end and motioned for Sophia to come and sit in his lap. "So, how was your first experience with wax play?" he asked.

"It was amazing. I hope we do it often," she replied.

"Oh, I'm sure we'll do it more, but I'm not sure how often. I have to keep you on your feet, so I'll try to change things up." he promised.

"I am totally okay with that, Sir," Sophie agreed. She lay back against him and just enjoyed the wonderful scent and warm feel of the water and the strong beating of Bryan's heart. Yeah, she was pretty sure she could live like this forever if she was given the opportunity.

Bryan leaned his head back and just listened to the sound of Sophia's steady breathing. He wanted forever with this woman and he had a plan to hopefully convince her to give him that chance. He was going to put himself out there and hope that she was on the same page as he was. He wasn't going to ask her to marry him—he wasn't sure either of them were ready for that—but he was going to try to get her to commit to staying for a long time. Sometimes when a person got comfortable with their situation long enough, it turned into forever before they ever really realized that it had happened. He was hoping that would happen for Sophia.

Two days later, in the early afternoon, Bryan instructed Sophia to go downstairs and wait for him in the play room. Sophia eagerly went downstairs and removed her clothing and placed it on the bench. She stepped into the room and took her position. Immediately, her mind started thinking about all that they had done together, and other than the whole losing her panties for the waxing thing, Bryan had never really seen the brat in her. She didn't always get the temptation to be a brat, but it was definitely a part of her. She had kind of been cautious about it because she knew that in order to truly curb bratty behavior, the Dominant needed to be both mentally and physically strong. It wasn't that Bryan hadn't been those things, but she had been worried about Larry at the start of this relationship and worried about Bryan's rib in the more recent weeks of the relationship. But if she was truly going to know if they were compatible for the long haul, he needed to see her at her worst and know what he was getting himself into. She also needed to know that he could handle her brattiest behavior. It was for that reason that she decided to be her absolute worst for him today and see where it landed them.

When Bryan walked into the room, he immediately sensed that something was different with Sophia. She was in her position, but not as perfectly as she had been the times he had seen her this way before. She was slightly slouched. He wasn't sure why, but he had a suspicion. "Your form is lacking its usual perfection, Sophia."

"Well, I don't see what all the fuss is about. I mean, is it really necessary that I strain my back just to look pretty?" Sophia said with sass.

"I see. Well, no, we wouldn't want you to strain your back, now would we?" Bryan agreed. He saw the quick glance from Sophia. That wasn't the reaction she was hoping for, and he knew it. But he was going to see just how far she was going to go with this. "You may rise, Sophia," he said while walking over to take one of the long lengths of rope he had cut from the spool. When she stood, he instructed her to get into position so that he could tie her to the spanking bench. She positioned herself on her stomach on the bench, but again, she lacked the form that would usually be expected. Oh, she was needing some very specific attention today obviously. He tied her hands to the metal rings on the sides of the wide sawhorse-like contraption. Then he placed leather cuffs on her ankles and attached them to the rings at the back. "You seem to lack your usual enthusiasm today, little one. Is there a problem?" He picked up one of his leather paddles and without any warm-up, he gave her one good swat across the fleshiest part of her ass. Nothing that was over the top for a first hit, but still, a pretty good sting. "How was that, Sophia?"

"Son of a bitch, that hurt," Sophia proclaimed loudly.

"Do you need your safe word, Sophia?" If she did, he would realize that she wasn't being a brat, she was obviously just not in the right head space to play today. If she continued to mouth off, his suspicions would be confirmed. "You do remember your safe word, don't you, Sophia?"

"Of course I do." She sounded rather irritated.

So, brat it was then. One more good swat to see where she was going to take this.

"You're a bully, do you know that?" she proclaimed.

"Oh, I know exactly what I am, Sophia, and I think you need to be disciplined," he said, hitting her one more time. "I also think you have decided to be a righteous brat today."

"I'm not a brat, you're just a brute."

"A brute am I? Did I hurt you, Sophia?" he asked.

"Of course not, you hit like a girl," she declared.

"A girl is it? Hmm." He hit her one more time. "Was that more to your liking, Sophia?"

Sophia just rolled her eyes. He could take care of that issue. He walked over to the drawer and pulled out a blindfold. He placed it over her eyes and then leaned in close to her ear and said, "I don't like little girls rolling their eyes at me, Sophia. It's disrespectful."

"Yeah, whatever." Sophie was really liking where this was going. He was obviously up for playing her game.

"I know how to curb that sassy mouth of yours too, little one," Bryan stated. "Open up, Sophia." She opened her mouth and he inserted a ball gag and fastened it at the back of her head. He stepped back a few feet and looked at her. "Now, Sophia, would you like to say anything more?"

Sophia obviously couldn't actually say any words, so she just growled at him.

"That's what I thought. Now I can have my fun," Bryan said. He paddled her several times in succession. He knew what he was doing could not have hurt Sophia; he was really playing more than anything. The hits were nothing serious, and they weren't causing anything more than a mild sting at most. He moved from side to side, striking one cheek then the other. He alternated with no specific pattern, as he had her warmed up, his hits became progressively harder. He kept checking the one thing that couldn't lie. Sophia was getting wet, which meant the pain wasn't too much; it was at the exact right level to make her aroused. He stepped away and got one of the vibrators he had bought for her. He inserted it into her wet pussy and turned it on to a low speed. He picked up the riding crop and began small flicks against the flesh at her inner thighs, coming close to hitting her pubic area, but not close enough. Again, Sophia growled, but this time he was pretty sure it was out of frustration that he wasn't hitting close enough. He turned up the speed on the vibrator and continued making little taps with the crop. "Is this more to your liking, Sophia?" he asked. Of course she couldn't answer, so she just sort of let out a muffled scream behind the ball gag. "Hmm, I guess not, I must not be doing it right. Maybe I should just stop." At that, she let out an even more frustrated scream.

Bryan stepped up and pulled the blindfold up to look Sophia in the eye and asked, "Am I not doing this right, Sophia?" She adamantly shook her head. "I'm not? Would you like me to hit harder or softer? I wouldn't want you to continue to think that I hit like a girl." Sophia was trying to say something but of course the words were just muffled noise. "I can't understand you, Sophia. Let me try again." He began the little flicks of the crop again, Sstill knowing there was no way it was giving her all of what she needed. When he did come close to her pubic area, the taps were so light that they couldn't possibly be aiding in her desire for an orgasm. He kept this up for several long minutes, Sophia getting more and more frustrated as he prolonged her actual enjoyment. Finally, he was ready to show her just who was in charge of their play time, and it wasn't her. "I think I have figured out what you are asking for, Sophia. So I have one question for you." He aimed the flap of the riding crop directly at her exposed clit and gave it one good hard flick. Sophia almost rose off the bench from the slapping pain that triggered her orgasm. Bryan leaned closer to her ear as he unhooked the ball gag. When Sophia focused on him, he asked "Did I pass my test, Sophia or do you need to push me further to see if I can handle you?"

"Yes, Sir, thank you, Sir," Sophia said, panting.

"Very well, little one," Bryan replied. "Now I get to do what pleases me." He removed the vibrator and his pants, quickly put on the condom that had been in his pocket, and entered Sophia from behind. He reached over to the small table next to him and picked up the anal plug he had used on her in the garage their second night together. He covered it with lube and began slowly working it in and out while holding himself still inside of her. Soon she was rising to meet his movements, and the plug slid into her easily. He kept his thumb on it while holding on to her hips. He pulled her back to meet his body as he thrust forward. He pounded into her as hard as his rib would allow. With the plug buried deep inside of her it was a very tight fit. He felt like her pussy was barely large enough for him to fit. It was too much to handle, and he came with a shout.

Sophie slowly drifted back to full realization of where she was and what had happened. She was lying on the couch that Bryan had set up at one end of the playroom. Bryan was nowhere to be seen. She remembered hearing him say that he could do what pleased him once he felt he had passed her test. Did that mean that what she had done by being bratty had displeased him? She didn't want to think about that, but she needed to. Being a brat wasn't a full-time thing for her; it wasn't even really something she did frequently, but it was a part of her at times. Had Bryan disliked her behavior and her attitude? She sat up and pulled the fluffy blanket tighter around herself. She wasn't sure if Bryan had gone upstairs and she should join him or if she should wait for him where she was. She was just starting to stand up when Bryan walked back into the room.

"What are you doing, Sophia? Where are you going?" he asked.

"I just didn't see you, so I thought maybe you had gone upstairs and were waiting for me to join you," she said rather sheepishly.

Bryan sat on the couch and lifted Sophia onto his lap. "Talk to me, little one," he said quietly, nuzzling into her hair.

"I don't know, I just know that I was more bratty today and then you said something about being able to do what you wanted finally, so I thought maybe I had displeased you," she said softly. "I thought maybe you just wanted to be done with me."

He cuddled her closer. "Oh, Sophia. I really do need to be careful with you, don't I? I didn't mean that what you had done displeased me. It was more about hoping that I had passed the test you were obviously giving me." He turned her so that she was straddling his lap, he had put his pants back on, but she was still fully naked under her blanket. "I don't think about the fact that you haven't really ever had a relationship like this before and that you are testing your waters and the way I said what I said probably came across as a displeased statement to you. I will try to be more careful of that in the future, Sophia. Can you forgive me?" He leaned in slowly to kiss her, but he gave her the opportunity to draw back from the kiss if she wasn't ready to forgive him yet. She fully responded to his kissing. "This is all new for both of us, and I'm not liking my own failures at this point. Part of what made you wonder if I was done was the fact that you didn't see me when you started to become more aware of your surroundings. And that is the fault of my rib," he explained. "Normally, after a session like we have had down here, I would want to carry you up to my bed and hold you while we both enjoyed the aftermath of our play. Unfortunately, I still don't feel strong enough to carry you up two flights of stairs. I needed to use the bathroom and dispose of the condom. Again, something that I would have done as we made our way upstairs together. It's sort of a learning curve for both of us, Sophia, but I can promise you that right now I have no thought or desire to be done with you, and I can't see myself being at that point anytime soon. Just give me your trust, Sophia, and know that things will progressively get better. Can you do that for me?"

She could definitely do that for him. She nodded her agreement and they began kissing again. Soon, Bryan set her aside long enough that he could pull his pants back down. He was just getting ready to set Sophia back on his lap when he remembered that he didn't have a condom; they were in the cabinet across the room. She tried to climb back in his lap but he said, "Hang on Sophia, I need to go get a condom."

"No, you don't," Sophia said and moved more fully onto him.

"What are you saying, Sophia?" he asked, still holding her from being able to actually get fully onto his lap.

"I'm saying that when we first talked, I told you I was on birth control, but I wanted the condoms as extra protection. I know you now, Bryan, and I trust you. If you say you are clean, then I believe you," she began. "It highly unlikely that I would get pregnant, but I know you well enough to know that if I did, you would step up and support me in whatever decision I made about that pregnancy."

Bryan wanted to argue with that point. He would support her in any decision except an abortion; that just wasn't something he was okay with. He knew that some would say that made him wrong, but if he created a child, he would do whatever it took to have that child in his life, even if it meant that the mother no longer was. He would raise a child alone if he had to. But that didn't seem to be what Sophia was saying, so he let that part drop and helped Sophia lower herself down on him. This was one amazing woman. When they had both been sated, Bryan helped Sophia up, and they walked hand in hand upstairs to take a shower together.

Chapter Seventeen

A few days later, Bryan asked Sophia to join him for breakfast at a diner a few small towns away. He wanted to take her for that ride in the country that he had promised her weeks ago. "Are you sure you're ready for that?" Sophia asked.

"Sophia, I promise that I will not ride overly fast or do anything that could potentially cause my rib to be damaged. Please, I just want to take you for a ride and enjoy the day with you. I'm going to be going back to work full-time soon and I just want a day with you before I get tied back into the whole real life thing."

"Okay, okay, I'll go get ready," Sophie agreed. Bryan had already gone to the garage a few times in the last week. He never stayed gone long, but Sophie could tell that he was working his way back into his usual routine.

They had a nice comfortable ride out through the country and ended up at a small restaurant with a sign proclaiming it to be "Pop's Diner." Bryan opened the door for Sophia, and they walked in. There was a young woman behind the counter that looked up when they arrived.

"Hey, Bryan," she said, coming around the counter to give him a hug. He kissed the top of her head, and Sophie immediately wondered if she had been a former girlfriend or even a former submissive play partner, although she was very young.

"Hey, Trina, is your grandpop here?" Bryan asked.

"Is that really a question?" the young woman asked with a laugh. "Is there a day that we are open that he isn't? I'll go tell him you're here." She walked back into the kitchen and soon an older man came through the same door she had used.

"Bryan, you finally decide to come see an old man?" he said as he walked over and did the handshake one-arm hug thing that men often did.

"Hey, Pops," Bryan said, patting the man on the back. "I had a bit of an accident a few weeks ago so I was laid up for a while. But I have someone I want you to meet." He turned to Sophia and drew her closer to him. "Pop, this is my girlfriend, Sophia. Sophia, this is Pops. He owns this place."

Sophie started to put out her hand to shake hands with the man, but he drew her in for a hug and a kiss on the cheek. She was a little taken aback, but it kind of seemed like that was probably just his way of greeting someone. When he pulled back, she said, "It's great to meet you."

"So you are the woman who will make this one settle down finally," the old man said.

"Well, I, um, I don't know that he's going to settle down." Sophie chuckled.

"Pop she's my girlfriend for now," Bryan cautioned. "Remember me telling you we were going to be doing a body guarding job for a young woman? Well, this is her."

"Yes, yes, I remember," the old man agreed. "I also know what happened. Trevor was here a couple of weeks ago and told me that you had been shot."

"I'm fine now," Bryan said. Again, he turned to Sophia. "Pops here was my dad's best friend for years. He was the one that really helped me be able to keep us kids together."

"Well, the court had no business stepping in to try to take you apart," Pops said.

"But I wouldn't have been able to convince them of that without your help," Bryan stated.

It was obvious to Sophie that this man was much like a surrogate father to Bryan. They sat in a booth, and Pop went to prepare their breakfast. The young woman that had greeted them when they walked in came to bring them coffee. "This is Pop's granddaughter, Katrina. She goes by Trina, though," Bryan explained.

When the young woman walked away, Sophia quietly asked, "Why do you call her Trina when you wouldn't ever call me Sophie? You made it very clear that you were going to call me Sophia. I thought you just had a problem with nicknames, but you do it with her."

"That's different, little one," Bryan stated. The tone in his voice signified that from the very start he had seen Sophia as a submissive and therefore, he was going to act as a Dominant.

They enjoyed a wonderful breakfast, and when Pop wasn't busy in the kitchen, he came out to speak to them and learn more about Sophie. She had no doubt that he was sizing her up to see if she was good enough for his 'son.'

They took the long and scenic route to get back to Bryan's home. Bryan was just enjoying having Sophia behind him on his motorcycle and he needed to buy Summer some time to do what he had asked her to do. One of the days that Sophia had assumed he had gone to the garage, he had actually taken a trip out to meet the breeders and had chosen a puppy.

When they got back to Bryan's house, Sophia got off the motorcycle and removed her helmet. "Was that Summer's car we passed down the road a ways? It looked like her," Sophia asked.

Bryan didn't want to give away the surprise that would be waiting inside for Sophia, so he just said, "It could have been, I guess. I didn't notice. Sometimes she comes out to ride a horse, or she may have just dropped off some mail from the shop or something. I don't know."

"She should have stayed. I could have made her lunch. Although I don't think I will be hungry anytime soon. Pop definitely serves big portions," Sophia said.

"I think he's just trying to fatten you up. He thinks you're too thin," Bryan joked.

Sophie unlocked the door and quickly disarmed the alarm. Bryan had given her the keys to his home and his truck until she could decide what she wanted to do about a car. Her car in Colorado was nothing special, so she wasn't sure if she wanted to go get it and drive it back or if she was just going to leave it there until she made a final decision about moving. Bryan had also offered to help her find a car if she wanted something smaller than his big four-wheel drive truck. Sophie thought she heard a strange noise coming from the corner near the breakfast nook. She walked over there and in a fairly large crate was the sweetest little puppy she had ever seen. It was a small ball of fluff and curls, a pale blond color. She was pretty sure it had poodle in it and maybe Lab or golden retriever. It was jumping up the side of the crate and whining. It very obviously wanted out of its confinement. Sophie leaned down to pick it up as Bryan walked into the room. She turned to him as the puppy licked her face. "What in the world? Where did this come from?" she asked.

"I believe she has a note," Bryan said, pointing to a small paper attached to the collar. He had asked Summer to not attach it until they were almost home because he didn't want to take a chance on the puppy eating the note.

Sophie removed the note from the collar. She shifted the puppy to her side so she had a free hand to open the folded paper. All it said on it was, "Please stay with us and love us forever." It was signed "Bryan and puppy." She had tears in her eyes as she cuddled the puppy close to her and threw her other arm around Bryan's neck. "A puppy, you got me a puppy." It was all she could think to say.

"I did, and you need to give her a name," Bryan said, holding his two girls close. "I am hoping for an answer to the request on the note, but if you aren't ready to give me an answer that's okay, I can wait. Either way, she's your puppy, Sophia. I'm just hoping you both want to stay."

Sophia looked up into Bryan's eyes and asked, "How did you do this?"

"Well, the other day you said that a family needed a puppy. I went online and started looking. One of the days you thought I was going to the garage, I went and picked out this little girl. Although if you would have preferred a male, they do have one left and are willing to let you swap."

"No, no, she's beautiful," Sophie cried. "I want her; you picked her out for me. I want the one you wanted to give me."

"Then she needs a name, Sophia," Bryan said. "You can't call her puppy forever."

Sophie pondered that for a while, still in Bryan's arms with the puppy going back and forth between licking her and licking him. It said a lot to her that the puppy licking him didn't seem to be fazing Bryan at all. He just allowed the puppy free access and even tilted his head to nuzzle the furball at times. That gave her the answer to both questions she had been pondering. "I think I have a name, but you may hate it," Sophie said. "It's not really a name so much as a phrase."

"What is it, Sophia? You can name her anything," Bryan insisted.

"I think she should be called Semper Fi," Sophia said. "Because of what it means."

Bryan knew exactly what those words meant. He had said Semper Fi for years. Those words meant always faithful. He looked at Sophia with a raised eyebrow. "Does that mean?"

"It does," Sophia confirmed. "My answer is yes, I will stay here with you and love you both forever."

Bryan drew her in even tighter, trying to be careful to not squash Semper Fi.

Epilogue

It had been four months since Sophie had returned to Michigan to be able to attend her brother's marriage celebration. It had been about three months since she had agreed to love Bryan and Semper forever. She was finding more and more reasons every day for that to be an easy thing. The hot humid days of August had finally taken a break for a few days, and the entire family was in Bryan's back yard for a cookout. Semper was running from person to person expecting everyone to give her all of their attention. And for the most part, everyone was. They all loved the energetic little puppy.

Autumn looked about ready to burst, although her due date was still a couple of weeks away. Sophie had been thinking about babies a lot lately. Not that she wanted one anytime soon, but the longer she was with Bryan, the more the possibility of marriage and family was in the back of her mind. She and Bryan had gone to Colorado two months ago and packed up everything she owned. They had hired a moving company to drive the big van across the country. She had sold her simple plain little car. She had always hated it but had convinced herself that she needed to be as drab as possible to not attract attention to herself. She had used the money from that to put a down payment on a car that she loved, a Ford Mustang. It was a little over the top, but even Bryan and his brothers had approved since it was Detroit Muscle. Her house was up for sale, with a very interested party currently working on the details. She really didn't care if the house sold for what she was asking or not. She didn't need the money really. Apparently, Bryan's house was paid for, and he refused to let her pitch in much on the bills. He did let her buy groceries, but she was pretty sure that was only because he really liked her cooking and wanted her to be able to pick out whatever she wanted to have in the house.

Summer had brought Jeremy to the cookout. From what Sophie could tell, they had been seeing each other ever since the party in April.

Her parents had even come to the cookout. They didn't usually do a lot of backyard barbeque things, but Sophie had noticed that her being back in Michigan seemed to have brought all of them closer together again. They had lived through a lot in the last several years. It made them all appreciate being together more.

Bryan had agreed to teach Sophie how to ride her own motorcycle, although he said he still preferred for her to ride his with him. She liked that more too, but learning how to ride was something she was committed to doing, even if she rarely took a solo ride.

The investigation into the circumstances surrounding Larry's death had been long closed. The police went through every detail and interviewed many of the family and even some of the guests that had been there that day, but no one other than Trevor and Riley could say exactly what had happened in those woods. Eventually, her father had gone to the prosecutor and the case had been closed. Sophie had no doubt that her father had taken the police reports from her beating years before. He had obtained a copy, and she was sure he had held on to it in case Larry ever came close to her again.

Evening was starting to set in when Sophia]e's parents bid everyone a good night and headed home. Pete and Autumn had left shortly after. Even though the days were a little cooler than they had been, being out in the hot sun had exhausted Autumn.

When it was down to just the Lawson family and Jeremy, Riley said he need to talk to his brothers about something. They all settled in at the large table on the back deck.

"So. BACA has a new assignment, and I'd like to take it. If you guys can spare me for a while," Riley began.

"Sure, man, I'm back to full speed at the shop and we don't have anything huge on the books. The PI aspect is mostly quiet for now other than some surveillance shit that Trevor can handle. Go for it." Bryan said. Trevor nodded his agreement.

"What's BACA?" Sophie asked as she leaned down to pick up Semper, who was trying desperately to jump up on her lap.

Riley turned to her and explained. "BACA stands for Bikers Against Child Abuse. When there is a child that has been abused or molested that needs to go to court, they assign a pair from the group to be that child's team. We befriend the child, they have our number and ways to get in contact if they just need someone to talk to or if they are scared. We go to court with them if they have to testify. Depending on the judge it's sometimes just the two, but if the judge allows it more people from the group go so the child sees the support they have behind them. It makes the accused person seem way less scary when you have your own team of bikers sitting there in leathers looking all bad ass." He smiled.

"Yeah, I can see where that would be a little intimidating to the accused," she agreed.

"It's not really about intimidating them, though," Bryan continued. "We never say a thing to them or really even have any contact with them. We could be in trouble if we tried to interact with them. It's more about the kid. They know they have these people on their side. When they look up and see the perpetrator there, they also see their own guardian angles sitting right in their line of sight. It's not about intimidating the accused, it's about the kid feeling like 'my team is stronger than you and I'm a part of that team.'"

"That makes sense," Sophie said.

Trevor chimed in, "When's the ride?"

"Tomorrow at ten," Riley answered.

"We'll be there," Bryan said.

"I'm in," Trevor added.

Bryan turned to Sophia to explain. "The ride is how we meet the child. As many of the group that can do a ride by of the child's home. So they see the strength in numbers. The first two riders are the actual guardian angels for the kid. They meet the kid and introduce themselves and then they tell the child that even though they have direct contact with the team of two, all of the group is there for them if they need it. And then the whole group rides by. The child feels like they have two close friends, but a hundred or more people waiting in the wings if needed."

"That sounds amazing. Can I ride with you?" Sophie asked. "I know I'm not a part of the group, but I'd like to be."

"I'm sure that will be fine, Sophie," Riley said.

The backyard gathering broke up soon after and everyone headed their separate ways. Sophie put Semper in her crate in the bedroom; she had one in the kitchen and one in their bedroom. When Sophie came back out of the bathroom, Semper was laying on the bed at Bryan's feet. "You're an old softy, you know that, right? She has you wrapped around her little paw." Sophie giggled.

"Yeah, well, she whines and yelps in the crate, and I'd never get any sleep," Bryan grumbled, but Sophie knew he wasn't really upset. He spoiled the puppy worse than she did. "As long as she lays down and is good, she can stay up here."

"Um-hmm," Sophie said skeptically. When she got in bed, Semper came up and tried to lie between Sophie and Bryan.

"Oh, hell no, you don't get to be between us." Bryan said. He scooped up the pup and put her back at their feet. "Stay there or you go in your crate," he said sternly. The puppy looked at him with her big sad eyes, but she settled in for the night. Bryan had been so good with the puppy. Between him hearing her rustle around if she got up in the night because of his super military hearing, as Sophie like to call it, and Sophie being home most of the time, the pup was pretty much house broken, so they really didn't keep her in the crate much except when they both left the house. That had far more to do with the fact that puppies like to chew on things than it did with her having accidents in the house.

Sophie cuddled up to Bryan and drifted off to sleep with the puppy at their feet. In her mind, life didn't get much better than it had been today. Family surrounding them and having fun, a man who loved her so much he had gotten her a puppy, and freedom from her past. Yeah, she was pretty sure this was what she wanted her forever to look like.

One day prior

Riley opened the email that had come in from the local BACA chapter. There was a new assignment, and they were looking for two people to step up and be guardian angles for a little girl. It explained the case, but Riley would read that later. He clicked on the attachment that had a picture of a little girl and her mother. They both had soulful brown eyes. The little girl's showed sadness and fear. The mother's showed concern and uncertainty. There was something about little brown-eyed girls that always tugged at his heart. He understood why. It wasn't a mystery that he always felt the need to save little brown-eyed girls. It was something that he had been trained to do. It was ingrained in his psyche.

Three years earlier, he had saved a little brown-eyed girl in Iraq. He hadn't seen her since he had walked out of the building, carrying her away from a life of torture and pain. Something inside the building had exploded and pieces of building and shrapnel had hit his entire back side. He had made it several more yards before the pain and loss of blood had gotten to be too much, and he had found a ditch to hide in. He only planned to stay there for a few minutes to catch his breath, and then they would move on. That was the last thing he remembered until he woke up in the military hospital several days later. It turned out that he had saved the little girl from the brothel she had been forced to live in, only for her to turn around and save him by guiding the team of Marines sent in to find survivors from the explosion to his limp and close to dead body in that ditch. She had been treated for malnourishment and dehydration and moved to a home for orphans. He had planned to go see her when he was released, but his injuries had been severe. He hadn't been released in the traditional sense. He had been sent stateside when he was able to travel, and his body had been slow to mend. Several weeks after he was released from the hospital, he was given an honorable medical discharge from the Marines. He had been told that the little girl was doing well, but he had never been able to find her again.

He responded to the message, immediately signing up to be one of the team of two that would be the close contact for this little girl. He didn't really care what her story was, although he would read it so he was prepared for the ride by and meet and greet the following Sunday. He was sure his brothers would be okay with him taking the assignment. Bryan was totally healed, and they weren't super busy. Either way, he was taking this one. A little brown-eyed girl needed him. He received a text from the chapter president thanking him for taking this one, and then he sat down to read the little girl's story.

Read Riley's story in Sizzling Triskelion Motorcycles 2, coming soon.

Fallen Rayne
Five Sloths Brewing book 1
By Robin Andrews
Now available!

Walt cleared his throat to get the attention of the young woman who was sitting staring out the window. Apparently, she hadn't heard his knock on the door, so he had pushed it open slightly to see if anyone was inside. She appeared to be lost in thought. When she heard him, she turned toward him, and he realized he was looking at the single most beautiful woman he had ever seen. Her skin was pale olive, her hair was a long wavy auburn mass that flowed most of the way down her back, her cheekbones were high and perfect, but her eyes, although a beautiful rich amber, were haunted, almost like there was no life in them. It took him aback for a moment to see someone so beautiful yet so lifeless inside.

He cleared his throat again to try to regain some control of the voices inside his head, the voices telling him that this woman needed him, and as more than just an attorney. He suddenly wanted to help her find life again. He just wasn't sure how to do that. He stepped into the room, reaching out his hand to her as he drew closer. "Hello, Ms. Davis. I'm Walter Jensen, your attorney." She took his hand, but again, he almost felt like there was no life in the woman sitting in front of him. Yes, obviously, she was alive, she was breathing, and she spoke softly when she said, "Hello." But there was no life there, not really, no vibrancy that he would expect from a woman so young and so beautiful. "I'm here to ask you a few questions so that we can get started on your case, if that's all right with you."

"That's fine," she said. "The sooner we get this taken care of, the sooner those bastards pay for what they did to me."

Ah, there was the life, at least a small spark of it, although not in the way he wanted to see her eyes light with emotion. This was pure loathing, utter hatred for the persons involved in the lawsuit he was hopefully going to win for her. Maybe that would give her some happiness. He very likely could make her a very rich woman with this case. After all, the defendant was obviously negligent. For some reason, though, he got the sense that money wasn't really going to do anything to change her demeanor. He also got the sense that those eyes would be almost like a slow burning flame if she were truly passionate about something. If she were truly passionate about someone. He briefly pictured those eyes staring into his with a different type of passion.

Whoa!! Walt, what the hell, dude? Totally not appropriate to be drooling over the client. Even if she was the most beautiful woman he had ever seen. He had seen his share of women and had probably dated more than his share. Being an attorney, a part owner of a microbrewery and a former frat boy at a prestigious law school, he had always seen beautiful women and truth be told, he had taken several of them to bed. But there was something about this woman. Maybe it was her sadness, maybe it was her physical beauty, and maybe it was the fact that she was a victim of a horrible injustice, but whatever it was, he was reacting to her like he had never reacted to someone before.

Get your head back in the game, Walt, he silently scolded himself. Yeah, it would seem totally professional to be drooling like a school kid for the initial interview with a new client. The thing was, though, that even though his body had definite thoughts about her, there was something else too. It wasn't a sexual draw, not that he would say there was nothing sexual to this, but there was something about this woman that made him want to put a smile back on her face, to see her lively and vibrant again. He had no doubt that at one point she had been vivacious and happy. Her case file said she had been a dancer all her life, so she had obviously had a deep passion for something—well, something other than revenge, that is.

He hesitated, not quite sure how to move forward. He had seen plaintiffs before that were bitter, he had seen ones that were in pain, he had seen ones that were angry, but he honestly didn't remember ever seeing one that seemed like the incident had literally taken the life from her. Finally, he shook his head to get his mind back on the matter at hand.

"Yes, well, of course," he said, trying to figure out how to move forward with the questions he needed to ask her. "First of all, thank you for taking the time to talk to me today. I think we have a great chance of winning this case. I believe it's pretty cut and dried that the construction company was negligent. I am very optimistic that we will get a very generous settlement."

"How much can they possibly pay? There is no amount that will get my life back. Life is over for me; no amount of money can fix that. But yes, I do want to make them pay, I want to make them pay to the point that they have to go out of business, I want to ruin their lives as much as they have ruined mine." The words came out almost like venom; there was pure hatred behind them. He had been wrong, it wasn't that there wasn't any life there; it was just that the life that was there was so bitter and hateful that she couldn't focus on anything but making someone pay for the situation she found herself in.

"Yes, well." Again, he found himself not knowing exactly how to respond. This petite beautiful woman was so hateful, so spiteful, so….so…. and that was when he saw what she really was. She was so hurt, so horribly, completely broken that she did not know how to even function in a normal manner. Maybe his best bet would be to try to find out from others what they felt had happened to her. Not the details of the accident, he could read those in the reports, but what had really happened to her, to the lively young woman that he could tell had been in there at some point.

"Actually, maybe it would be best if I get you to sign some release forms for me so that I can talk to your doctors and the other medical staff involved in your case, I might be able to get a better idea of what we are dealing with from them, before you and I sit and talk strategy for the case."

"That's fine. Whatever you need from me. I just want to get this over with," she said softly.

He gave her the usual forms, the retainer naming him as her attorney in the case of Rayne Davis vs Charmichael Construction, releases of her medical files, permission to talk with doctors, therapists, police, and anyone else who might have any insight into her case.

She signed paper after paper, pretty much before he had a chance to explain to her what she was signing.

"Are you sure you don't want to read over any of these before you sign them?" he asked.

She looked up at him and again, he was touched deeply by the lifelessness of her eyes. "I'm sure that there is nothing in here that can harm me any more that what this incident has already done. If you are worried that I may be signing away things that I shouldn't, trust me, Mr. Jensen, I don't believe I have anything more to lose than my life and the future I dreamed of."

Walt walked out of the room at the rehabilitation facility almost in a fog. He felt something so deeply for that young woman. It wasn't pity, not really. Although he did feel extreme sorrow, it wasn't pity, it was a deep and utter sickening at the pain and loss that he had seen in that young woman's face. He vowed that he would do whatever it took to bring life back to those eyes. He knew it wasn't about money for her, so he had to figure out what it was about. And then he needed to fix whatever it was. He wouldn't stop, he wouldn't rest until he saw some spark of life in her eyes again. He just wasn't sure how he was going to do that.

Rayne sadly shook her head as the attorney left her room. That was one handsome man. She had never really had much experience with men. She had always been so involved in her dancing, from lessons to exercise to choreography planning, that she had never really had time for boys when she was younger and definitely not for men once she got old enough to start working toward becoming a member of the New York City Ballet. She had always thought there would be time for that later. Most prima ballerinas didn't work much past the age of thirty or thirty-five. She was only twenty-three. She'd thought she had plenty of time for dating and marriage and children, later, after her career had peaked. Now, though, she would never know that life. Who would want to marry a woman who was so sad, so utterly broken that she didn't see the way to ever be happy again? Life was just throwing her all kinds of hard hits lately. She'd lost her dream to dance and then she lost her dream to have a family someday.

No, she knew that she would always be alone. No one would find her attractive, no one would want to be involved with someone like her. A woman that was possibly never going to get out of a wheelchair or at best would have a horrible limp. But still, she couldn't help but think about how gorgeous that man had been, with his deep black hair and those emerald green eyes. Well, at least she would have a good-looking man around long enough for her lawsuit to finish. Even if there was no hope of having someone like him in her life forever.

Opaque Skye
Five Sloths Brewing book 2
By Robin Andrews
Now available!

Zak sat drumming his thumbs on the steering wheel and glancing around while waiting for whatever it was that had traffic at a standstill at 8:50 a.m. on this sunny Monday morning. He was going to be late for work, as usual. Not that it mattered. When you were the son of a senior managing partner at a law firm, no one really had the balls to say anything about you strolling in to the office at 9:15 or even 9:30, for that matter. Although lately his parents had both been getting on to him about being more responsible, taking some initiative, maybe even settling down a little from his playboy ways. But at 29, who wanted to settle down? Although his life had been what some would call "charmed," he still had some living he wanted to do.

Sure, he'd had all the best things in life growing up; sure, he had gotten into all the best schools because of his last name and his father's status as alumni. That didn't mean that he hadn't earned his good grades. He had studied hard to graduate at the top of his class in both high school and college. His grades at Harvard Law had proven that he did what it took to get the job done. But now that was over and he had passed the bar exam, it was time to live a little.

Zak's eyes caught on a woman getting out of an SUV parked alongside the road. Man, she was hot, with long blond hair that was not curly, but not really straight either. It framed a beautiful face: high cheekbones, gorgeous lips, and those eyes. He couldn't tell exactly what color they were from this distance, but definitely something light, like blue or maybe gray. Either way, they looked like eyes a man like him could get lost in while he sank deep into her body as it writhed in pleasure under him. A body which, from what he could see, was built for pleasure. She wasn't pencil thin like so many of the women who came on to him in the clubs, but she wasn't fat by any means either; she did have just enough curves that a man could get lost for hours exploring them.

He watched as she opened the back door and leaned in to get something out of the backseat. That was when his suspicions were confirmed: she had an ass that was meant for a firm slap now and then, maybe even a bite or two. His mouth suddenly watered at the thought of sinking his teeth into that luscious flesh. That was a woman that he could definitely invest hours and hours of his time getting to know, inside and out.

Skye felt like someone was watching her as she reached into the backseat of the SUV. She tried to glance over her shoulder to see if there was anyone there. Of course, with traffic this time of morning, it could be anyone. She didn't feel intimidated by it, just sensed it. It didn't set off alarm bells like it was someone with ill intent, just this feeling that there were eyes burning into her flesh. She shook off the feeling. If she didn't get moving, she would be late for her 9:00 yoga class and she still had to check Cassie into the daycare center the health club offered to its members and staff.

As she pulled the little girl out of her car seat, Cassie gave her the biggest smile as she grabbed a fistful of Skye's hair. Despite all that had happened in the span of her short life, she was always so happy and full of energy and life. It made Skye smile too, just to see her niece so carefree and secure. As she turned toward the road, juggling her gym bag, the diaper bag, and Cassie, she couldn't help but continue to smile at the joy this little girl could bring to her day. That was when she spotted him, the guy in the bright yellow sports car staring at her. Their eyes locked and at first she wasn't sure what to think, but then he seemed to look away like he had been caught staring, or like maybe he didn't like what he saw. She was used to that; most men didn't like women with a little "meat" on their bones. *Oh well, his loss.* She was comfortable with who she was and how she looked. Besides, she had way too much going on in her life right now to even think about a man being any part of it. Although she did have to admit for a minute there, she had felt the heat of his gaze. She felt the way their eyes locked for a brief moment, and from what she could tell from the limited view looking into his car, he was hot as hell.

Encouraging Autumn
Five Sloths Brewing book 3
By Robin Andrews
Now available!

When everyone was done eating, they worked together to clear the table. Then Pete took his place next to Autumn, turning his chair so that he could look more directly at her. "I know that you don't want to talk to me about this. But I believe I have some ideas that may help you if you will be honest in your answers and keep an open mind to my suggestions. I promise you that whatever you decide, nothing that I already know nor anything that you tell me today will go any further than this room unless you decide that it does. And I will assure you that none of what I am asking will result in any kind of judgment or condemnation."

Autumn could see why Pete was considered a good attorney. He was very professional, and he seemed very ready to argue whatever case it was that he was going to try to make. "I understand," she agreed.

"First, how far along are you?"

"About a month," Autumn said quietly.

"Good, that's great," Pete encouraged. Autumn did not see what was so great about it all. "Correct me if I am wrong, but this is the way that I see it. With your family, if you had eloped and gotten pregnant on your honeymoon, while being disappointed that they didn't get to throw you a huge wedding, they would at least be happy that you were not an unwed mother?"

"I suppose, yes, that's true, but it's also irrelevant," Autumn protested.

"Not necessarily," Pete stated. "Here is what I propose, no pun intended. I think we should head to Las Vegas for the weekend and get married." He saw the protest already rising in Autumn's mind, so he held up a finger to keep her from saying anything just yet. "A marriage in name only. I'm not expecting you to sleep with me. Although I do think we need to live together to keep up appearances. For now, we can live in my apartment, or yours. We would start looking for a house together. If your family still wants to have a wedding, I am not opposed to it as long as they understand that we ran off to Vegas because I just couldn't wait the time it would take to put a whole wedding together."

Was this man crazy? "I can't marry you; we aren't in love," Autumn protested.

"We know that; they don't. You got pregnant on our trip to Vegas. I know it's close to a month off timing wise, but we will work on that as we go along. First babies are often late anyway, so if this one holds off a week or two, it just helps support our story. If it doesn't, babies are also known to come early sometimes, which wouldn't not support our story. I will be the father of this child in every way as far as anyone outside of this room knows. And when the time comes, if you will allow it, I would very privately and discreetly adopt the child and, regardless of what happens with our relationship, this child would always have my support as a father." Pete continued, "As far as not being in love, no, I suppose we aren't the picture of romantic love, but people marry for all sorts of reasons, social status, money, companionship—why not for this reason? All I want to do is support you and help you in this situation."

Autumn looked around the room, Skye looked pretty much as gobsmacked as Autumn felt, but for some reason, Zak didn't seem to be surprised about this crazy idea. Most likely, Pete had talked to him about it before. "So, even though we aren't in love, and you know nothing about the real situation, you just want to step in and be my husband and the father of my child, why?" Autumn asked.

"First, yes, I know we aren't technically in love, but we got along well when we were dating. We can be friends and keep this completely platonic other than having to appear as a real couple when we are out in public," Pete encouraged. "As far as the other aspect, as a man and as an attorney, I will admit that I want the man who did this to be appropriately punished, but it will remain completely up to you whether or not you want to tell me. I will guarantee you that if you tell me, I will do everything in my power to protect you from any backlash of what he did to you."

Autumn just nodded her understanding so Pete continued, "I know that this is not a situation you would have ever wanted to find yourself in, and I know that this isn't the proposal of your dreams, but I am trying to be practical and help you in any way that I can. If it doesn't work, when you feel it's appropriate and safe to do so, you simply tell your family that we have decided to divorce and go our separate ways.

I don't know your family; you do. I'm committed to this for the rest of my life if that is what you want. If not, then I will make sure that any separating is done on your terms."

"Why, why would you do this?" Autumn pleaded. "It's crazy to even think about."

"I can't go into them right now, but I do have reasons, and some day, I promise I will tell you. Right now, what I would like to do if it's okay with everyone is go home and let you discuss this with Skye and Zak. I think everyone will eventually agree that this is the best plan of action. I have a flight scheduled for ten in the morning to take the four of us to Vegas. I will be at the airport. You have three choices of how to handle this. You can just not show up at all, and I will know that you do not want my help. You can show up with Zak and Skye, but ask me to not get on the plane and I will know that you want to have a fun weekend with your friends but you don't want my help. Or you can come and get on the airplane with me and we will all work together to make the best of this weekend and I will help you with all of it," Pete promised. "Since I am leaving, I give Zak permission to answer general questions about me. You know a lot about me from dating, but if you have questions, you can ask Zak." He looked to his friend and they shared some sort of eye movement, head nod, non-verbal conversation and then Pete headed for the door and was gone.

Triskelion
A spin-off from Five Sloths Brewing
Coming Fall 2020

Bryan...big brother...first to become a Green Beret... first to serve his country, first to protect his siblings.... first to step up and make a place for his brothers to come home to.

Trevor... middle kid.... wasn't the oldest, wasn't the youngest, so he became determined to be the smartest. When he joined the Green Berets, it was because the Marines would rather he was hacking for them than into them.

Riley... little brother...baby of the family. When your only family is already Green Beret, what else are you going to be? Sometimes he wishes he had died with his squad....sometimes he's glad he didn't, but all the time, he wishes he could really walk away... not from life, not from reality, not from the only blood he's got left... but from the pain and the memories... yeah, those he wishes he could walk away from.

Triskelion is a series about Bryan, Trevor and Riley Lawson. Three brothers, all former Green Beret.

Triskelion Motorcycles, their bike shop is their 'every day' job. It's also the location for the offices of their bodyguard and private investigating services for people that need their skills.

Triskelion turns the heat up a few notches from my Five Sloths Brewing series.

About Robin Andrews

Robin Andrews still lives in the same small town that she grew up in. She began college headed for a legal career. While she still went into the legal arena, she set aside the idea of becoming an attorney for the much more rewarding life of a mother and grandmother. She has been married for thirty-five years. She lives with her husband and her miniature Labradoodle, Hope.

She is the mother to three adult children (two boys, one girl) and grandmother to three grandchildren (two girls, one boy). She loves taking her family to the local fitness center for family swim days.

Her greatest joys in life are writing, reading and spending time cuddling with her grandkids.

* * * *

Website: www.robin-andrews.com

I would love to have you join my readers group on Facebook: Robin's Readers Nest.
https://www.facebook.com/groups/898899640504649/?ref=share

Other books by Robin Andrews

Fallen Rayne, Five Sloths Brewing Book 1
Opaque Skye, Five Sloths Brewing Book 2
Encouraging Autumn, Five Sloths Brewing Book 3
Resistant Summer, Five Sloths Brewing Book 4, coming soon
Embracing Sunni, Five Sloths Brewing Book 5, coming soon

www.ingramcontent.com/pod-product-compliance
Lightning Source LLC
Chambersburg PA
CBHW032135170626
46808CB00006B/2244